JOSEPHINE LIGHT

EVERNIGHT PUBLISHING ®

www.evernightpublishing.com

FOR ALL MY EFFORT

Copyright© 2025

Josephine Light

ISBN: 978-0-3695-1192-8

Cover Artist: Jay Aheer

Editor: CA Clauson

JOSEPHINE LIGHT

DEDICATION

To all my boys: Your love is a distraction I easily accept.

JOSEPHINE LIGHT

FOR ALL MY EFFORT

Not All Omegas, 2

Josephine Light

Copyright © 2024

Chapter One

Every protest I'd ever been to was different. My first was a simple march down the street leading to the private road of the local Omega Compound. I had also held signs outside of buildings where terrible decisions were being made, chanted in circles, worn a dog collar around my neck and tape over my mouth—my favorite.

I'd been protesting since the day I bloomed into an omega at thirteen and was forcibly admitted into the local Omega Compound for my supposed protection. Just playing in the snow, the proud thirteen-year-old that I was and bragging to my friends that I'd already gotten my period and designation.

I had no idea who had called the OC, still didn't, since that information was considered sensitive. But I remembered begging my parents, my friends, anyone to save me. No one did. Even as the workers told me I was safe, that it was simply my hormones making me act out, I knew that what was happening was wrong.

They told me all about alpha ruts, something uncontrollable in the more dominant designation that was only triggered by an unbonded omega. For my safety, I needed to be taken away. To me, it had always seemed like an alpha problem.

My body went into heat, but I wasn't dangerous. Alphas were.

Omegas were the ones taken from our families, pulled out of schools to learn how to be a proper omega. It was all bullshit. How to nest, how to cook, how to nurse, and watch children. All the things that supposedly came naturally, yet we had to learn.

Just the idiocy of that thought had me snorting out loud, breaking up the awkward silence of the sit-in.

A sit-in didn't feel nearly as effective as all the other protests I'd been a part of. Honestly, it was boring, not speaking, holding myself still. I preferred the protests where I could yell, my throat aching for the next few days from screaming so loud I'd lost my voice. The only reason I kept my ass firmly planted on the cold hard tile flooring of the restaurant was for the sole reason that I believed in the stance we were taking.

Omegas' rights were already limited. We weren't allowed to live on our own, needing to be bonded to alphas in order to move out of the OC. Higher education was basically impossible since the institutes never accepted omegas on the idiotic basis of our heats forcing us to miss too many of the classes. And of course, there was the fact that we needed a chaperone if we left our homes. Alphas were dangerous to omegas—that much I agreed with.

The restaurant we were protesting in was owned by an up-and-coming politician. The alpha—because of course it was an alpha—claimed society needed more protective stances for omegas. Specifically, he wanted to age omegas out of the OC, forcing them to bond with alpha packs to help them through heats after a certain age.

Considering his pack didn't have an omega yet, it was easy enough to see his true intentions.

That was why I, and this random group of betas, had shown up eight hours ago, immediately at the restaurant's opening, taking up all the seats, including the floor space, and refusing to move or order. Despite never having met the group before, my natural designation meant I knew I was the only omega. Fortunately, that also meant I was able to participate since an alpha would have been able to detect my omega perfume.

Just the thought of some strange alpha scenting me made my perfume spike in agitation. I forced myself to take a deep breath, ignoring the cold bite of air down my throat from the rapidly lowering air-conditioned room attempting to force us out.

I thought of my own alphas—Jackson, Sebastian, Han, and Zeke. They rescued me from the OC two years ago. I'd already loved them when I decided to bond with them. When they learned my secret, and wanted to help me? I knew I was going to spend the rest of my life with them, happily.

My mates were anxiously waiting for me on the other side of the shopping complex this restaurant was located in. When this protest eventually got shutdown, I'd make my way to them.

I wasn't supposed to be out alone. That crime alone would get me sent back to the OC, potentially taken away from my mates. Hiding my designation was usually possible among betas since their ability to smell perfumes, designations, and heightened emotions was weaker.

The front door swung open, making me jump, and revealing the exact reason I never made it to the end of the protest. Peace officers.

Dressed in protective gear around their chests and backs, their job was all about designation handling in public. Usually, that meant pulling alphas out of public ruts, stopping alphas from bullying betas, even pulling freshly perfumed thirteen-year-old omegas from their homes.

Since more protests had been popping up, they were the ones answering the call.

They were usually a mix of alphas and betas, which meant my time was officially up when they arrived. Outside, I was usually safe long enough to run the planned route as soon as they showed up. Inside, it would take a bit of finesse to manage not getting arrested as they blocked the only exit.

"Okay, folks," one of the officers said, already sounding bored. "You've made your point. Now it's time to leave."

No one moved, but my muscles tensed.

This was my least favorite part. No matter the good I felt like I was doing by showing up for the cause, I never got to follow through. When the peace officers showed, I took that as my opportunity to leave.

It was a compromise. Commit to the amount that meant I could go home every night and be with my mates. Even if it meant I didn't make the grand declaration I always wanted. To be the first omega arrested. To prove that omegas weren't happy with the way things were.

Even my best friend, Koda Tucker, was doing more. She was an omega who somehow presented as a beta, meaning she was able to attend college, and actually get a degree. And she had bonded with a pack of alphas. The girl was getting knotted and educated in the same week.

The same peace officer sighed, adding, "Anyone still on the premises that's not an employee or is unwilling to purchase food, will find themselves in a cell overnight and charged."

I wish they'd given me more time. In my own mind, I had refused to get up. In my mind, I'd seen the inside of the cell or the center without fear. Only, I couldn't get myself to risk my pack.

Here I was, at a protest, slowly standing up. Around me, I heard the mutters of the betas who thought of me as weak for leaving.

The entire restaurant watched me move, step by step closer to the door. I could scent at least seven peace officers, almost all of them betas. Except one. They didn't fully move out of the way of the door, attempting to force me to walk between the two rows they'd created in order to leave.

My heart was pounding, partly from all the silent attention, and partly because I hated the peace officers. They might not have been the exact ones that took me from my home, but their uniforms were the same. It was enough to make me feel thirteen again, making me lose all the confidence I'd actually gained in the last eight years.

Each thud of my boots seemed to be the only noise, and much louder than shoes had probably ever sounded before.

One of the officers opened the door, the bell chiming—

Then I felt it. A hand on my upper arm. The sheer fabric on my sleeves wasn't enough to hide the warmth from their touch.

I knew immediately, before their scent even reached my nostrils. Only alpha assholes grabbed whoever they pleased, and the old, dusty scent only confirmed their designation.

"Are you an omega?"

Maybe his question was rhetorical. Maybe he was only barely able to scent my omega perfume in the clouded room of beta stress.

Panic looped in my stomach until I thought I might throw up right there. Their touch wasn't painful, but my instincts demanded only my alphas be allowed to touch me. The aggressive behavior would definitely get me some mandated lessons back at the OC.

Instead, I swallowed down the growl, the need to bare my teeth and claw at the hand that had still been touching me. And I screamed. Not the kind asking for help, the loud high-pitched kind that made the officer drop my arm in a startled reflex.

Then I ran.

My feet took me toward my alphas without even thinking.

The restaurant was in the middle of the fashion center, a prime commodity spot considering the amount of foot traffic it gets from shoppers. Unfortunately, the fuck-ton of people didn't work to my advantage.

No one seemed willing to move out of my way. I tried shoving and squeezing through crowds, but I could still feel myself being chased like prey.

My entire focus was on the path in front of me. I couldn't see over the shoulders of basically everyone, which meant I couldn't tell if I'd passed the turn I should have made between the two stores that was a shortcut to the back parking lot.

Despite the fear coursing through my system, it wasn't enough to block out the burn in my lungs from how much I was heaving, or the strain in my calves as I tried to run with my thick heavy boots. I could tell I was naturally slowing down, but not even that knowledge helped me move faster.

Unlike my mates, I couldn't feel them through our bond. Omegas relied on our sense of smell to identify our mates' emotions which meant the bond was more one-way.

Maybe I was hoping that they'd sense my panic and come to my rescue? Except the longer I ran, shoving and stumbling, the more I realized that I wasn't going to be rescued this time.

I felt the tug on the back strap of my overall-denim dress, just enough to throw off my momentum. My feet stumbled as I tried to right myself. Then a sharper tug, this one with a full grip on my clothes. Rather than falling straight back into the alpha, the movement pulled me toward his side.

I was looking up at the alpha—knowing that something was wrong even without my instincts. The male was pale, and backing away?

Other faces started to crowd in around me, and I couldn't figure out how they were managing to look down on me. I was used to others sort of glancing down to talk to me, but this felt extreme.

Looking around, I realized I was on the ground. Something touched my ear, most likely a bug, and I lifted my hand to swat it away, feeling like it took every ounce of my strength to move my arm.

When I lifted my hand back up, I saw the red, and it took me several long seconds to realize it was mine. That I shouldn't be lying down.

The faces over me changed. These ones were much more handsome—my mates. Sebastian was at my head, completely upside down, and saying something if his moving lips was anything to go by. His indulgent smile was missing, the one he always wore as he called me princess and let me run wild. Han and Zeke, like always, were on either side of me, almost perfect mirrors of each other if you ignored their looks. Where Zeke was an artist in skill with his drawings, Han was the masterpiece of clothes, loving to try styles from around the world. And of course, Jackson, my grumpy mate, the one that was usually glaring at the world to protect me but was glaring down at me.

That's how I knew something was wrong. My other mates might overreact, not Jackson. He's my levelheaded alpha. The one that takes the pamphlets about keeping an omega happy very seriously. He made it his life goal to keep me safe and healthy and happy.

I reached out, visibly watching the shaking of my hand as I touched his cheek. His dark skin hid the stain of my blood. His hand caught mine, keeping it against his cheek, which was good because I couldn't hold it up anymore.

For just a moment, the world went dark—no, I blinked. My eyelids were like weights, and I was never one for exercise unless you counted every time I was on top of my mates, riding their dicks. That was a thigh workout for sure.

I wanted to ask something, only the words went missing almost as soon as I thought of them. Despite how light my body felt, it was impossible to open my eyes again. And then the world truly went to shit.

Chapter Two

I slept like crap. My entire body felt stiff, like rather than blood running through my veins, it was sand, weighing me down and making it impossible to get comfortable.

Plus, it was colder than I like my nest to be. The OC was filled with assholes, but they at least had independently separated controls for each omega's nest. I liked mine warm, so I didn't have to be wrapped up in blankets. Not hot, I didn't want to sweat. Just perfectly in the middle so I could spread out.

This was borderline torturous. I curled my legs up, trying to nuzzle under the thin blanket and get warm.

"She's cold."

Those words had me gasping in outrage. Someone was in my nest. Apparently, a bad night's sleep could mute my instincts, that's what they should be teaching me.

I sat up, my vision immediately swimming as I struggled to take in everything. It was all so bright—too bright.

"The lights," someone snapped. A different someone. How many people were in my freaking nest?

Shutting my eyes, I took a deep breath, scrunching my nose at the harsh smell of chemicals. It was almost overwhelming, but I managed to pull out four distinct scents. Four alphas.

Even with my eyes closed, I could tell the lights had been properly dimmed. By this point, I was starting to realize that something wasn't right. This bed was definitely not my nest, it was too boxed in and uncomfortable. The room should have been soaked in my scent and I couldn't imagine the OC allowing anyone into my nest. It was supposed to be a sacred place for omegas, the one place in the entire world that was solely mine.

Omegas had been known to go into rages when someone entered their nest without permission. Even their mates.

"Hannah, how are you feeling?" a third voice asked.

With my eyes still shut, I glared in the direction of the voice. Obviously, something wasn't right. I tried to think about yesterday, except I couldn't. What day was it? No one from the OC was knocking on my nest door demanding I get up to attend the mandatory sessions, so most likely a weekend.

Again, I tried opening my eyes. They were blurry at first, which was gross. I rubbed at the eye boogers and tried a third time.

I was right. Four males, alphas by their scent, standing all around me. Rather than stressing me out, my body seemed to relax at their presence, which was definitely not something that was supposed to happen. I'd met alphas before, and they all made me nervous. These ones, they actually made me stressed *for* them.

Dark circles under their eyes, their shoulders almost hunched, hair mussed, and the air around them was like they were at a 24-hour funeral.

Considering how fragile they looked, I didn't immediately snap at them for being so close. "What happened?"

The alpha by my feet, the smallest in the group, though definitely larger than me, spoke first. "That asshole officer raced after you. He tried to stop you, but he apparently overestimated his strength because he flung you back so hard you smacked your head on the stone walkway."

I looked at the other alphas, their anger increasing with each word the male said. On my behalf?

Reaching up, I wanted to touch the back part of my head where the pain seemed to be. The cool texture of my scalp, along with the feel of staples—I screamed.

Regretting it almost instantly as nausea boiled up from my stomach. I threw up once in my mouth and the second time over the side of the bed and into a pan.

"I got you, princess, let it all out." The nearest male's words were soothing, and he petted my shoulder which was weirdly comforting as he held the pan for me.

When I finally finished, sitting back against the bed, I felt worse. It was like I could finally recognize the thudding in my head, how much effort it took to move my neck, even the cold. My legs were still curled close to my body, but it wasn't enough with just the thin blanket on top.

"Blanket," the large male on my left side snapped. His voice was deep, with a natural growl that had me shivering with just that word.

I must have closed my eyes because I missed whoever set a blanket on top of my lap. I petted it, feeling the familiar weave of the sarape blanket which had me opening my eyes again.

Most omegas preferred super soft blankets, ones that were fluffy and warm. But I'd always preferred the slight roughness of sarapes. I felt like I sweated too much in traditional nesting fabrics, and these were more breathable. Great for keeping me covered without making me too hot.

The design was beautiful. A dark green and brown, the diamond in the middle a light tan. It definitely wasn't one of mine, except when I brought it up to my face, I could scent myself—the lavender floral of my natural omega perfume.

I guessed that meant it was time to ask, "Who are you?"

No one spoke right away. I looked between the four males, each one radiating fear and sadness and worry to the point that my instincts were demanding I comfort them. I didn't, though, because comforting strangers while I was in a hospital bed seemed too ironic for even me.

"I'll get the doctor."

The male who'd comforted me while I vomited basically ran out of the room, the bright lights from the hallway making me slam my eyes shut until I heard the click of the door shutting again.

"You really don't know who we are?" one of the others asked.

I looked at the male. His skin was naturally tanned, his features sharp, and his eyes tilted in a way that made him look classically handsome. Even his clothes were good-looking. His white shirt was tucked into his pants, the buttons done up except for the top two, exposing his chest. At some point, he'd curled up the sleeves over his arms, showing off his sexy forearms. Had I ever thought forearms were sexy before?

And his scent. Pumpkin. Not like the dessert, like autumn. He reminded me of fall nights and candle lights. Cozy to the core.

Opposite him was an alpha with a completely different vibe. This male wore a sweater, the V of his collar just barely ripped and proving he wasn't wearing a shirt underneath. His sleeves were scrunched upwards, bunched at his elbows and showing off ink tattooed into his brown arms. He had his hair shaved close to the scalp with some sort of design on the sides.

His scent was like berries. A whole mix of them together that I'd like to grab a handful of and eat. It made my mouth water and my stomach rumble.

Then there was the final male. He was everything that society thought alphas should be. Large and strong. Built in a way that would have other alphas admiring him. Despite his intense stare, he seemed laid back. No, maybe that was the wrong way to describe him. He was the kind of male that didn't give someone the time of day if he didn't care for them. And those he considered his? He'd do anything.

He smelled like crisp apples. Delicious and juicy. Healthy yet even better when dipped in chocolate. His dark skin was an almost shocking contrast to my paleness.

I wanted something to jog a memory. Something that I could tell these men to make them feel better. But I didn't know them. Not their names, or what they did for a living. I didn't even remember seeing them before, because I knew that I wouldn't have forgotten these males if I'd passed them on the streets or spotted them through a window.

"I'm sorry." I looked between all three. "I don't know…"

A knock on the door couldn't break the awkward tension in the room as a doctor came in, followed by the fourth male in this group. "All right, all right. It looks like you're finally awake. How are you feeling, Hannah?"

"Why is my head shaved?" Not quite what I'd meant to ask, but same gist.

The beta doctor smiled like I'd made a joke. "You took quite a hit to the head. We had to clear the area in order to properly put you back together."

I huffed, looking away from the doctor's kind gaze. My own immediately caught on the large male's next to me. He was still watching me, a sort of intense look on his face like he thought I might disappear if he so much as blinked.

I blamed my instincts for reaching out and squeezing his forearm. Then my arousal for mumbling, "shit, you're hard."

Someone laughed which had me yanking my head away from the male.

The doctor cleared his throat, pulling my attention back to him as he asked, "How's your head? Can you tell me what you last remember?"

My lips parted, ready to say something, except no words came out. What did I last remember? Maybe trying to fall asleep in my nest? I couldn't tell if that was last night or just a memory of a bad night from a few weeks ago.

"I'm not sure." I hated how confused I felt. And I especially hated the pain that seemed to form between my eyes as I tried to remember anything. "These guys said I was attacked? I don't remember that at all?"

Something I said seemed to truly get the doctor's attention. He'd been content to stand near the foot of my bed, asking his questions. After my answer, he moved two of the alphas away, a brave move for a beta.

"Can you tell me your name?" he asked.

"Hannah Zeal."

"And what about over there on your left side. What's his name?"

"If I had to guess—"

"No, don't guess."

I rolled my eyes. "Fine, then I don't know."

"What about any of the alphas in here?"

"Without guessing?"

"Yes."

"No." I bit my bottom lip, feeling the tension rise in the space. Something behind me started beeping, which made me jump, attempting to turn around and see what it was.

"Just your heart monitor. Maybe we should finish this assessment alone."

Then the beeping started to go crazy. I was shaking my head, the idea of the men leaving sounded like a terrible idea. They were protecting me. They cared about me. Not knowing their names didn't mean they should abandon me like everyone else had—

Warm fingers wrapped around the back of my neck. Distantly, I heard the doctor tell the alpha to be careful, but I was fully focused on the dark brown eyes in front of me. "Calm down, rebel. We aren't going anywhere."

I felt the stress drain from my body. I inhaled deeply, taking in his apple scent mixed with lavender. No wait, that was me. Leaning forward, the male let me inhale by his neck, where scents were the strongest. I hadn't noticed it before. He's been claimed already.

"Are we mates?" I asked.

"Yes."

Guilt. That was a new emotion for me. At the OC I refused to make any friends. For starters, their families came to visit, whereas mine stopped being welcome after I went into a teeny tiny rage the first week after my imprisonment. Then there was the fact that I snuck out of the facility to attend protests, and I didn't trust a single omega in the compound to not tattle. I was bitter, refusing to trust anyone.

I never considered that I'd find a mate. My plan was to live at the OC until I figured out how to survive on my own. I hadn't figured out how to do that yet, nevertheless it was in my plans.

But knowing I had mates. And forgot about them. It felt like I had abandoned them. Treating them worse than my parents had me. I'd claimed them. I could scent my perfume embedded in their scents.

Tears burned my eyes, making my head hurt even worse.

Then I felt it. A vibration in his chest that stopped the tears in their tracks. A purr. I'd heard them before in my mandatory omega lessons. In the OC shoppette, you can actually purchase recordings of the sound in blankets.

Those always felt wrong. It was just a noise like any other.

This one was like the best drugs in the world. Not that I'd actually ever taken drugs. But I would do terrible, sinful things for him to keep going.

"Well, it seems even if bits of your memory are missing, your instincts are still intact." The doctor's voice ruined the blissful state I was in.

Pulling back, I reached up to wrap my fingers around the male's wrist, keeping his hand around the back of my neck where I wanted him. I was starting to think I should get everyone's name if I was going to be so dramatic in front of them.

I would've sworn my emotions were more stable than this. I couldn't even remember the last time I cried—outside of enduring painful heats by myself.

Coming to stand next to me again, the beta doctor started flashing a little light in my eyes. "I'm going to get a technician ready for some scans of your brain. Memory loss isn't uncommon with head injuries. Unfortunately, there's no way to know if it's permanent or not."

"What about other side effects?" the blond alpha asked. He wasn't close enough that I could take in his scent fully, but I was getting something tropical. Not beachy, more foodwise.

"Let's not borrow trouble, yeah?" the doctor said. "I'll leave you all alone for a bit to get your images all scheduled. If you need anything, Hannah, there's a button on the bed rail you can press for a nurse."

The doctor left, and that time, I didn't flinch from the hallway lights. Progress.

"So…" I started. "I kind of need to know your names."

The alpha with the berry scent and tattoos spoke up first. "I'm Zeke."

"Han," the handsome, pumpkin scented alpha added.

Fingers tightened around my neck slightly, physically turning so I was facing him. "Jackson."

I blushed. Heat rushing to my cheeks at the intensity of Jackson's gaze. When I turned away, he easily let me.

The last male looked like he was in pain. He was the lightest of all the alphas with his dirty blond hair, perfectly unperfect like he'd purposefully ran his fingers through the length in order to style it. As he stepped closer, his tropical scent became stronger, letting me pull out notes of pineapple and guava. Mostly the latter.

In some ways, he was similar to Han in the way both alphas held themselves, prim and proper like they'd been trained to walk with sticks up their asses. Only this alpha, he never relaxed.

"Sebastian," he finally said. "My name is Sebastian. But you usually call me Seb."

His voice almost broke. And it felt like my heart was breaking right along with him.

"Should I call you that?" I asked. That instinct to comfort them, to give them what they wanted was pulling at me like the memories were simply hiding inside my head, attempting to fight their way out. I tried, imagining hands inside my brain clawing their way toward the memories, ignoring the pounding in my head that was getting stronger.

"Hey, no, don't hurt yourself." Seb said, rubbing his fingers against my temples. It wasn't where the pounding was, but it still felt good to have his fingers on me. If there was any doubt that he was my mate beyond our marks, the fact that my body simply obeyed his command was proof enough that I instinctually trusted him.

"Well," someone said, clapping their hands. I turned away from Seb to look at Han who kept saying, "I feel like we've had our morbid moment but it's time to look at the positives. Hannah is awake, and so far, only her memory seems to be hurt. As far as I'm concerned, we can make new memories."

Next to Han, Zeke started nodding. "A few hours ago, I would have agreed to memory loss if it meant you woke up."

It was weird. It was like the air in the room physically changed. Becoming something softer, lighter. Shoulders lost their tension, lips turned up naturally at the ends. Everyone seemed to get closer to me—Zeke and Han barely sitting on edge of the bed, Jackson keeping his hand on the back of my neck, and Sebastian reaching out to hold my hand.

Having all four of them so close, without the morbid air distracting me, it gave me a weird mix of calm and arousal. With my one free hand, I reached out to the blanket over my lap, petting it, pretending to arrange it around me as if it needed to be tucked under my legs just right.

For the first time in my life, I wished I'd paid attention to the classes at the OC about flirting—yes, that was an actual mandatory lesson.

Unfortunately, I wasn't feeling very confident. Especially when I thought of the patch of missing hair. Was it vain? Sure. But it made me worried that the males wouldn't want this version of me.

Fuck this.

I bottled up the emotions, grabbing onto the negative tail ends and shoving them so deep inside me that I could ignore them. Pulling my shoulders back, I sat up straight. I was letting my instincts run the show right now, that was why I was so trusting. But I didn't want to get lost in them.

"We're all mates?" I looked at each male, watching them nod along to my question. "You're all hot, so that's good, at least. How long have we been together?"

"Two years," Han said.

Zeke glared at the other male before turning his focus back to me. "Two and a half."

"That would make me ... how old exactly?" I couldn't remember the last birthday I celebrated.

"You're about to turn twenty-two," Seb said. His fingers were starting to trace invisible designs onto my hand and wrist. With how much attention he was giving the area, I was surprised his claiming mark wasn't there.

It would be interesting to figure out where all my bites were. Weird, too, exploring my own body.

Someone knocked on the door, peeking in through the crack. I could just make her out between Seb and Han, giving me just a sliver of a view of the room. Considering the scrubs, it was obviously a nurse. "Hey, Hannah. We have time now to get your images taken. You ready?"

"Sure." I tried to get out of the bed, which was hard enough since the side railings basically blocked me in like a crib. Only none of the alphas moved. Even when I scooted down to the foot of the bed, expecting Han or Zeke to get out of my way, neither did.

The nurse basically shoved her way between

them, giving me a wide smile. She looked remarkably happy, as if she was having the best day of her life while working in the hospital. Her smile was definitely contagious.

"Oh, you can stay lying down." She patted the top where the thinnest pillow in existence was. "I'm going to push the whole bed out of here. Doc says you shouldn't be walking."

I literally wasn't going to argue with her until she'd added that last bit. "I can't walk?"

Someone groaned, it sounded like Zeke, but I couldn't be completely positive since I didn't look away from the nurse.

"Just for a bit. Once we get your head all scanned and cleared of any brain injuries, no doubt you'll be up and running."

I could run now. I didn't say that, but if the muffled smirks were anything to go by, the sentiment was understood through my mating bonds. Not even physical exhaustion was stronger than my spite.

"Be good, rebel," Jackson called out. The command seemed to wash over me, but it didn't encourage me to do anything I would have considered good. And his deep chuckle as the nurse pushed me away told me that he knew it too.

Chapter Three

Apparently, there was a difference between sleeping and being knocked out. After all the scans of my head, I was pushed back into my room. All I had done was basically lie still, and yet I was exhausted.

I didn't remember falling asleep, but I noticed the whispered shouting that woke me up. It was weirdly comforting to hear the voices of the familiar alphas and being able to recognize them. At least until their words finally managed to penetrate the heavy fog of sleep in my mind.

"Tell them to leave me the hell alone," I mumbled before adjusting on my other side so I could fall back asleep.

With the stitches along the back of my head, and the gap of missing hair, I couldn't lay on my back. Usually I slept on my stomach, needing the perfect mattress to caress my boobs, not smash them, so I hadn't even tried that position with this hospital one.

A hand ran along the side of my face, gently tracing my features. The spiced pumpkin scent told me it was Han. "Unfortunately, I think you're going to have to talk with them. It isn't a great look if we deny them access. They'll just send a mandatory appearance in the mail."

I groaned, ensuring the sound was loud and emphasizing how put-out I felt.

I was more tired than when I had first woken up. My head wasn't thumping anymore, but I would've sworn the stitches were too tight with the amount of pressure I felt on the back of my head.

The room was dark, with just a sliver of light

coming from the attached bathroom between the cracks and the floor. Even with the black-out curtains over the windows, I knew the sun had already set. In late winter, that made knowing the time slightly more difficult since the sun went down before dinner.

Everyone seemed to stop talking, obviously realizing I was awake. Just barely peeking open my eyes, I could see Han in front of me, giving me an amused smile. It made him look impossibly more handsome as dimples appeared on both of his cheeks.

"If you talk to them, I'll sneak out of here and bring you a shake." He whispered the words softly and he suddenly had all of my attention.

"A shake?"

"I guess you don't remember. But we have a secret place that we like going to. The others don't know where it is, so they try to bring you random ones. It's usually just a little game we all play, although now that I'm trying to describe it—"

"Will you get one too?"

The sad look that was creeping onto Han's face disappears at my question. "Sure. I'll let the others know that you're willing to meet with the OC rep."

Han stood and left, taking Zeke with him. The two alphas seemed unusually close, not just because they were leaving together, but in how physically close they walked side by side. It wasn't impossible for alphas to be together, although omegas were known to be territorial. That was not my feeling about the idea, however, if my blooming scent of arousal was any indication.

Jackson basically prowling toward me didn't help the growing scent of lavender either. He stopped at the foot of the bed, leaning over the end with his fists on the mattress looking like the predator he was. "I'll tell them to leave. You don't have to speak with them."

Behind him, Seb moved closer. "It's better to just let them in. I don't want them making a visit to the house and ruining the safe space Hannah's created there."

"She doesn't have to see them at all. It should be her choice."

Seb sighed. "It should. Unfortunately, that's not the way it works. They're following protocol. It'll raise flags if we deny them."

"What sort of protocol?" I asked.

"You came in with a severe head injury. The hospital called the center to talk to you about abuse."

Jackson growled, pushing off the bed to start pacing. "Absolutely ridiculous."

"What do you say, princess? Seb asked. "We won't be able to stay in here with you, but we'll be just outside the room."

I agreed, mostly because I knew saying 'no' wasn't truly an option. The OC always got its way. Their decisions controlled the peace officers, the law makers, the social rules. It wasn't just a place to home unbonded omegas, it was a neatly packaged form of control. Their 'scientists' made claims that turned into laws and with such a beautiful working relationship with enforcement, it wasn't a surprise that our society was heavily regulated by their influence.

Seb basically had to haul Jackson out of the room. No doubt, the other alpha was letting him, but there was something special about the way Jackson wanted to protect me. I wasn't oblivious to both males doing what they thought was right. I just loved seeing someone stand up for me, even against someone else who they also loved.

My moment of quiet almost had me falling back asleep.

It seemed rare that I was actually left alone.

Technically, I knew that I'd have to have a nest at the house I was living in with the alphas. Since I couldn't remember that, though, I thought about my nest at the compound. It was private, but it hadn't given me comfort. From the rest of the omegas living nearby, sure. From my life? No.

I winced when my fingers found the stitches on the back of my head. It wasn't even a conscious thought to touch it, something just kept drawing my hand to the square bald spot.

When I left the hospital, I was planning on getting my hair fixed. I didn't remember dying it purple and as much as I imagined it looked cute, it didn't feel right anymore. Maybe a burnt orange. Or a red. And shorter. Definitely shorter.

As I was lost in thought, someone entered my space. I hadn't heard the door—it was their scent that drew my attention. Sweet, just not naturally. Some betas used a chemical perfume to create a distinct scent to cover their softer, natural one. Either for the purposes of blending in with omegas, or for trying to attract an alpha.

Some of the beta employees at the compound wore fake perfumes because they thought omegas worked best with other omegas. That we'd be more likely to trust them, seek them out, that sort of thing.

"Hello, Hannah." The beta was leaning against the door, a notebook pressed tightly against her chest. She was dressed in a long, tight pencil skirt and a blouse tucked in. Flats rather than heels which added to the beta-wanting-to-be-an-omega vibe since omegas were stereotypically short.

"Hi."

"My name is Eve. I'm with the Omega Center. I was hoping to speak with you for a few minutes, would that be okay?"

"Sure."

She gave me a soft smile, and I couldn't help wondering if it was the same one she'd give a child. No matter what betas said, I'd never met one that liked me. Some pretended to be kind, gushing over me or my scent or something else that they thought would make me their best friend. This type of beta was easy enough to spot because they were strangers that constantly touched me, hoping to get enough of my scent on them that they'd attract the attentions of alphas.

Then there were the kinds of betas who didn't even pretend to tolerate me. All they saw were the courting dates, the private rooms, and the fact that we didn't work—if you didn't consider mandatory lessons on pleasing your mates, work.

Those betas didn't get it though, the concept of a golden cage. They *wanted* an easy life, and they could have it. It would be hard, but the only thing stopping an alpha pack from mating a beta were social norms.

Omegas weren't allowed to work. They weren't allowed to go shopping without an escort or attend higher education beyond whatever they learned once they presented. We had no choices. Not even about whether we wanted to live at the OC.

Eve moved all the way around the room since the chairs were all pushed to that side. She tried to make small talk as she opened her notebook, finding a free page without even needing to look since all the used pages had been bent inward.

"I know you've been through such a traumatic ordeal," she started. "The doctor on rotation filled me in and I spoke with the emergency personnel who transported you here. Everyone seems to be in agreement that your injuries aren't conducive to a simple fall. I was hoping you could shed a light on what happened, from your own perspective."

"I don't remember."

She immediately started writing in her journal. In a weird way, it was amazing to watch her two hands work together, one writing, the other guiding as she continued to stare at me, not even needing to glance down at the paper.

"The doctor said something about memory loss. Apparently, I've lost a few years."

"That must be quite disorienting. How do you feel with your alphas? They've all been to visit, yes?"

I nodded. "I don't remember them, but my instincts do."

"That's wonderful to hear. The bond between alphas and their omega is very special. Your instincts are definitely important in your relationship. That being said, you're currently in a unique situation."

Without even looking, she folded the top corner of the page she was writing on and started on the next. "With your memory loss, forgetting your mates, I want to make sure you feel comfortable going home with them."

"I do."

She nodded as if she expected that answer. "Can I be honest with you, Hannah? It's a very unusual case for a bonded omega to come to the hospital with such a severe injury."

No way was that true.

"I can see your disbelief. Illness is one thing. Small home injuries are another. But let me tell you what I see when I look at your file. A bonded omega with several alphas in her pack. She's out at the mall, either without proper supervision and gets injured, or she was with her pack and one of those members was responsible."

Words jumble against my tongue. Denials that I

don't know how to word properly because I couldn't admit what really happened. I didn't know.

My perfume turned bitter the longer I said nothing.

"I'm not trying to frighten you, Hannah. The truth is, we don't know what happened. Your mates are being unusually close-lipped about the incident which doesn't shine them in a good light."

"If they'd done something, my instincts wouldn't trust them."

"Maybe. Without your memories to verify, it's better to be safe, yes?"

"What does that mean?"

"One suggestion for you is to come back to the OC. We have guest rooms for bonded omegas who need to stay for a number of reasons. There, your pack will essentially court you again, giving you the chance to get to know them in a potentially more comforting and safer environment."

I snorted, the sound coming out before I thought better of it. "And the other option?"

"You're technically already mated. So, you're welcome to return home with the alphas, but I'd like to check in a few times, drop by and ensure you're safe and happy still. It's up to you, of course."

"I'll stay with my mates." The idea of having this female visit wasn't exactly an ideal situation, but if those were my only two options, it was the better one.

"If you're sure…"

I nodded and she finally glanced down at her book, making whatever final notes about my decision.

"Well, I'm glad you're okay, Hannah. I'll be going now, but I'll check in with you soon."

The moment she opened the door, Jackson and Sebastian were already there. Since my attention was still on her, I noticed the way she watched my mates warily, as if she expected them to attack me right then.

"I spoke with your doctor," Seb started, pulling my attention to him. "They think you'll be able to get out of here in a few days since your scans all came back as good."

I groaned. "A few days?"

Jackson was adjusting the sarape blanket around me, tucking the edges over my legs so that it was tight, although not to the point that the fabric over my thighs was taut. "No point arguing."

Again, I groaned, although that time it was mostly because he was right. I couldn't leave until the doctor discharged me, no matter how much I didn't want to be there anymore. The bed wasn't comfortable, the room still smelled more like chemicals than my mates, and I hated staring at these walls constantly. Not even the TV was enough to distract me.

Fortunately, Zeke and Han showed back up. My attention zeroed in on the clear plastic cups in Han's hands. One was a dark purple while the other was a dark brown. He came to sit right next to me, holding out both options. "One is a berry blast, the other is a chocolate pumpkin."

"Which one is yours?"

He smiled, almost like my question amused him. "Whichever one you don't want."

"Really?"

"Mhm."

I might not have remembered Han, but even I knew he was acting weird. Glancing over at the others to see if they noticed, I realized they were all sort of smiling. Zeke was actually looking down at the floor, his lips pressed tightly together like he was stopping himself from laughing. There was obviously some sort of inside joke that I was missing.

"Berry, please." Han handed over the purple drink. I could see the seeds from the mixed berries as I used the straw to stir it.

Still sitting on the edge of the bed, I watched Han take a sip of his drink. That one looked good too. Trying my own drink, I had to fight back the urge to spit it out, swallowing as quickly as I could. Even as I licked my lips, I almost shuddered at the echo of the taste.

Did I usually like this one? Was not only my memory broken but a fundamental part of who I was?

"Here." Han handed his drink over to me, taking mine without asking. "Try this one."

Obviously, I'd done a shit job of hiding my dislike. He didn't seem annoyed or concerned, though.

Trying his drink, it was so much better. The chocolate and pumpkin went together so smoothly, it was perfect. Mostly chocolate and sweet, the notes of pumpkin were minimal, just enough to diversify the cocoa from being too much.

"This is so good." I was chugging the drink. "Are you sure you're good with that one?"

"Yeah, I like berry. It's fine."

"Can't believe you're still keeping that place a secret," Sebastian mumbled. He was smiling though, even winking at me when I glanced in his direction.

I considered offering him a sip of mine. After all, Han hadn't gotten any for the rest of the pack. The words just seemed to remain on my tongue which was too busy enjoying my drink.

By the time I finished, my stomach felt bloated, and I was satisfyingly full. Turning onto my side, I watched the males talk, teasing each other, their voices becoming part of the background as I drifted off to sleep.

JOSEPHINE LIGHT

Chapter Four

Finally, after several days in the hospital, bound to the bed except for the few excursions to the bathroom, I was discharged. I was already dressed and sitting in the wheelchair a nurse had brought into the room, demanding I use it until I left hospital property, while the nurse went over the last few notes with my mates.

It was a boring list of what I shouldn't do, which was basically anything besides staying in bed. No stairs, no being left alone, no greasy foods, no intense exercise. The more she continued to list off my restrictions, the stronger my scent bloomed with my annoyance.

Jackson was behind me, ready to push my chair and stoutly paying attention to every word that left the nurse's mouth. One of his hands came down onto my shoulder, squeezing in a comforting way. It helped, offering me a distraction to focus on when he started to massage.

I couldn't remember the last time I'd been touched so casually. And the arousal that came from feeling the heat of his palm against me was stronger than it probably should have been. Just his touch had my stomach fluttering in anticipation. Then his thumb pressed into my back, pleasure spreading lower to my core, making me moan. My eyes shut and my head fell forward in case he wanted more access.

He chuckled, the deep sound only lasting for a moment.

"Well, I—um—I guess that's everything," the nurse stuttered along. "Have a nice rest of your day. I hope you feel better soon, Hannah."

I waved a hand in some form of goodbye as

Jackson lifted his hand off my shoulder to grab the chair's handles. Turning to look up at him, I pouted at the lack of his touch.

"When we get home," he promised.

I was pushed toward the elevator, Jackson refusing to enter any of the passing options until the box was completely empty. In the reflection of the metal doors, I stared at my mate. He was obviously handsome with his dark, flawless skin and strong facial composition. It helped that he was bulky in a way that made me think watching him work out would be an arousing experience.

More than just his appearance, he never took his hands off the handles, despite being forced to slightly hunch to reach them. Jackson was a protector. I knew that much just from the last few days of watching him.

We rode down in silence, and when the doors opened, he pushed me through with little effort. Just like they'd planned, a car was out front, the back door open and waiting for us. Sebastian was driving, already back from dropping Han and Zeke off at the house.

"Let me help you in." Without waiting for a response, Jackson lifted me from the chair like I weighed nothing. His easy strength, and the feeling of being against him, even for just a few moments, was enough to have my body become excited.

My imagination was taking off with ideas of exactly how he could put that strength to good use. Holding me against him as he thrusted into me. His hands around my thighs would help bounce me on his dick. I would've bet my life that he was proportional everywhere.

When I was in the car, he tried pulling away, taking his intoxicating scent with him until I reached out, my fingers tightening around his shirt. No way was he leaving me. I needed him to be nearby so I could convince him to fuck me.

"Do you smell that?" His voice was distant, which was weird because I could literally feel him next to me.

"Shit. It's probably just a spike. We need to get her home."

"Hear that, omega? We need to get you home—to your nest."

Nest. Oh, yes, I needed that. Because where I was at was no good. Too much was missing—the proper scents, the right space, and it was too bright, too open. Every blink took effort as I looked at my surroundings trying to figure out what exactly I was seeing. It was all a blur, and I couldn't figure out why.

A part of me wanted to panic, but I could scent my mates nearby, two of them. I whimpered for them to get closer, relaxing only slightly when I felt the warmth of one against my knee.

When the world finally seemed to come into focus, I realized we were outside. The sun was bright and shining down on us despite the coldness of the air. All of a sudden, Jackson seemed to appear, lifting me up so my side was pressed to his front, one arm around my back, and the other under my knees.

I wrapped my arms around his neck and pulled myself closer to him, nuzzling his throat. Pressed this close to him, the bite of chill in the air disappeared. My feet started kicking as I continued to suck in his crisp, apple scent.

As soon as we were inside, I was basically thrown into a state of euphoria. This—this place smelled of my mates. Each inhale was a mix of the four, somehow distinct, yet managing to blend in a way that settled something deep inside me. Like one scent with several notes all tightly pressed together.

I heard talking, my focus not strong enough to determine their words. Not that I cared. I was as happy as I could be, content to be near my mates. Then the lights seemed to dim—even better. I hadn't realized my eyes were closed until the brightness behind my eyelids disappeared.

One deep breath. That was all it took for my eyes to open and for me to launch myself from Jackson's grip, determined to get into my nest.

Home.

Safe.

This was my perfect place.

My mate didn't immediately release me as I attempted to scramble out of his arms. Once I felt the mattress underneath me, he finally let me go.

The nest was its own room. Draping from the ceiling were large pieces of fabric helping to make the room feel more closed. Every inch of the floor had a slight give of the mattress. Several rows of pillows were on the floor, pressed against the three walls and making the center of the nest feel closed in. Nicely folded near the base of the pillows were a bunch of blankets, all of them sarapes or at least similar in texture.

Laying down, feeling the give of the mattress under my head, was such a relief to finally be able to lie on my back. Under me, I felt the bizarre squares of the mattress gently cradling my body. No matter which way I turned, or squirmed, I was supported and comfortable and I was never going to leave.

A knock caught my attention. I had just enough strength to lift my head.

Zeke. His scent drifted toward me from the other door before my eyes fully focused on him. He had taken off most of his clothes, leaving him in just some tight-fitting boxers. The darkness of his brown skin seemed to lighten around his stomach and thighs, though he was still darker than any tanned white.

"Can I come into your nest, Hannah?"

I gasped, sitting up so quickly my head seemed to spin. That sounded like a wonderful idea. "Yes."

He chuckled, getting down onto his hands and knees to crawl into the nest with me. Watching his shoulders work, seeing his thighs flex, it was like he was seducing me just by walking—crawling—existing.

"Like what you see?" he asked.

I groaned, nodding my head, not even denying it.

He came to lay beside me, on his side with his head propped up on his hand. I didn't even think before I reached out to touch him, running my fingers over his heated chest. Under his baggy clothes, my mate was toned. The divide between his pecs with a slight smattering of hair, his stomach with the light markings of his abdominal muscles, and of course, the deep V of his hips disappearing under his boxers. He oozed sexual appeal.

One moment, I was just tracing him with my touch, the next I was pushing him back, crawling over him until my legs were on either side of his body. My center was directly over his boxers, so I could feel the thickness of him.

"Hannah—"

My name on his lips was like a beckoning call. I leaned forward, pressing our chests together until I reached his mouth, needing to taste him.

He groaned against my lips as I kissed him. I felt his hands come to my hips, pressing me harder against him as he sat up, never pulling his mouth from mine. Our heads almost touched the hanging fabrics, but I didn't care. My attention was on exploring his mouth, my hands on the back of his neck to keep him where I wanted.

At some point I had to pull away to breathe. Each inhale was full of our mixed scents—lavender and berry and arousal.

He leaned back in first, his fingers tightening around my waist as his tongue traced my lips, then went inside to play with my own. I felt him hardening even further against me, like a tease of what I could enjoy if he wasn't wearing underwear.

Then his lips moved, kissing down my jaw toward my neck, sucking on the skin like he wanted to mark me with a hickey. I never would've thought my neck was so erotic, yet I leaned my head more to the side, giving him more access.

When his lips moved lower, one of his hands moved to pull down my collar, giving him more access to my skin. I felt his tongue trace the bone there, moving toward the little dent at the base of my throat. He groaned, the sound vibrating from his lips, against my own skin, and exciting something deep in my core.

I started moving my hips, first forward and back, sliding down his hidden length, feeling how good it was to have pressure where I was starting to feel empty.

Then one of his hands moved between our bodies, stopping my movement when I had just started to feel the sparks of pleasure.

"Be good, omega," Zeke growled. "I'm going to give you pleasure."

I stuck my bottom lip out in a pout. What was that supposed to mean? I was always good. Like a fucking fairy and sweeter than chocolate that was melting on your fingers before you even lifted it to your tongue.

Any retort I had died on my lips when I felt Zeke's hand touch me. Not around my waist, or near my hip. Under my clothes. Over my center. Swiping through the dripping slick that I naturally produced buckets of every time I got aroused.

He didn't hesitate, shoving two fingers inside my core. Even with all the lubrication from my slick, his two fingers were still a stretch—the best kind in the world.

With the way his hand was positioned, the tightness from my clothes, each thrust with his fingers had the heel of his palm pressing against my clit.

I was trying to get words out, any words, praising him, begging for more, but I couldn't think past the pleasure. My thighs slammed down in opposition with his hand, increasing my desire even as my muscles began to ache. Only, the burn somehow made it better.

Zeke's free arm wrapped more tightly around my back, drawing me even closer to him. All the pleasure had me leaning my head against his shoulder, needing a break to breathe even though my movements never stopped.

I was planting kisses anywhere I could reach. His shoulder, his neck, his collarbone.

Throughout every part of my body, my pulse was pounding. Sweat was trickling down the sides of my head. We were both panting, breathing in each other's air. Even my stomach was tightening with my nearing orgasm.

The climax started in my core, reaching up and squeezing every muscle in my lower abdomen before tightening its hold around my lungs, forcing my scream to be quiet as the bliss wrecked every part of me. My head fell back, exposing my throat to my alpha in an ultimate sign of trust.

Until I realized that I couldn't seem to inhale. Immediately, my head sprang upward, banging my chin against my mate's head who'd been leaning down to kiss my neck.

"Shit. Fuck. Hannah, you okay, babe?"

Zeke lifted his head, and I watched his eyes

basically bulge as he stared at me. I knew my mouth was open, attempting to suck in any air I could manage, but my lungs weren't listening to me. My head was starting to become heavy on my neck, even as my thoughts were becoming harder to hold onto.

Then, Zeke started yelling. First the names of the other alphas then for them to call help as he moved me so I was lying on the mattress, on my side. I tried reaching for him, but he was too busy slamming a hand against my back, the other holding my shoulder steady.

Han was the first to arrive, just moments before Sebastian and Jackson.

Another set of hands started on my chest, rubbing circles, while someone else started pressing against my stomach. Blackness began creeping in at the edges of my vision before my neck was twisted at an awkward angle, and I was staring at Jackson.

"Breathe. Now." His alpha command rushed through me, and I finally managed to gasp in air, choking on the cold and dry feeling of it along my throat.

I heard Seb announce that he was getting me some water and then I was unceremoniously rolled onto my back as I sucked in lungsful of air.

"What the hell?" Han asked.

Zeke ran a hand over his head, his short hair not giving him anything to yank or pull on. He looked panicked—his eyes large, easily showing the whites, and his cheeks flushed with a slight red that was reaching down his throat. Even his chest was raising and falling a few inches with every heavy breath.

Trying to push my way to a sitting position was harder than it should be with Jackson attempting to forcefully push me back down. I swatted his hands away, glaring at the male before he finally let me up.

"She just stopped breathing," Zeke said. Then he

turned his attention to me, glaring at me. "What the fuck, Hannah?"

I threw myself toward him, wrapping my arms around his neck and inhaling his scent right at his neck where it seemed to be the strongest. "I'm sorry," I mumbled against his skin. His arms tightened around me so tightly that I could barely take a full breath, but I wasn't going to admit that.

"I'm sorry." Over and over again I apologized.

"You scared the shit out of me."

I felt the tears as they dropped off my nose and onto Zeke's chest. He was just barely rocking his body back and forth, taking me with him as he tried to soothe me. It was hard to feel comforted though when I could still scent the fear radiating from his skin.

"Here, princess, have something to drink." Sebastian ran a hand over my head, at least partially since I still had stitches on the back. The glass he offered had a lid with a straw, something I was grateful for since we were still in my nest and the fact that my hand shook when I reached out for it.

The ice-cold water was delicious, and I gulped probably half of it down before I came up for air.

"Now," Sebastian said, "what happened?"

Still on Zeke's lap, I leaned back and admitted, "He was fingering me, and when I came, I forgot how to breathe."

For a long minute, no one spoke. And then the alphas burst out laughing. Zeke didn't, but he did seem to lose some of his tension, his shoulders relaxing as a small smile tugged at his lips. When he rested his head on my shoulder, I ran my hands up and down his back, comforting him while also enjoying the freedom to touch him.

"You're okay?" Zeke whispered, barely loud

enough to hear over the others' laughter.

"I'm fine."

"Don't do that again."

That comment managed to get a chuckle out of me. Zeke lifted his head, moving in slowly to give me a soft kiss.

I sighed when he pulled away, completely content. "I think I had a small heat spike."

I hadn't noticed how fuzzy my thoughts had become until then. No longer completely blinded by any thoughts except being in my nest, it was obvious what had happened.

Sebastian nodded. "I'll call the hospital and ask about precautions."

There was nothing that could be done to stop my heat from coming. Suppressants only worked on heat symptoms—the biggest being pregnancy. If there had been something that stopped or even postponed my heats, I would've taken it.

"Do that," Jackson said, "then we'll have a proper pack meeting."

"Pack meeting?" I asked.

"We know you, rebel. But you don't know us. Until your memory comes back, we need to make sure you're feeling safe here. Like we did when we first started courting you."

It felt awkward, like this place was and wasn't my home simultaneously. But I knew their effort was with the best intentions. So I tried to shove down my irritation, making sure my scent didn't bloom with it, and agreed.

Chapter Five

As Sebastian was on hold, waiting to speak with my doctor from the hospital, a thought occurred to me.

"Do I have a phone?"

At the OC my phone was basically just used for everything except getting in contact with someone. An app for shopping deals? Yes. An app disguised as a social media platform to talk about omega rights? Also yes. Any phone numbers beyond my assigned doctor and all the required ones for the employees at the OC? Unfortunately, also, also yes.

"I'll get it," Han said. "I plugged it in, upstairs in your room."

"Oh, I can—"

Jackson bent down, gently pushing his shoulder into my stomach before lifting me up. He was surprisingly gentle considering I was essentially upside down. "No stairs."

Behind Jackson, Zeke winked at me, the male still only dressed in his boxers. The others were more dressed, at least slightly. Jackson wore a thin flannel jacket, unbuttoned so his stomach and chest were exposed. I swore I could feel the heat of his body where my thigh met his skin.

Sebastian was in a pajama set that almost looked like a suit as he paced between the kitchen island and the back of the living room couch. The two rooms were basically one considering how open they were. It made me wonder where the dining room was, but I guessed I would have a chance to explore properly later.

Carefully, Jackson lowered me off his shoulder, setting me down on one of the couches. There were three, all different, making a semi-circle toward the large brick fireplace that housed a television. The couches were silky and firm, and wide enough that they could probably pass for beds if needed.

In between each couch was a cute woven basket. When Zeke lifted the lid, I noticed it was full of blankets, more sarapes. Offering me one, I shook my head, and he took one for himself, gently placing it on his lap as he sat down on my left side.

Jackson sat on the low table set up in the middle of the living space. It was at the right height for someone to rest their feet on except the clues on the top clearly showed it wasn't meant to be a bench.

Someone had attempted to weave some fabric together, and considering how badly misshapen it looked, they weren't doing a very good job. I'd always wanted to be an artsy kind of girl, I just never actually sat down and did it. Maybe I could pick it up and try with my alpha. Could be a good bonding experience. Or maybe I'd already learned how to do it and I was teaching my alpha. Hopefully I didn't lose that skill and it was more instinctual than from knowledge.

Han came thumping down the stairs, his feet slapping against the hardwood flooring. He kissed the top of my head as he handed me a phone that was apparently mine.

It looked somewhat familiar. Just larger than I was used to, although not bulky. Tapping the screen, it showed a lot of notifications. Like, a lot. Some were from familiar apps, like the one where I found out where upcoming protests were happening. Most seemed to be messages though.

Dismissing everything, I stared at the photos as they appeared. So many. Full of a life I'd lived and couldn't remember. I looked happy, that was something, but it was weird to see me in a way I didn't know. Were we even the same person? Would that version of Hannah and myself react the same without knowing the experiences that made us who we were?

I jolted when hands touched my folded legs, having been so deep in my thoughts. Next to me, Zeke had reached over, his hand on my thigh and precariously close to my core. Han had appeared on my other side, kneeling in front of the couch and touching my knee. In front of me, Jackson had leaned closer, too, his elbows on his knees like he was a moment away from just grabbing me off the couch and pulling me onto his lap.

"We'll make new memories," Han said.

I nodded, trying to give him a reassuring smile. I didn't want new memories, though—no I did, I just also wanted my old ones too.

And worst of all, I couldn't seem to control my emotions. These pictures made me feel so disconnected with myself that I wanted to cry. It felt like my range of emotions were too extreme on either end, refusing to balance out and give me just a moment of peace.

I tried to find some inner happiness to pull on, something to replace the dissociation or to temporarily convince me that it was fine to forget large portions of my life. I found that happiness in remembering my first protest. It was a march, such a simple thing, and yet, I'd lied to the OC specialist assigned to me about where I was going. I'd slipped my alpha guard. The entire time I had been terrified, but it was so exhilarating.

That's who I was. Determined. Brave. Fucking intelligent beyond the means of any other omega in existence.

I forced myself to feel better, tucking away the dark emotions.

"You all good, princess?" Sebastian came into the

room, no longer on the phone and a deep frown over his features.

"Fine. Did the doctor give his permission for rough fucking?"

He chuckled, his gaze seeming to drop to the others. "We were recommended to wait as long as possible before giving in to your heat. Apparently, the trauma you sustained could cause your mind to react poorly to highly intensive situations."

His words jogged my memory of something I'd wanted to ask. "So, what happened? Like—" I raised my hands before gesturing to absolutely nothing.

"To put you in the hospital?" Seb asked.

I nodded. "You said I was pushed by an officer?"

"Pulled technically," Han said. The amusement in his tone died quickly, like he still couldn't even make the joke.

Sebastian told the story, at least from how much they saw. No one knew what happened that caused me to run from the protest, or why the officer was chasing me. According to them, they'd gotten so distracted by my injury that they forgot to notice the officer. Or the asshole running away.

Out of everything, what shocked me the most was that I was even at a protest. And these alphas didn't seem to care. They knew I was out in public without a chaperone.

"How come you all weren't there?" It was an innocent question. A genuine one, too.

That didn't stop the tension in the room from growing. I could scent the changes in the alphas, all of them, radiating guilt and shame. The dark emotions were turning their scents bitter, filling up the large living room until I felt like I was choking on it.

"Next time," Jackson gritted out, "we'll go with

you. We won't leave you alone again."

Um, that wasn't exactly what I'd asked. And despite the strong statement, both Han and Sebastian didn't seem to be on board. They shared a look, somehow a mix between worried and unsure.

"Jackson, we should talk about this," Seb said.

I tried to figure out what this division was. Were Sebastian and Han not in agreement that I should be allowed to go to protests? The two alphas did radiate a more prestigious vibe. Wealthier alphas almost required an omega in order to be taken seriously in society. Without one, alphas seemed too wild, too young, too poor.

Rather than wonder and pine secretly for an answer, I stared back and forth between Han and Sebastian, demanding, "You don't think I should protest omega rights anymore?"

Sebastian shook his head while Han immediately tightened his grip on my leg, saying, "That's not what he means. Of course, you should still protest. None of us agrees with the strict omega laws."

"What do you mean, then?"

On my opposite side, I could scent Zeke's emotional shift to amusement, but I didn't take my attention away from the other two alphas.

Seb adjusted his clothes, fidgeting slightly before managing any words. "My family—mine and Han's—are well-off. Not just financially, but socially."

My nose wrinkled in distaste which made everyone chuckle.

"Yeah, we know," he continued. "But at some point, we had decided it would be better to maintain the façade that comes from our family names."

Han squeezed my leg, dragging my attention to him. "We did it to protect you. Omegas are barely afforded any rights as it is, if the OC, the public, found out an omega was protesting, we don't know what that would mean for your designation. Most of the protests are done by betas. Whenever an alpha joins the forum in your app, you don't attend."

I frowned, unable to help it. How many protests was I missing because of this 'rule'?

"Plus," Seb added, "It also means we have the ear of certain important people."

That got my attention. "Really?"

"I work for a lab that's big with pharmaceuticals." He laughed when he saw my expression drop. "Trust me, it feels distant in the chain of power, but it's not nothing. And Han's family—"

"My family is rich. Old money. At the minimum, it helps convince people to look the other way. To accept a handshake filled with cash so we can get something done."

That made me feel … better. I'd apparently given up a little, but I wasn't alone anymore. And if we were negotiating new rules about being at protests or not, I had some thoughts to share.

It was Jackson who brought the conversation back on track, simultaneously pulling me out of my thoughts. "None of us knows what happened between Hannah being at the protest and where we found her. Did the officer mark her as an omega? Did she do something—"

"Hey." I glared at the alpha for the baseless accusation.

He just snorted. "Don't even bother, rebel. We know exactly who we mated. You're no innocent little omega."

Despite the words, I preened.

My hand started buzzing, more messages coming in on the phone. I felt bad ignoring them, but I wasn't sure how I was going to handle the other Hannah's friends. She might have had good taste in mates, I just didn't know if that would extend to random people. Anyways, I wouldn't get the jokes, the references. It was better to just wait.

"We've had this conversation a lot." Seb started pacing, staying in the room, just walking a few steps behind the little table Jackson was perched on. "Going with Hannah alerts everyone that there's an omega protesting. It'll cause a social epidemic."

"She can't go alone anymore," Jackson argued. "If they'd grabbed her, we'd have never known."

"We just need a new system." Zeke's words caught everyone's attention. Leaning back against the couch, the hand not touching me laying on the top of the cushions, he looked completely relaxed in this conversation. "Maybe we go but pretend to not know Hannah. Arrive at different times. Someone can protect her, and it might even act like a fake confirmation that no omega is present."

I nodded my head so hard I had to stop because the pain in the back of my head almost gave me an instant headache. "I like that idea."

Sebastian and Han seemed to consider this option, having their own private conversation. It must be nice to know someone so well that you could communicate silently with them.

"We're not saying no," Sebastian started. He stared right at me as he said the words before turning his attention to Jackson. "But I would like to remind everyone that all four of us are easily recognizable."

I glanced down at my clothes. They were still the same borrowed pajamas that I wore out of the hospital, so definitely not my style. Still, I couldn't imagine my style as one that blended in. Unless...

I gasped. "Am I boring now? Do I wear sad beige clothes like the beta counselors tried to convince me was somehow better on my instincts? Color theory is bullshit, by the way. There's no way that rhinestone bras and fishnet mittens make any difference in my temperament."

Still sitting on the small table, Jackson leaned closer, pinching my chin between his thumb and fingers. "Take a deep breath, rebel." He waited, actually waited until I'd done as he said, even if my breath was more of a puff of annoyance. "You're still you. Putting together crazy outfits that we tear off you because we can't stand not fucking you when you beam at us, so full of pride at whatever you've made that we actually get jealous of the fucking clothes you bedazzled and shit."

"Oh." His words were nice, probably, but it was his grip on my face, his stern glare, the way his crisp scent seemed to become stronger—

It happened faster than a blink. One moment, I was sitting on the couch, indulging in my mate, and the next, I was in Jackson's lap, my knees spread on either side of him as my lips hovered just a breath away from his. I wanted to taste him. He was mine, after all. I'd claimed him.

Except it wasn't *me* that claimed him. So, this last bit of distance made me hesitate.

Jackson didn't.

He wrapped his hand around the back of my neck and pulled me that last inch to his lips. Kissing him was different than Zeke. Jackson's bottom lip was thicker, giving him a perfect pout that I kissed and licked and bit. He let me explore, taking my time, but I wasn't under any illusion that I was the one in control.

When I pressed my tongue into his mouth, tasting him, I groaned, pressing closer to him like I could somehow fuse our bodies together, wanting to get closer than was even possible.

On and on the kiss went, my arousal growing stronger, until I had to pull away just to breathe. I rested my forehead against his, enjoying the feel of his length, hard and pressing in between my thighs.

I wanted more. My perfume was filling the air, letting everyone know how much I enjoyed that. I felt my internal muscles twitch, clamping down on nothing, reminding me that I was empty. Obviously, my body wanted more, wanted me to act on my arousal. This make-out session was a tease, and omegas never do well with that.

Leaning back, I stared at Jackson's brown eyes. Their color was dark, almost blending into the black part of his iris, yet still vibrant, almost like the color was glowing. I traced my thumbs under his eyes, admiring his masculinity.

He leaned forward, giving me one last kiss on my lips before resting his head on my shoulder. I felt his arms tighten even further around me.

For just a moment, I swore I could scent grief in his scent, just a hint of it before I lost the slight tendril.

As he sat up straight, I tucked my head against his chest. It felt … normal. My entire body relaxed into the position as if it was something familiar.

"Out of all of us, I think I'm the least recognizable," Zeke said, bringing the conversation back on track as if they hadn't just watched me learn the taste of one of my mates. "I could go with Hannah. Might even be able to appear like a beta?"

Lifting my head off Jackson's chest—and ignoring the grumbling sound of annoyance—I looked over at Zeke. He might be the smallest of all the alphas in this room, but that didn't make him any less alpha. It was more than just his ripped body or his height. Sure, alphas were typically strong and tall and whatnot. But omegas were usually quiet and fragile and small.

I was only one of those things. Unless I was wearing my platform boots, then I was none.

Zeke had the type of dominance that you'd only overlook once because you wouldn't get the chance to do it again. His size wasn't a weakness, it was camouflage. One look might have you dismissing him, but as soon as you looked away, you'd feel the pinprick warning on your neck that a predator was behind you.

Shaking my head, I admitted, "You'd never pass as a beta."

His chest seemed to puff up slightly, like he was proud of that statement. I hid my smile against Jackson's chest, enjoying the silent rumble coming from the large male.

"Do we even need to figure this out now?" Han asked. "It'll be some time before Hannah goes to another protest."

Since Han was almost directly behind me, I couldn't turn my head to see him, and I was way too comfortable with Jackson's purring to glare at him for his comment.

My silent annoyance didn't go unmissed though.

"You're still injured, Hannah," Han continued. "Not to mention your heat will be soon. Both of those factors aren't to be taken lightly. These protests are important, but not more so than your health."

I mumbled out an apology, hiding the blush on my cheeks from the chastisement. When he said it that way, it all sounded so logical. It seemed like I kept getting overly defensive of everything. Yet at every turn, these alphas proved they cared about me. It was startling and disjointing.

"There's something else that I think we've

forgotten to mention," Sebastian said.

I turned my head so I was leaning my opposite cheek on Jackson's chest and could see Seb as he spoke. He was closer now, no longer pacing.

"One of the reasons you haven't been to a lot of protests recently, was because you've been taking some online classes. You didn't want to risk getting detained to the compound and not being able to finish."

It took my brain a while to make the connection. School was never really my thing, hell, I barely even attended the mandatory classes at the OC. Plus, omegas weren't allowed to continue school after they packed-up. Technically it wasn't a law, although anyone who had heats wasn't allowed in a classroom, so it basically was. Designation bigots didn't need to use the proper terms to make unjust rules, they easily attacked the symptoms, claiming innocence afterward.

"College classes?" It was a question, a clarification, because I didn't understand how that was even possible.

Seb nodded. "We told you. Our families give us a sort of pull, a safety net of sorts that allows us to weave lies right above it. The classes are online only, and you're technically labeled as a beta, but you're a student at the local community college. You have a real profile backed by fake lab results that I submitted. Your first name is the same, but we changed your last name so you're not completely traceable."

I didn't truly understand how any of this was possible—and I didn't care. I was taking college classes. Maybe even able to get a degree as a beta. What that would mean for the omegas' rights movement ... I wasn't exactly sure, but it would be substantial, it had to be.

Excited energy was rushing through my body until I was squirming to get out of Jackson's lap. He growled playfully before letting me go.

I couldn't hold still, wanting to pace, wanting to look at my classes, needing to know more. At some point, I'd grabbed Sebastian's shoulders, needing to go up onto my tip toes to do so. "What degree plan am I on?"

"You haven't decided yet."

That didn't make any sense. I'd looked at colleges before. Hell, I'd even applied, over and over again, constantly being denied because of heat-protection laws, or because my previous education grades weren't good enough, or because my supposed application got lost. It was always something that stopped me from being able to legally attend—beyond my basic designation.

Apparently, a no wasn't bigoted if it wasn't directly stated that designation was the reason why. What a fucking joke.

Still, I'd looked at plenty of course catalogues. There were so many options! Art or science or math or literature or technology, it was so open to possibilities that I understood being overwhelmed.

"Can I apply to a major still?" I asked, unable to keep the hopefulness from my voice.

"Of course, princess. You'll just have to wait until the start of the next semester, apply like everyone else."

My smile was so wide that it was burning my cheeks, the muscles in my face straining to hold the happy composure. I bounced on my toes, ignoring the slight pounding that was starting in the back of my head.

I wanted to look at the options right then. I looked around for a laptop, quickly giving up when my attention snagged on my phone. Good enough.

Throwing myself back in between Zeke and Han, I started on my phone, trying to work it out so I could search through my options.

Options. It was my new favorite word. I'd been so

unfamiliar with it for so long and now it was like a rainbow, the colorful lights arching in a smile, representing beautiful possibilities at their ends.

I was still trying to figure out all the apps on my phone when my screen popped up with an image of a random female. And then, in my panic, as the ringtone started, I tossed the device across the room.

JOSEPHINE LIGHT

Chapter Six

As soon as the phone left my fingertips, I regretted throwing it.

I scrambled after it, glad that it seemed to land on the couch to the left rather than breaking against the brick fireplace or actually hitting anyone.

It was still ringing as I stared at the screen. Rather than a picture, I could actually see the female as she was apparently talking to someone behind her phone. She was pretty, slightly disheveled, though, and looking a little panicked every time she glanced down at the phone like she couldn't see me.

Then I realized the buttons suggesting I answer or end the call were still there. She was waiting still.

Holding up the phone to the alphas, I asked, "Who's this?"

"Koda Tucker," Sebastian said. "You just met her last month, but you've grown very close since. Talking every day, basically."

"Do I answer it?"

No one seemed to have a good response to that. Then, all of sudden, I was pressing the button to accept the call.

"Hannah, holy shit—guys, she finally answered. Hannah, where have you been? Are you okay? Why are you looking at me like that? Do I need to come over? Guys, I need to go see Hannah."

Zeke plucked the phone from my hand when words continued to refuse to come out. "Koda, Hannah is fine."

That made me snort, effectively helping me out of the trance from all the rapid-fire questions. If 'fine' meant memory loss, scalp stitches, missing chunks of hair, and a despondent feeling like I'll never belong, then sure.

I leaned over the arm of the couch, not in the view of the camera, but so I could still see Koda.

"Fine?" Koda shrieked. "She was attacked and sent to the hospital—"

Her words sent every alpha in the room on alert.

"How do you know that, Koda?" The demand came from Jackson.

His barked tone had someone on Koda's end growling in response. I watched a male pull Koda back against his chest, two other males appearing off to the sides like they were trying to see what was happening.

I whispered the question, "She's an omega?"

Zeke nodded, then shook his head, before turning to Sebastian. My blond alpha just mouthed the word 'later' which felt more ominous than comforting.

"Apologies, Koda," Jackson gritted out, not sounding sorry at all.

"It's okay," the female said. "Honestly, if what they're saying is true, I bet y'all are stressed over there. I've been trying to check in with Hannah and when I couldn't get ahold of her, I was starting to worry."

"We don't know what you're talking about," Han admitted.

Through the screen, her jaw actually dropped open. "It's literally all over the news, like trending right now. Hold on, let me pull up the article Jen showed me. Uh … here it is. *Omega gets attacked by so-called omega activists*. They're claiming a bunch of beta protestors attacked Hannah because she refused to join them. It also says that her injuries had her in the hospital."

"They got part of that right," I admitted.

"You were in the hospital?" she shrieked.

Zeke turned the camera in my direction, and I half

turned so they could see the back of my head.

"Oh, Hannah, your hair."

I had the same reaction when I saw the monstrous square of missing hair that made me look like a botched haircut gone wrong. It didn't help that the dark black stitches against the paleness of my scalp made the whole thing look even more extreme.

"What really happened? You told me you were going to the protest, and you'd text me later. Well, it's later."

"Um, I don't know," I told her. "Apparently the injury to my head caused some sort of memory loss."

I adjusted myself over the back of the couch, half leaning on Zeke's shoulders so I could better talk to Koda.

"Wait, hold on. You don't remember anything at all?"

"Nope. I lost a few years apparently."

"Years?" She screeched the word, making me wince even as I chuckled. "But how, I mean ... if you ... what does that mean exactly?"

"It just means I can't remember anything that happened in the last few years. Like meeting you or my mates—"

"You don't remember claiming your alphas?" Through the screen, I could see the whites of Koda's eyes turning red as she tried to stop herself from crying.

I shook my head, unable to admit the words out loud.

My mates all seemed to shuffle closer. Zeke turned so he could rest a hand on my shoulder. Jackson touched my ankle that was up on the couch's arm. Han adjusted so he was sitting sideways on the couch, facing Zeke, and stretching his arm out to press against my forearm. Even Sebastian moved out of the living room, into the hallway space so he was behind me, gently pressing against my back.

"Sebastian," one of the men behind Koda said. The alpha had blond hair, and an air to him like Han and Seb that made me think he probably came from money too. "They haven't identified you all yet, but there's photos circling with the four of you hunched over her. Someone is going to recognize y'all soon. Especially at the rate of popularity this is getting."

The concern in his voice had me turning to look at my mate, almost falling off the couch and making every single alpha lunge for me. I giggled, then gasped when Jackson slapped his hand down on my ass. It didn't hurt—the opposite actually, my mind instantly giving me delicious ideas of exactly how my heat will go.

My perfume bloomed, and Jackson chuckled.

"Has anyone reached out to you?" Seb asked the other male.

Some sort of private conversation happened on the other end before the blond sighed. "Yes, actually. My mother reached out. She said nothing that should be repeated, but she's at least seen it, I know that."

Sebastian nodded as if this information was helpful. I felt like I was somehow in the middle of the conversation despite having been the one to answer the call.

"Not to continue giving you bad news," Koda said. "But the news is also saying that the OC is currently investigating the circumstances. Like, right now."

Jackson and Seb both started searching the living room space, most likely for a remote. Han pulled me off the back of the couch, resettling me between him and Zeke. His arm rested over my shoulder, his hand squeezing the back of Zeke's neck.

The move was easy, like he'd done it a bunch of

times. I watched Zeke's face, looking for any signs that the move did something more to him than a simple gesture from another alpha packmate.

Then my attention was pulled toward the screen. Sebastian was frozen with the remote in his hand and my phone in the other.

"Again, our latest report on the victim of this devastating beta protest. To you Chelsea." The woman on the screen was replaced with another. "Thanks, Veronica. I'm still outside the restaurant where the protest took place just earlier this week. Both the local Omega Compound, and this district's peace officers, are unable to tell us what exactly happened since the issue is still under investigation."

I didn't recognize the restaurant behind the reporter, although it wasn't really what I was looking at. Next to her, a male in a suit stood, diligently waiting for his turn to speak. He was an older male, not so old as to have a full head of gray hair, but old enough that the fact he had no gray hairs was probably due to him dying it.

When she turned to him, resting her arm on his shoulder like a casual acquaintance, I knew the drama was about to start, my body leaning toward the TV in anticipation. "Representative Adam, what do you make of the protest that happened in your restaurant which led to the nearly fatal injury of an omega?"

Someone tried to speak, and I shushed them, waving a hand in the general direction of the noise.

"Obviously, something like this should never be allowed to happen again. Omegas need protection, we all know this. I'll admit, I too was blinded to the fact that even betas posed a threat to our gentlest designation, but this is just undisputable proof. Change needs to happen. Safety needs to be ensured."

She just let him prattle on, basically spouting his

entire political intentions for the news audience. Who was this guy?

"Will you be shutting down your restaurant?" the reporter asked.

"Of course not. This is my livelihood, and I won't let a failed mob control my decisions."

"And what about the omega that was injured? Anything to say to her?"

He looked directly at the camera. His eyes seemed to find mine through space and time and cameras and internet and pixels on a screen. "I would recommend she stays with her alphas, if she has some, or to claim a pack of alphas soon. For her safety."

Not even the pretend worried face he put on looked genuine. Honestly, it kind of creeped me out.

"Who is this guy again?" I asked.

"This is the asshole you were protesting," Koda said.

Sebastian handed my phone to Han who gave it back to me so I could still see Koda and her men on the other side. They looked distracted, too, like they were also watching the shit-show that was happening.

"He wants to start an age limit where omegas have to be mated by like mid-twenties or else they'll get assigned an alpha pack." Koda's words were surprisingly fierce, drawing my attention down to her and away from the ongoing reporter recapping the situation. "That doesn't even include the ridiculous motion he wants to add that all new packs should be alpha only."

I shake my head. "Aren't betas the majority of the populace? How can he just cut them out of packs?"

"Most betas don't join packs. We're raised with a sort of disdain for pack life. Not good enough to be an omega. Not good enough to be an alpha."

"That's ridiculous."

"I agree. But it's very real. Which means most betas aren't offended by not being allowed in a pack they never intended to join."

The number of our potential supporters was shrinking at an alarming rate. Still, that wasn't what my brain chose to focus on. "You're a beta?"

Koda chuckled. "Uh, kind of?"

My next question about what exactly that meant was lost when Han spoke up. "The question is, what do they mean by 'under investigation'? That rep already spoke with Hannah in the hospital. Either their sources are slow, or there's still shit going on behind the curtains that we're unaware of."

I groaned, a disgustingly familiar conversation coming to the forefront of my mind. "That beta. From the compound. She told me she was going to be randomly dropping in. Do you think that's what they mean?"

"I doubt it," Sebastian said, coming to kneel in front of me despite the limited space between the couch and the little table. He plucked the phone from my hands, tossing it off to the side for another alpha to catch. "She told us, too, that she'd be stopping by, so don't stress."

"They haven't said anything in a while about an update on the omega," Han pointed out. "It's all the same images, the same information about you needing to go to the hospital. Nothing after that. No status on if you're going to live or not."

Just the mention of my death had Jackson glaring at Han.

"Do you want to reach out to someone?" Koda asked, barely getting the words out before several alphas, both mine and hers yelled, "No."

My eyebrows raised at the vehement response from Sebastian and Han. The former quickly explained,

"Media work is tricky. At the moment, keeping them in the dark is the only option until we figure out the best route we're going to take."

"What does that mean?" I asked. "What routes are there?"

"Right now, they're using you as a tool to push forward their own agendas."

"Exactly. I need to stop them." Even more, I needed my mate to see that.

"I know. And we will. But I promise you, if you reach out to a reporter, they might talk to you. They'd be sympathetic and give you a temporary voice. Then the cameras would shut off, and they'd switch back to the newsroom. You have a documented case of memory loss, which they'll point out. On top of that, all it would take right now is a little investigative work to confirm that you are a bonded omega that was out, at a protest, without your alphas. They'd force you back to the OC, pull you away from us."

Every instinct in my body rejected the words. Not the truth, the idea of being pulled from my alphas. We were bonded. It wouldn't just turn them feral, but me too.

My words were caught in my throat, wanting to come out to argue yet stuck.

Sebastian didn't have the same problem, continuing his speech. "If I'm honest, this representative is doing us a favor. He's turning the attention away from you. He might be using your designation, but not you specifically. It's like hiding in plain sight."

"If he wins…" I whispered, just barely able to get my voice to work.

"He won't. We won't let him. But we have time. Time to fight this battle on a different front, using your designation, not you, specifically. Let us try, princess."

"What do we do, then?"

Sebastian pinched my chin, his gaze a mix of sadness and determination. "I don't know yet. But I promise you, we won't stop trying to protect you and other omegas. Trust us."

He was looking for my agreement, for reassurance that I wouldn't go around him and talk to the media anyways wielding a metaphorical sword to this very real battle. As much as I hated it, I easily agreed. Old Hannah trusted these alphas, and so far, I did too. They weren't keeping me out of the decision, just telling me to wait.

As much as I felt like the power of my honest words would be enough to persuade everyone to believe me, to believe in my cause, I'd learned the hard way it wouldn't be enough. What would an interview on TV do that a protest didn't? That a sit-in didn't? That a march or provocative dress didn't?

"Okay," I told him. "I'll wait."

"Good girl, princess."

A delicious shiver ran through my body at his words. I felt the hairs on my arms raise, also excited by his tone.

"So," it was Koda's long, drawn-out word that finally pulled my attention from my blond alpha, "does this mean I can come see you. I'd really like to check you over with my two eyes."

She had a bit of a whine in her words, something her mates seemed to notice too since they all squeezed closer to her and more in frame.

"Hannah is going to be starting her heat, soon," Zeke said.

"I'll be really quick."

One of her mates growled, "I don't like the idea of you near alphas whose mate is about to go into heat."

Koda and I both looked at each other, mentally mapping out his verbal route.

"My mates don't mind, do you?" I looked around the room, expecting four nodding heads. I found none. Their scents were already rising, becoming territorial. "Uh, maybe after my heat?"

Then everyone seemed to nod.

Koda and I hung up after I promised to stay in touch. I could tell by the look on her face that she was worried I wouldn't. Maybe it was wrong, but I wasn't feeling as disconnected with Koda as I was with my mates. I still hadn't remembered her. It was just easier to accept a new friendship with her than forever with four alphas.

Although, easier, didn't mean easy.

My finger hovered over the button to delete all of my saved messages. Jokes that I wouldn't get, and references that would confuse me, or plans that I'd forgotten. I didn't want them there, lurking over me like a possibility that may never happen. Memories were impossible to see in the brain, so no one knew whether I'd get mine back. And it was that bastardly speck of hope that had me backing out, keeping all the messages and pictures of another life.

Annoyed with myself, I shoved my phone into the couch cushions, content with the little phone prison.

"I'm hungry," I declared, getting up to make my way to the kitchen.

All four of the alphas spoke at the same time, asking what I wanted, demanding I sit back down, wanting to know what I was craving.

I had to press my lips together tightly to keep from laughing. Considering they were bonded to me, my attempt at hiding my amusement was impossible. Still, I answered, "Something savory. Like a potato but smothered in cheese. Or maybe some of that round pasta with a cheese sauce? Oh, oh, maybe breaded cheese that we can fry up?"

"I'm sensing a theme," Zeke said. He lifted me up onto the kitchen island, standing between my legs like it was a totally casual thing for him to do.

Han was looking through the massive fridge while Seb opened a door that went into a walk-in pantry. My jaw dropped at that.

The alpha in front of me chuckled. "There's five of us in this house. We eat, a lot."

After shutting the door, and getting a shake of the head from Seb, Han said, "Unfortunately, we don't have a lot here. How does delivery sound?"

"Well, I want—"

"We know, rebel," Jackson said, already scrolling on his phone. "Something with cheese."

I huffed, turning my nose up, feigning a propriety I didn't have.

When a hand forcibly turned my face toward Jackson again, I could see the feral gleam in his eyes. This was an alpha, dealing with an omega's attitude. It made me want to run—not out of fear—to be chased.

My perfume bloomed, hinting at the excitement that I was almost shaking with.

Slowly, so slowly, Jackson leaned closer. Between my legs, I could still feel the firm body of Zeke, but the alpha didn't move as Jackson lowered his lips near my neck. His hand around my jaw turned my head again before I felt his lips finally press against my nape.

And then my entire body seemed to relax. My muscles losing every inch of tension.

When he pulled away, still close enough that I felt his breath against the little hairs on my neck, I whimpered. I wanted more. That spot was perfect.

"That's where my claiming mark is, rebel," Jackson said.

I was nodding along to his words, already agreeing to everything, nothing, anything if it meant he would kiss me there again.

"Do you know why it's on the back of your neck? Not the side?"

Words didn't exist. What did he want? Yes. No. I wasn't sure.

"Because you like to run. And I like to chase you. Then when I catch you, I make you present for your alpha. Head down, ass up."

Slick was leaking from my core. I tried to press my hips closer to Zeke, hoping he'd give me the friction I needed, or even better, touch me like he had before. His hands were on my thighs, his thumbs so close to where I needed them.

Still, neither was committing. The tease thrumming through my body didn't make me compliant. No, it was like a spark over the liquid in my veins.

I growled, reaching out with one hand to pull Jackson that last inch that separated us, and with my other, I dragged Zeke's hand right where I wanted him.

Jackson took over the kiss, demanding all my focus and attention to give him as good as I was getting. Each nip, lick, suck had more slick pouring from me. I had no idea whether it was because my heat was so close, or if it was just always like this with my mates.

My attention was so focused on my lips, I jumped when I felt the cool press of a finger against my clit. I was pretty sure I had never been so sensitive there before, but the anticipation, the need, was building tension in all my nerves.

I wrapped my legs around Zeke as best I could without seeing, ensuring he didn't pull away until I was done with him.

I think he chuckled? The sound was a rumble I

felt up my legs like a vibration on the lowest setting.

When I pulled away from Jackson, just an inch, needing to breathe, I inhaled the scents of four aroused alphas. All of them mixed together, an array of mouthwatering smells that I wanted to pour onto a pillow and inhale constantly.

Was it possible to become addicted to an alpha's scent?

"What happened to waiting until her heat starts?" Sebastian demanded. "Or going over limits?" The male had his arms crossed over his chest, attempting to look stern despite the obvious arousal bulging in his pants. It was an impressive bulge, too.

I hadn't kissed Sebastian yet. Or Han. And I really wanted to.

Jackson was demanding. Zeke was all-consuming. How would my other alphas touch me? Would Sebastian let me take the lead? Did Han like to play any sort of game? They were my mates after all, and if I was going to spend the rest of my life bonded to them, it was important to know how we all interacted sexually, right?

My body was craving my alphas. Zeke's touch, Jackson's kisses, I needed more. I was already aroused, my body taut with the anticipation of more. The pressure on the back of my head was barely noticeable. If that was my only injury, I was sure that sex would be fine so long as no one pulled my hair.

"See something you like, princess?" The question was cocky, and I wasn't even ashamed to realize I was still staring at Sebastian's bulge in his pants.

"Definitely." My mouth watered like it was already anticipating the taste of him.

"No can do. A conversation still needs to be had about what everyone's preferences are and then we're supposed to be waiting until your heat starts."

That brought my attention to Sebastian's face. I glared at the smirk on his lips.

"All right." Han clapped his hands together, the resounding smack catching all of our attention. "Let's take a breath. Jackson, did you order the food already?"

"Of course, I did."

"Then maybe a tour is in order before the food gets here."

"She's not supposed to go up and down stairs," Seb said.

Between my legs, Zeke turned around. He grabbed my arms, winding them over his shoulders before holding onto my thighs as he lifted me off the table. Despite the wetness between my thighs, Zeke pulled me as close as possible to him. Resting my chin on his shoulder, I was completely content, enjoying the heat radiating from his bare back.

I was still aroused, but that excitement was being overshadowed by my curiosity—just barely. Not only was I curious about the home I had supposedly been living in, I was also wondering if something had the potential to rejog my memory.

"Be careful," Jackson snapped.

Turing around, I gave a finger salute that had the alpha glaring at me.

"Mind if I join the tour?" Han looked at the two of us, his scent spiking as if he was imagining something more. Was it just watching Zeke and I together? Or the possibility of the three of us?

"Sure."

The first floor was what the alphas had coined, the family space. It had a dining room on the opposite side of the kitchen, hidden away from the living space and making it more private. A large wooden table with decorative black stained metal legs was the main focus of the room. Benches on the long sides and regular chairs on the short ones, it was set up for double the number of members of this pack.

Outside the dining room there was also a gathering room, which, according to Han, was like a living room but rather than the pack relaxing there, it was for whenever we had guests. There wasn't a TV in this space, but it had a bookshelf full of boring literature and even a little bar full of alcohol that made me wrinkle my nose.

"Where's the blender?" I asked, as Han was raising different bottles up for me to see. "Or something colorful. Everything is brown. Don't you have any mixers?"

"This is mostly for show," Han said like having dozens of bottles of hard drinks and wine was typical. "Your fruity little drinks are in the pantry back in the kitchen."

I nodded, expecting the answer. I still didn't understand what the purpose of this room was, but I didn't say that as we continued the tour.

There were two bathrooms down here, both massive with their own little room inside for the toilet so there was a separation while someone showered. Was I slightly disappointed that there wasn't a bath? Yes and no. At least the showers were massive, probably meant for three people at a time with the number of showerheads attached to the walls and ceiling.

Finally, we made our way upstairs. The second floor was full of offices. Han apparently was the only one that worked from home, but the others had an office for the times when their work followed them home. This floor also had the laundry room, which I'd thought was odd.

And then, the third floor. All the bedrooms and

my nest were up there. This level didn't have any windows, completely relying on the warm orange glow from the dangling fixtures to provide any sense of light. Now that I noticed it, all the lights had a dim sort of hue to them rather than the bright whites from the hospital, or even at the OC.

Up here, I loved the scents that had soaked into the walls. The second floor smelled good too, but there was also stress on that level. And the first was so open and mixed with scents of cooking and cleaning that it just didn't hit as strong.

On this level, I was content to lay down on the hard flooring if someone just gave me a blanket and a pillow. Before I could suggest this, however, I heard a faint chime ringing up from the stairs.

It was an elegant noise, even if I could barely hear it. "What was that?"

"Doorbell. Food must be here already," Han said.

My stomach took the opportunity to rumble in excitement at his words, making Zeke laugh who must have felt the demand for food against his back.

Zeke took his time down the stairs, careful not to jostle me too much. As soon as he landed on the first level floor, I wiggled to get down, absolutely desperate for the food I could already smell. I moaned, my stomach rumbling again for the greasy goodness.

All of my hunger seemed to disappear at the sight of the front door, open, my mates standing just barely inside the house. Between them, I could make out a female, a red bag under her arm that she must have used to carry all the food Jackson was holding.

It wasn't that she was a female, or that she was exceptionally pretty with her tall stature, tight shirt that shaped around her breasts, and the perfect curl to the tips of her hair tucked under a hat. It was her smile, the way she was leaning toward them, her foot, crossing the threshold of the doorframe like she was *expecting* to be invited in.

I wasn't even aware of Han and Zeke, the two attempting to pull me back toward the kitchen. Then Han stood in front of me, blocking my view, and making my imagination go wild—

What if she touched my mates?

I just seemed to snap.

JOSEPHINE LIGHT

Chapter Seven

I had no idea how I got out of Zeke's grip, or how I managed to get around Han, but suddenly I was lunging for the female, soaking in the scent of her fear as it overpowered her very obvious arousal toward my mates.

It was Sebastian who managed to catch me before I did any real damage to the female. His arms were tight around my stomach, my attention not willing to part from my retreating prey for long enough to figure out how to get out of his hold.

When the door slammed shut, blocking out my view from the retreating beta, I still hadn't calmed down.

Claim them. Remind them they're yours. Remind everyone.

I listened to my instincts, turning around in my mate's arms and climbing him until I was close enough to press my mouth to his. He needed to be aroused. I wanted him to be hard for me and only me.

My mouth was desperate on his and he let me explore. I felt him adjust his grip around my ass, squeezing each cheek as he held me against him. I ran my hands up to his hair, feeling the short blond strands between my fingers.

I felt a dull pain in my lower stomach which reminded me just how empty I was.

Kissing wasn't enough.

I started pulling at the fabric over his body, ripping where I could, yanking at other spots, unbothered by the burn on my thighs as I worked to get my mate naked. When his chest was finally bare, I leaned forward and licked the space between his pecs, humming at his taste on my tongue.

Behind me, voices were nothing more than noise, no more indistinguishable than a bunch of motionless vibrations.

Limbs seemed to be getting in my way, I couldn't figure out why I wasn't moving down to reach my alpha's cock. Every time I reached for his hardness, it was like my arm found its way back to my mate's shoulder.

My annoyance bubbled out of me with a growl as I tried, again, to reach my alpha's knot.

When I was denied, my temper flared. Already the dark haze in my mind was blocking most of my conscious thought, but my anger made me close to feral.

I felt my arms being pulled tight behind my back, my front pressed against the delicious hard scent of a tropical fruit. Beating hard against his chest, his heart was a strong steady presence.

At some point, I'd closed my eyes. Another pain in my core had me groaning, trying to bring my arms back around to curl against my stomach except I couldn't break whatever hold kept them locked behind me.

Cool tears ran down my cheeks, letting me know how hot my body was. I didn't want space though, no, I needed my alphas closer. They could take away this pain. I needed them, all of them, and more importantly, their knots.

Once this cramp seemed to pass, I took a deep breath, realizing we'd changed locations. I could smell my nest. The sense of safety it invoked meant I could instinctually recognize it with my eyes closed.

The room was dark, the lights even dimmer than the rest of the house. I squirmed out of my mate's grasp, landing on the floor to my nest just past the door's threshold.

I knew the others were nearby, but right now, my focus was on my nest. Of course my mates hadn't satisfied me yet, I hadn't made a nest. This was our safe place. No one could give over to their instincts until I'd prepared it properly.

First, the pillows. I started with the back walls, yanking all the pillows away and fluffing them before setting them back. The stuffing inside a particular pillow refused to even out, and that one got tossed from the bunch.

Then, onto the next wall. Working through the heat cramps that bowed me over, each one getting stronger and longer. And the next wall. Around the entrance to the nest, it was a little more difficult, but I prepped the pillows near the door for when it was finally closed.

Once the outer layers of the nest were set up how I liked, I made my way into the middle. Before I fixed the blankets onto the ground in the perfect half wall, I made the final adjustments to the pillows.

A square nest was not ideal. Round. Not circular, ovular. Corners needed to be shaped properly. The whole thing should be wide enough for my mates to sit in comfortably while waiting to knot me.

I was sweating by the time I finished all the pillows.

For the blankets, I folded them longways, wrapping one on top of another on top of another, until they were halfway up the pillow's height, bordering in the perfect shape of the nest.

"This is a very nice nest, omega. Can we come in?"

The voice belonged to my first alpha. He liked my nest.

"Yes, yes, in."

Apples, green ones, juicy and fresh that had water dripping down your chin with each bite.

Guava, sweet and airy, the perfect concoction for relieving any stress.

Pumpkin, spiced with cinnamon, a comfort equivalent to being calm and safe and free.

Berries, a mix of so many, sweet and tart and diverse yet completely mouthwatering.

Just the scents of all my mates nearby had even more slick leaking from me. My stomach cramped again, this time more painfully than before. It eased slightly when I felt one of my mates pull me tight against their body, his hand sliding down to rest on my lower abdomen.

I groaned at the tease. I wanted him inside me.

Attempting to scramble off his lap, I pressed my chest against the floor's mattress, lifting my hips so high that I could feel the deep curve of my spine to accommodate the position. I was ready to be fucked. My nest was made and safe. All my mates were inside. And I was presenting like a good omega.

Against the back of my thighs, I felt my first alpha press against me. Even without my nose telling me it was him, I knew he'd demand the first rutting in my heat.

His hand ran down my spine, admiring my position for him. I felt his hands wrap around my hips, squeezing like he was trying to get his fingers to touch all the way around me. This waiting was killing me. More slick was leaking out of me, and I could feel the tell-tale signs of another heat cramp wanting to begin again.

I tried wiggling my hips, whimpering, anything to get him to act, to stop hesitating. If he was demanding anything, I couldn't hear it. My ears felt stuffed, my thoughts only existing about my mates, and my body internally weeping for the pleasure I knew would come from my mates.

Whatever was holding him back, he finally aligned the head of his cock with my entrance and shoved his way in, not stopping until he was fully inside me.

I clawed at the bedding, loving the feeling of complete fullness from my mate.

He didn't hesitate, leaning over me so I felt his stomach flush against my back, one of his hands releasing my hip to hold my nape down, and then he started thrusting into me.

His cock was so large, it took effort for him to push inside me. I did my best to push back against him, adding to the friction and the force of the pleasure.

Now that he was inside me, I needed more. Needed him to come. To knot me.

Pleas were falling from my lips. I clenched my internal muscles to try and force his cock to come inside me.

The hand around my nape tightened, not squeezing my breath, just letting me know that he was feeling his own pleasure. A smile pulled at my lips, loving that my alpha was enjoying himself.

A loud smack followed by heat on my ass had me groaning. There was no pain, only pleasure. Again and again, I felt a hand come down on my cheeks until my mate groaned, rutting into me without any hesitation.

I was so close to an orgasm, my body naturally holding it off until he finally pressed into me again, his knot expanding inside me, and I exploded over the edge, pure bliss reaching every muscle in my body and wrapping around my entire being.

Stuffed inside my pussy, I could feel each jerk from my mate's member, each flood of his cum.

My body relaxed, no longer primed to beg and plead, temporarily content to feel locked against my mate. His knot made his cock even larger, swelling against the walls of my inner being and pressing until there was nowhere else for him to go. We were linked, bound to each other for this temporary blissful moment.

He turned us so we laid on our sides. Another of my mates came to my front, his guava scent barely registering as he pressed in close. I was surprised that my first alpha let my other mate near while I was still on his knot, but I loved having more of my mates close.

A slight rumbling came from my own chest, pleased that I was surrounded, bound, and blissed. I fell asleep, content to let my mates watch over me as I was stuck on my alpha's cock.

Sometime later, my body started to ache again, letting me know that my mate's knot was about to loosen, and I would need to take another. I grabbed at the alpha in front of me, kissing him in preparation for his knot next.

When I reached down to feel his length, something caught my attention. I forced my eyes open, staring down at my alpha's dick and trying to figure out what was different. A piece of something was attached to the tip and the under part of his mushroom shaped head.

My fingers carefully traced over each round piece, and my mate groaned. I almost pulled my hand away, worried I'd hurt my mate until his scent hit me—full of arousal and amusement. He liked this.

I wiggled away from my first alpha, ignoring the rush of cum that leaked from me as I pulled off his knot completely. He was still hard, his length wet from our mixed arousals and pressing against my cheeks.

This new alpha pulled me until I was on top of him, my legs spread on either side of him. Leaning forward, I rested one hand against his chest, feeling his heart pound under my fingers, and the other I reached in between my legs, helping to guide my entrance onto his considerable length.

Each inch I lowered myself down, it was—I felt the two round pieces inside me, pressing against my inner walls like a goddamn internal massage. I whimpered, unable to explain how good he felt.

My mate wasn't as large as my first alpha, but those pieces on his dick made his length just as fun to take.

As soon as he was all the way inside me, I squirmed, trying to figure out the best way to move. My knees were spread wide on either side of his body, just barely reaching the mattress. I couldn't put enough force down to ride him like I wanted.

The words asking for help were lost in the cloudiness of my mind, in the thickness of my tongue. I whined, the sound begging for help and making all four of my mates growl.

Under me, I felt hands move my legs so rather than my knees on the mattress floor, my feet were. It spread my hips wide, like the most intense squat, and the presence of my mate inside me only became stronger—fuller. Hands grabbed my wrists and moved them from my mate's chest to his stomach, better supporting my position.

Then I felt it, his hands on my ass, helping to raise me up and drop me back down. I immediately figured it out, using my thighs and hips to bounce on top of him.

Someone grabbed my neck, turning my face toward lips demanding a kiss. Their apple scent and thickness immediately told me who it was.

Against my first alpha's lips I begged my mate under me to knot me. No matter how good he felt inside me, my ultimate goal wasn't to get fucked—it was to milk my mates' cocks for all of their cum.

"Please knot me, alpha. Please, I want you to fill

me with your cum."

I felt the vibration of my mate's groan under my hands. Tearing my mouth away from my first mate, I leaned over so I could kiss my alpha under me, needing him closer to his climax.

He opened his mouth for me, letting me explore and tease my tongue against his. Together, our pace started to become brutal, his hands helping to slam me down against him as he thrusted up into me.

Slick poured from me, running down my mate's hips as my body made more in preparation for his knot. Someone was catching just enough to wet the tip of their finger and press it against my clit.

I screamed in pleasure, just that little bit of pressure enough that my body wanted to come but held back until my mate started knotting me.

My head fell onto his chest as I continued to sink harder onto him. Words that I hoped were pleas came pouring past my lips until he finally moved his hands toward my hips and held me down, his knot forming.

The pleasure had my climax shattering me until I was more a lump of bones and muscles and nerves than an actual conscious person.

I was heaving in air, trying to remember how to breathe as I rested on top of my mate. Each pulse from his cock had my inner muscles tensing to keep as much cum inside me as possible.

Hands ran over my thighs, rubbing them and moving my legs so my knees were back down on the floor. I sighed, feeling completely comfortable and safe in that moment. My eyelids fluttered shut as I inhaled the tropical scent. Mixed with arousal, it was basically sex on the beach.

More time passed as I waited for my mate to finish filling me with his cum. I wanted to trace my fingers down his chest and stomach, but just the thought of moving my arms or even my fingers, felt like too much.

Eventually, the knot inside me was shrinking, the mixed cum from our arousal making me sad as it dripped out from my core.

I barely had time to mourn the loss of another knot when my body warned me it wouldn't allow me enough time to do anything but find another cock to mount. My lower abdomen clenched in a small cramp, reminding me of my body's demands.

"Knot," I demanded.

Before I could position myself back on my mate's cock again, I was lifted off, the scent of pumpkin keeping me calm and arousing my excitement. My mouth began to water, like it was excited for a taste of something to come.

"You'll get your knot, omega," the alpha behind me said.

We were both on our knees, my alpha positioned behind me. He wrapped one arm around my hips and the other around my chest, keeping me pinned against him. His mouth came down to plant kisses against my neck and shoulder until I went pliant in his grasp.

Someone traced a finger along my cheek, and I snapped my head up, not knowing when I relaxed it against my mate's shoulder. There was a dull ache coming from there and I ignored it. Nothing would hurt more than the cramps if I didn't get knotted soon.

The scent of berries was in front of me, their mix of sweet and sour already burning my cheeks with the delicious flavor.

"Want to taste me, omega?" my alpha asked.

Yes. I lunged for him, desperate for a taste but was stopped by the alpha still pinning me against him.

"Patience, omega."

I whimpered.

"Yes. Now, do as you're told. Get on all fours and open your mouth for your alpha. Tongue out."

His words were hard to fully understand, yet my body seemed to move of its own accord. This time, rather than lowering my chest to the ground, I stayed up on the palms of my hands. Even though my knees remained on the floor, I spread them a few more inches apart so my mate behind me could easily press against me.

As soon as I stuck my tongue out, I tasted the precum leaking from my mate's cock. It was so delicious, like someone had blended up a bunch of different berries and I was able to drink it down.

I licked at the head, demanding more of the taste.

"Take him deeper," a voice recommended.

I obliged, pulling off first to lick all around his dick, getting him nice and wet before taking him back into my mouth. As I worked on taking him deeper, suddenly craving the feel of him at the back of my throat, my mate behind me started to play with my body.

He gripped both of my cheeks in his hands, spreading them like he wanted a full view of every inch of me. Then he dipped his fingers into my drenched core, his barely curved fingers pressing against my inner walls. It took my blurry brain a few extra moments to figure out what he was doing—dragging out all the cum left inside me from my other mates.

When he finished, I heard him say something that had my mate in front of me pulling away. I tried to reach for him but was distracted by the fingers suddenly waving in my face. I could see the wetness dripping between the two tightly pressed fingers and I knew what my mate wanted. Leaning forward, I took them into my mouth, tasting my slick and my mates' cum.

I cleaned off the fingers until he pulled them away. I mewled at the loss, the sound cutting off when he pressed himself against my entrance and then slowly pushed all the way inside.

Tapping against my lips, I felt the head of my other mate's cock, not even hesitating as I licked it again, taking it into my mouth.

That taste of arousal on his tip made me suck harder, wanting more.

My two mates and I were pulled into a vicious cycle. I sucked on the berry flavored cock, making my alpha groan and flex his hips for more, effectively turning on my mate behind me, thrusting harder into my core which forced me to take my alpha deeper.

The scents of berries and spiced pumpkin somehow complemented each other. They weren't too sweet or too fruity.

"I'm almost there," my alpha behind me said.

Every muscle in my body seemed to understand those words, clenching down harder and releasing more slick to encourage his knot.

"Listen to me, omega." A hand touched my cheek and I leaned into it as best I could with my head still on his cock and my neck unable to move too much. "I'm going to knot your mouth. That means you won't be able to pull away, understand?"

All I heard was the word 'knot' and I was nodding my head. I wanted a knot, his knot.

The alpha growled, his frustration tainting his arousal. I didn't like that at all.

When he tried to pull out, I felt my own panic start to rise, my instincts telling me that my alpha was rejecting me. Then he stopped pulling away just as the tip of his head was still in my mouth.

Around me, male voices were talking, and even

though I couldn't truly understand their words, I recognized all the voices as my mates'. I worked even harder to please my alpha, licking and sucking and just barely scraping my teeth along his glands, taking him deep in my throat again like I knew he enjoyed.

Some decision seemed to have been made because my pumpkin scented mate behind me started taking me roughly, his hands around my hips helping to pull me back harder onto him. I was pushed and pulled between the two cocks, and I loved every minute—every second of it.

My mate between my legs came first, knotting me and making me call out around my other mate's cock in pleasure. Then I felt it, the slight increase against my tongue, forcing it flat against the bottom of my mouth as my alpha's knot grew. He was locked in place behind my teeth, forcing me to breathe through my nose.

This orgasm truly did reach every part of me. From my tongue and cheeks to my stomach and even down to my toes. I was just a body of pleasure, completely relaxed and unaware of everything except the two knots and the electric bliss occasionally shocking my nerves.

Carefully, and so, so slowly, both mates seemed to move in unison, lowering all three of us against the nest's mattress. My head was gently placed on my alpha's thigh and the rest of my body turned sideways as well, the alpha behind me curving his body against mine so that both our heads were resting on the same leg.

I loved feeling my alpha's cum settle in my stomach even if I wished to taste it. As my eyes closed, I enjoyed the feeling of so many hands touching me. Petting my hair, squeezing my ass, fondling my breasts, even peppered kisses along my face as if the pair of lips was drawing each of my features.

A purr started up in my chest, and four answering ones responded. This moment was the best in my life.

Unfortunately, knots didn't last forever. I lost both eventually and then I was ready for more. My heat demanded only knots and cum.

When one of my mates waited too long to start fucking me, my lower abdomen and core would spasm with painful cramps, reminding me that I needed to be filled.

There was no time for sleep except when I was knotted onto a cock. If my mates took me two at a time, however, my orgasm would be so strong that it would knock me out for even longer. And on the rare occasion that I got three of my four mates at one time, I completely blacked out after that.

I had no idea how much time passed—and I didn't care.

And then, what felt like randomly, with a knot lodged into my core, I felt the fog of my heat officially clear.

JOSEPHINE LIGHT

Chapter Eight

I didn't want to leave my nest. Despite my heat being over, my instincts were telling me it was a terrible idea to leave the safety of my nest. All my mates were together, their scents clinging to the room that forced me to taste them with each inhale.

"C'mon, rebel, I've ordered food." Jackson's cajoling didn't intrigue me the way he'd probably anticipated. When he exhaled loudly, I knew he was feeling my emotions turn bitter.

Remembering everything that happened in a heat was nearly impossible when it took so many days. No one ate or drank anything during that time, which was technically fine since our bodies had gone into a sexual hibernation of sorts.

As soon as that cloud cleared our minds and bodies, I remembered everything before that—not my actual memories, just the way the delivery woman flirted with my mates. And more importantly, the way they didn't tell her to fuck off.

The physical part of my heat might be over, but my hormones were still going crazy. Logically, I knew it would only take an extra day or two for all the emotional demands to finally seep from my system … until then, I was screwed feeling wildly extreme.

I had a sarape wrapped around me, my fingers playing with the tasseled ends.

A part of me wanted to yell at them for letting her touch them and the other part wanted to cry because they hadn't stopped her. Somewhere, in the furthest part of my conscious thoughts, there was a tiny logical voice that said they hadn't actually done anything. That voice wasn't loud enough to drown out the shouting of my worries.

Was it because I was no longer the same Hannah they'd bonded with? Were they happy with this new, potentially permanent, version of myself that meant starting over? Would they rather just start over with someone else?

Fingers grabbed my chin, pulling my face alarmingly close to Jackson's. His natural features already looked stern, but it was amazing how dangerous he appeared when he was actually glaring at me, anger radiating from him.

"Knock it off. You're our mate, Hannah. You. It doesn't matter that your memories are lost because you're still the same little rebel omega."

"What if I'm not?" My question was whispered so quietly, I was actually surprised that he could hear it, let alone anyone else.

Zeke came up next to me, rubbing his cheek against mine in a soothing gesture. "Then we'll love this new version of you."

"Why don't you come out of the nest, and we'll talk about everything that's concerning you?" Sebastian recommended.

I glared at the male for his suggestion.

"You need food, Hannah," Han said. "And the sooner you get out of the nest, the quicker this need to stay in here will leave, too.

I grumbled under my breath as I made my way to the nest door. I moved as slowly as possible. Mostly out of spite, but also because I barely felt strong enough to crawl to the door.

Jackson reached over me, opening the door that led to the hallway on the third floor. Despite the typically soft orange glow, it felt too bright against my eyes. I tried turning back into the nest, content that I'd failed in leaving when I ran directly into my alpha. He lifted me up, letting me hide my face against his chest as he carried me away from my nest.

I was already shaking my head, complaining that this was an absolutely terrible idea. The stairs were even brighter than the hallway and when we reached the bottom floor, I had a headache from how bright the lights were—or maybe it was about how strongly I was scrunching my face to block out the bright lights.

The sound of the front door opening and then quickly shutting did make me feel better. No delivery person this time.

Jackson sat down, keeping me in his lap as the others moved around. Zeke was getting drinks, Han was separating the food, and Sebastian was updating the outside world that my heat was officially over.

My mouth watered at the smells. When Han lifted the lid off the cheesy pasta in front of me, I groaned at the delicious tendrils of heat rising from the food.

Before Zeke had managed to come back with all the drinks, Han was handing Jackson a fork. I watched my mate's hand spear a few cheesy shells before lifting them up to my mouth.

The feeling of being fed probably would be weird any other time except in my post-heat phase, so I didn't even hesitate in enjoying the food.

"It's the start of the weekend," Sebastian said once everyone was sitting in the dining space. "We'll have the next few days to rest before we have to go back to work."

A growl curled out from my throat at the idea of my mates leaving anytime soon.

"Not until you're ready," Sebastian agreed.

Jackson continued to feed me food, the heavy

meal settling in my stomach with each bite. The need to return to my nest was still buzzing through my body, like an itch I tried to ignore. When Jackson's chest vibrated with a purr, my body finally settled.

We mostly ate in silence, the alphas needing all the energy they could get. When we finished, I could barely keep my eyes open any longer.

"Nest?" I asked through a yawn.

"Not yet, rebel. We need to rinse you off."

If I had more energy, I would have argued against removing their scents from my body. As it was, I couldn't even keep my eyes open, let alone muster up the strength to speak.

I felt my body shifted from one set of arms to another. Pumpkin and spice and cinnamon had me pressing my nose harder against Han's throat for more of his scent. He smelled so relaxing, making me want to wrap myself up in a blanket as I cuddled against his chest.

Even as he climbed the steps back up to the third floor, the gentle rocking motion had me nodding off to sleep for a moment. It was the sound of water pouring that jostled me awake again.

The lights were bright, but I managed to open my eyes fully after lots of blinking and rubbing against my eyelids. This bathroom was a dark gray and gold mix, making the whole space appear very elegant. Dark cabinets with bright handles, little streaks of that tawny yellow through the floor's grout.

What stood out the most was the tub, its bright white surface not matching the vibe of the rest of the room. It was huge, though, definitely made for two people to relax in. As it filled up, the room began to fill with steam.

"Usually, I would ask if you wanted me to stay

with you," Han started. "But this heat was longer than usual, and I can tell you're wiped. I'm going to stay in here with you and make sure you don't fall asleep in the water, okay?"

"No. Join me."

Han chuckled and I took that as his agreement.

He set me down on top of the counter, making sure my blanket was under my thighs so the cool surface didn't bother me. After checking the temperature, adding a few drops of some sort of oil, and then using his hand to stir the water, he picked me back up, letting my sarape drop to the floor.

With how warm the space was, only my arm hairs seemed to rise in response to the slightly different temperature.

My alpha stepped into the water first, sighing even as the warmth only rose to his knees, and then helped me in. I almost cried with how good it felt to be in the water. Behind me, my mate leaned against the tub, letting me lean against him. As we settled, the water lapped at my neck before calming.

Now that I was closer to the water, I could smell the mint drops Han had added. It overwhelmed my senses, in the best way, seeming to clear out the primitive part of my thoughts that demanded the scents of my mate and the comfort of my nest.

It was a good choice that Han joined me because at some point, I did fall asleep in the water.

****

The next few days, the pack mostly slept and ate. I found myself falling asleep with one alpha only to wake up with a different one. Every day I felt a little less antsy about being away from my nest until eventually, I let my mates help me clean out my private space.

Air purifiers set up in the room for the permanent

drapes that hang from the ceiling, blankets in the wash, pillows deep cleaned with a fancy nozzle that used hot water and soap.

Then a huge pack cuddle with all the freshly cleaned items to get everyone's scent back on them.

By the end of the weekend, I was officially out of my post-heat phase and the alphas were all preparing for work. I learned that Sebastian was a scientist, currently testing betas and the effects of bonding them into a pack. Jackson owned his own company which was a bunch of long-term security teams for famous people. Zeke was a tattoo artist at a prestigious studio where the wait to get a single piece by him was a six-month period. At least Han worked from home, his job letting him be anywhere his computers were since he worked on breaking into security systems and then refortifying them until he couldn't.

When the morning came that three out of my four alphas were supposed to leave, I started to spiral. We had been so focused on regaining our energy and cleaning the nest that we didn't actually have time to talk about what happened.

The flirting beta, sex during the heat, all of it was making me unable to hold still. Jackson, Sebastian, and Zeke were all eating breakfast, a meal my tastebuds craved but my stomach threatened to revolt if I so much as took a bite of it.

I knew my mates could feel the anxiety burning through my system, but no one seemed concerned as they ate away at their meals. Or maybe they were just chalking it up to my opinions on my missing mate.

"Where's Han?" I demanded.

I was pacing back and forth, walking a few steps out of the dining room, wanting to look for my fourth mate before my body demanded I turn back around and be near my present mates.

"He'll be back soon," Zeke said.

"But where is he?" If I clenched my jaw any tighter, it would be a miracle if words still managed to make it past my teeth.

"Don't worry, Hannah. He'll be home before any of us leave."

I glared at him mentioning the 'L' word.

"What are your plans for the day, rebel?" Jackson asked.

Shrugging, I admitted, "I don't know." Leaving the house wasn't technically legal, and I was still injured. Reaching a hand to feel the strange section of missing hair, I add, "Maybe I'll make a hair appointment."

All three of my mates perked up at that, their excitement blatantly obvious.

"That sounds like a great idea, princess," Seb said. "Are you thinking of a new color? You've had purple for a while now."

"You don't like the purple?"

"I like any color you do. I think my favorite was when you did the half and half green and black."

"Very femme fatale," Zeke agreed. His arousal just barely caught my attention.

I blushed even as I shook my head. I wasn't sure what I was going to do, just that I wanted a change.

"Whatever it is, you'll look perfect, rebel."

My thanks was forgotten when I heard the door open. I wasn't ashamed to admit that I ran, determined to learn why my mate had left so early in the morning without a goodbye. With a drink in each hand, he used his foot to shut the door behind him.

"Good morning," he said, smiling widely. His positive demeanor was so distracting that I forgot to respond as he came up and kissed both of my cheeks before handing me a drink. Like the one from the hospital, it was in a clear plastic cup.

Mine was a dark purple color, similar to the last one I'd had.

"Thank you." I took a sip, the sweet taste I was expecting turning out to be bitter. My nose wrinkled in disgust before I thought better of it and tried to school my features. It sort of tasted like the last one I had, only they must have screwed it up when making it.

"Here, try mine." Before I could argue, Han switched our drinks. His was a soft white color, and when I tried it, I could actually taste the authentic vanilla beans blended in it. "Keep it. I don't mind this one."

It was probably bad, but I didn't argue. This smoothie was so much better and if he was offering to switch drinks, I wasn't going to stop him.

In the next few minutes, the rest of my alphas left, and Han went up to the second floor to work.

For the first hour, I enjoyed my drink, even reheating some breakfast to eat. Then I tried walking around, exploring the house on my own, ignoring the very specific instructions not to use the stairs. When I was bored of that, I went back to the living room space, wondering if I should just sit and watch some TV. My attention caught on the bag of yarn and hooks on the small table.

Pulling everything out, I noticed only a single bit had been attempted, although it appeared to be already coming apart. Deciding to start from scratch, I undid the loops and knots and whatnot and grabbed the folded instructions.

Seemed easy enough. Knot the yarn on the hook then do some loopy-loops and bam—a stuffed dog.

The first knot, getting the yarn to stay on the hook was misleadingly easy. When I tried to actually make the yarn exist in any way that was more complicated than unrolling it, I failed. I kept grabbing more and more length, unspooling the ball in an attempt to make this project work. It was impossible.

At some point, I had to stop and rewind all the yarn back around itself. Then, I tried again.

I was concentrating so hard my head was beginning to thump, especially the back part where the stitches were aching, making it difficult to think properly. Still, I tried to power through, taking a deep breath, rolling my shoulders so I wasn't hunched over the little table, and started again.

"It's fucking impossible." Throwing the goddamned yarn and hook on the table, I didn't even bother putting it away. The instructions sucked. They didn't even fucking make sense.

"You good, Hannah?"

Han's voice appeared from the stairs, my alpha standing on the bottom step, leaning against the wall as he smirked at me.

"This is impossible." I pointed to the broken yarn and unusable hook. "There's no way this was something I've ever done."

"Actually, the last time you tried, I came downstairs just in time to stop you from tossing it into the fireplace. You said something about wanting to hear it scream in the fire of everlasting pain."

I shrugged. Past me definitely had the right idea.

"I'm taking lunch, want to join me?"

To be honest, I wasn't really hungry, but I went into the kitchen anyways, not bothering to put away my unfinished project. Han made his food with ease, letting me help grab him what he needed. It was a quick pasta with some heated-up seafood and a delicious sauce that apparently he makes at the beginning of each month and stores for pack use.

Rather than walk all the way to the dining room, Han just ate over the large kitchen island. I made myself comfortable on top of the counter. Each time he offered a bite, I took it without hesitation, moaning at how good it was.

"So." Han scraped the last bit of sauce off his plate before continuing. "What's the plan?"

"Plan?"

"Obviously, that—", he gestured to the living room, "—wasn't going well. And you're supposed to be taking it easy."

I groaned, unable to help it. "I'm so bored."

"Why do you feel so guilty about that?"

"Because. I mean, look at this place. There has to be something I can do. I can't imagine I just waited around for everyone to get home."

"Of course not. Usually you did your classes—"

I gasped, the sound seeming to startle Han who sat up straight. "I totally forgot I was taking classes. I got so distracted with everything. Can you show me how to access them?"

"Hannah, you're supposed to be taking it easy. Sebastian has already been in contact with your professors about giving you more time."

"Time for what?"

I realized in the silence what he meant. Not just time to heal physically, but time for my memories to come back. My mates were waiting for their version of Hannah to return. Despite the doctors saying that it was potentially impossible, they still wanted her back. It was weird to think of myself almost like 'the other woman'.

It felt like a betrayal. Like every time they told me it was fine that I didn't remember, every time they said they would still love this new version, was a lie. My heart felt heavy in my chest, aching with a dull pain.

Sitting on top of the counter suddenly felt too vulnerable. I hopped down, ignoring the jarring pain in the back of my head from my heavy landing.

"No, wait, Hannah."

I stopped, despite the burn starting behind my eyes that I didn't want him to see, because I wanted him to make it better. I wanted his words to fix the problem.

He didn't turn me around or move to stand in front of me. Staying behind me, I could feel the heat from his body, could smell his pumpkin scent becoming distressed. My own instincts wanted me to comfort him, so I did, unable to fight it. I turned around wrapping my arms around him and trying to get myself to purr.

It stuttered before finally committing.

"I'm sorry, Hannah," he said. I knew he meant it, could smell his guilt and regret getting stronger with each of my own sniffles as I tried to stop myself from crying. He didn't offer any other words or explanations. "I'll teach you how to log in, okay? It's your decision if you want to continue classes or not."

"Okay. I'd like that."

For the first time since I woke up in the hospital, it was awkward with one of my mates. Together, the silence was almost painful as I followed him up the stairs to the second floor. He led me to his office, the majority of the room taken up by his desk with multiple screens and thick hardware underneath. In the back corner was a giant round one-seater couch with a sleek silver laptop beside it. My lavender scent was all over the wool upholstery.

"Here." Han handed me another blanket, not a sarape, but not something so soft that it would stick to my sweat.

I folded my legs underneath myself as I sat down,

draping the fabric over my lap. Han's computer screens were easily visible from where I was sitting, although I had no idea what to make of most of it. One just had a website for some sort of energy company. Another was all black with typed words I'd swear weren't actually readable. Next to that was a weird screen that had the company logo in the corner and was magically typing by itself.

The alpha crouched next to me, showing how he logs into the little computer and then how to get to the college website. "These are the two classes you're taking right now."

I nodded, my excitement struggling to grab a foothold against the sadness still coursing through my body. I didn't want my other emotions tainting what was a first time for me, so I did my best to grab onto the happy feelings and ignore the negative ones, pretending, at least temporarily, that all was fine.

In all honesty, I was struggling.

"Hannah?"

I looked up at the sound of my name, the word seeming loud since I'd been so focused on myself.

"I just wanted to say, that what happened downstairs was a misunderstanding."

Just like that, the sadness in my system disappeared to anger. "Oh, yeah? How so?"

Despite the tone in my words, Han smiled. "I know you, Hannah. We all do. You're the only one that's forgotten. You're still a rebel, determined to fight for omega's rights. Still love the idea of changing your hair and I know you absolutely hate that missing piece from your surgery. You have zero artistic skill despite how much you want to. You've forgotten the little things, but you're still the same."

"But what if I'm not?"

"You are."

"But what if?"

"Then we get to fall in love with you all over again. Is that such a bad thing?"

The words came out without letting me think them over first. "What if you don't love this version of me? What if I'm not the same Hannah you fell in love with the first time and you can't love me?"

There was no cure for what happened to my brain, and there was a very real chance that I would never recover those memories. Inside jokes, gifts, bonding moments, all of them gone.

"You're not getting it." Han reached out with both his hands, cupping my face and bringing me so close that each of his words had him puffing a little bit of air over my own lips. "You're not different than you were with those memories, Hannah. The only reason we want you to remember is for your benefit. And a little to assuage our own guilt."

"What do you mean?"

"We didn't protect you." His voice broke over those words, his hands dropping from my face as his head bowed. The guilt and sorrow pouring from him clogging my nose with how strong the scents were. "Of course we want your memories to come back because then it won't feel like we failed you so badly. Being so far away that you had to run, terrified, from a peace officer, who fucking hurt you. And look how much you're struggling. Your life is already hard enough with your designation and all these political bullshit laws going into place."

My heart ached as I reached out to my mate, trying to comfort him. His forehead was on the edge of my little couch, his arms spread like he wanted to reach for me, but wasn't actually touching me. Warm tears fell down my cheeks as my nose became inexplicably stuffed as it always did when I cried.

I curved my body over him, gently lying on top of him like I could protect him from his own dark thoughts. While his words helped to soothe my own internal aches, it was like he'd ripped off his own emotional scab before it had time to heal, and now it was bleeding inside him.

As best I could, I ran a finger over his hand, pushing out my own calming pheromones to help him. My scent became so strong that I almost lost track of any traces of pumpkin.

"Please forgive me, Hannah," Han said, his voice still muffled. "I didn't mean to hurt you."

His words were like magic, healing my wound from earlier and making me wonder why I'd even overreacted. I snuggled impossibly closer to my alpha. "I forgive you."

I felt the muscles in his back lose their tension, and I couldn't help turning my face to kiss him. If he felt my lips through the fabric of his shirt, he didn't say anything.

Eventually, Han and I broke apart. He needed to get back to work and I was officially excited to take a look at my classes.

Before he returned to his chair, he leaned close, kissing me gently. Han's lips were soft, only I didn't want something tender then. I pressed harder against him, sucking his bottom lip before gently biting it. He groaned, the sound going straight to my insides like he had a direct line to my pleasure center.

"Later, Hannah. I'll make it up to you."

"Promise?" I meant it to be a raspy, flirty question. Instead, it sounded almost desperate and worried and slightly breathless.

His gaze met mine as we stared at each other. Han's eyes were naturally heavy-lidded and thin, making him look like he could model just his eyes. Sure, his jaw line was sharp and good looking, and his cheek bones were prominent without making him appear gaunt, but his eyes were the showstoppers. "Promise."

He kissed me again, and then we spent the rest of the day in a comfortable silence.

JOSEPHINE LIGHT

Chapter Nine

A few hours later, my head was throbbing, and not even the icepack Han had gotten for me was really relieving the pain. Still, I wasn't stopping.

My position on the large chair in Han's office was incredibly awkward since I needed both hands to type. I was leaning against the couch, using my head's weight to keep the icepack pinned in place over the stitches.

Han kept looking back over his shoulder, obviously feeling the pain from how hard I was concentrating and the apparent repercussions from that. It was a weird effect of doing school, but one I was intent on ignoring.

The door to the room flew open, just barely managing to miss Han's computer screen that was nearby. I gasped loudly, my hand slamming over my chest like my heart was actually preparing to leap from my body.

Jackson didn't hesitate at the door, coming to gather me against him, uncaring that he almost dropped my laptop on the ground. "Time for a break, rebel."

"I didn't get anything done. I have assignments past due."

"Sebastian handled all of that for you."

Jackson carried me down the hallway toward his office, adjusting me so I wasn't cradled against his chest but wrapped around him like a frontward backpack. One of his arms went under my butt to help keep me up while the other pressed against my back until I was leaning my head against his shoulder.

"I want to do my classes now," I said. "I told Han earlier that I wasn't going to wait for memories to come back that might be lost forever."

A blast of cool air made me shiver as Jackson carried me into his office, his scent soaked into the room. Unlike Han's multiple computers, Jackson's space had one. A silver, three-tiered cabinet was against the back wall along with several cork boards. It took my brain a moment to realize all the boards had roughly the same information, including a list of names, a map of a city, multiple pages of paper tacked together outlining a 'SOP', and even a random address on a sticky note in all the top right corners.

"Is that what made you upset earlier?" Jackson asked.

I was too distracted by the room to answer his question properly. "What is all this stuff?"

"It's a complete copy of my office at work. All the important information about where I have teams, their safety plans, and whatnot. In case an emergency happens, I need to be able to find them. So, what upset you earlier?"

"It was just a misunderstanding."

"Explain it to me, then."

Jackson sat me down on the only chair in the room, standing against the little bit of wall next to the door. His thick arms were crossed over his chest, and despite his naturally stern expression, his scent was patient and calm. The chair was wide, letting me cross my legs in the seat. To stop myself from turning around from the momentum, I reached out to the desk to settle.

"It was private," I tell him.

He shakes his head. "Nothing in this house is private. Nothing to do with this pack is private. Especially not to me."

We stared at each other for a long minute, my attitude versus his calm. Part of the reason that I didn't want to tell him had to do with the fact that I was embarrassed. I let my negative emotions win rather than just talking it out. Was I allowed to have feelings? Sure. But my mates weren't rude alphas, they genuinely cared about me. And I kept assuming the worst with them.

I broke our eye contact, half deflating as I admitted what had happened. The words just flowed out of me, and I didn't look back up toward Jackson until I finished.

"I think we all messed up," he surprised me by saying. "It didn't help that your heat came on much quicker than anticipated, but we can rectify that now. Let's go on a date."

"A date?"

"How else are we supposed to make new memories? Get to know one another again? The issue is that you're worried about belonging in the pack. The solution is to prove to you just how compatible we truly are."

It made sense. Was logical. Honestly, it even made me excited. My instincts loved the idea of being pampered and spending time with my mates.

My hangup was the term dating. Did that mean exclusive? Were we no longer a pack as we got to know each other so there was a potential for us breaking up? I didn't like that idea at all.

With one hand on the desk, I pushed myself side to side in a comforting gesture while I tried to think through accepting the proposal or not.

Pushing off the wall, Jackson stepped closer. He grabbed my hand so I couldn't turn the chair away from him and then kneeled down in front of me. "Talk to me, Hannah. Don't keep your worries to yourself. I can feel you starting to panic."

"I don't want to break up."

The words were barely out of my mouth before

Jackson growled, his scent spiking with anger. "We won't."

I raised my hand about head level, explaining, "Bonding is like here. Top tier, forever." Lowering my hand to my stomach's height, I added, "Dating is here. We'd be going back a step."

"Wrong. We will always be here." He placed his fist under my hand, raising it up back to the imaginary line I drew for bonding. "We're dating you in name only. I won't let anyone take you from me, not even you."

"You're crazy," I whispered, even as my stomach tingled at the aggressive compliment.

To that, he just grunted.

"So that beta…"

"Which one? Koda?"

"The one who flirted with you and Seb that sent me into a heat."

"Is that what caused all these doubts you've been having since your heat? You think we might want someone else? Oh, rebel," he tsked. "I will happily prove to you every day that you're the only one I want."

"Even if I never remember?"

"One day, you'll become so confident in my love and adoration for you that you won't ever doubt me. That's my goal. So yes, even if you never remember. You're mine. And I can't wait to watch you fall in love with me all over again."

His words were honest, but I still snorted a laugh at his phrasing. "You're cocky, huh."

"With good reason, rebel."

When he winked, another round of tingles started at my stomach and spread upward to my cheeks, pulling my facial muscles into a wide smile. Flashes of memories from my heat reminded me how good it felt when he'd knotted me and I squirmed on the seat, the chair making my movements more exaggerated.

"C'mon, I want to clear the air with the others." It must have been a rhetorical question because Jackson picked me up and carried me out of the office and back down to the first floor. "Pack meeting. Living room. Now."

Jackson's alpha bark had me straining to beat him to the couch even though he hadn't let me go. As soon as I saw Sebastian and Zeke, I wanted their scents on me. When I tried to get out of Jackson's arms, he just squeezed me tighter.

"Let go."

"Kiss."

I rolled my eyes at the demand even as I leaned in, teasing him with a short, quick kiss to his bottom lip before pulling away. He didn't let me go. Growling, his hand came up to the back of my neck, pulling my face against his. This kiss was overwhelming, my alpha was completely in control, devouring me, tasting me.

When he pulled away, I tried to follow, wanting more. I tightened my legs around him, at least as far as they reached around the large male, clinging to him in the hope that he would finish the tease he started.

Instead, he just chuckled, easily pulling my limbs off him and settling me on the couch between Zeke and Sebastian. I snuggled close to both alphas, and everyone simply ignored my hint of lavender arousal in the air. Mostly.

Seb chuckled, even going so far as to press his face close to my neck and take a deep inhale of my scent. Which, of course, only made my arousal bloom more. Han was sitting on the couch's arm next to Zeke, and he leaned against the back of the couch to reach out an arm and touch me. And Zeke was just barely touching me, his fingers gently tracing a random path along my inner knee and upper thigh.

"Let's get down to business so we can do dinner," Jackson started. He stood in front of the fireplace—unable to sit on the little table since my deformed art project was still there—and looking completely relaxed as he surveyed his pack. "Hannah hasn't been feeling stable in the pack, so it's our job to step up."

Just like that, the lazy, arousal-filled air seemed to disappear. Tension replaced it with a hint of sadness and anxiety.

Jackson continued, "We're going to start taking her out on dates. We've already talked about it, courting her again, but now we need to actually make plans—"

"I call dibs on first date," Zeke said.

"Now, wait a minute," Sebastian started. "That's not even fair. Jackson wasn't done talking."

Zeke shrugged. "You snooze, you lose."

"Maybe we should let Hannah decide," Han suggested.

"She can decide the second date, I already called first," Zeke said.

Around and around the playful arguments kept going. I hid my smile by biting on my inner cheek, enjoying the way they fought to spend time with me. Looking up at Jackson, the male was already watching me, a smug smile on his face. He winked, sending a thrill through my body.

"Enough," Jackson said, not unkindly. "I think it's only fair that Hannah's first alpha gets her first date. Just makes sense."

That comment just got the whole argument started over again.

Eventually progress was made when Han admitted, "I can concede to not being the first date since the shit I ordered hasn't arrived yet. But when it does, I want that immediate weekend."

"What did you buy?" I asked.

"You'll find out when it gets here."

That didn't sound like an ideal solution. "Why not just tell me?"

"It'll be a surprise."

"No, thanks. Just tell me." Waiting weeks to figure out what Han had planned sounded like torture.

Sebastian chuckled behind me, pulling me onto his lap even as I maintained eye contact with Han, demanding an answer. He didn't tell me anything. Huffing, I crossed my arms over my chest, officially pouting as my mind offered no ideas as to what Han could be waiting on.

"So, it's settled," Jackson said. "Zeke first, then Seb, then me. Han will take whatever weekend is closest to his items arriving."

Everyone nodded.

"Next, I think it'll be good for us all to verbally reassure Hannah that she will be the only omega we'll be dating. The incident with the beta delivery driver has her rightfully worried."

Still holding me in his lap, Seb swore, somehow pulling me tighter against him. "I promise, we were not accepting of her advances, Hannah. We always order for the food to be left so we didn't bother to check when we opened the door."

I snuggled harder against Seb's chest, his tropical scent and beating heart truly reminding me of the ocean. "She tried to touch you."

"I didn't want her to. Didn't ask her to. Didn't lean into her. She tried to come into my home, where my injured omega was, she was lucky my mother had trained me to control my emotions, or I'd have properly gone into a rage."

Jackson grunted in agreement. "I'm used to high intensity situations. I practice keeping myself centered. It's the only reason I didn't let my instincts take over."

I felt the tiny kernels of tension in my body disappear. My emotions had been so blinded by how angry and hurt I was, I'd forgotten my alphas. They didn't want to be touched by a random beta. They didn't want a delivery person coming into their private home.

"Should we tell her supervisors or something?" I asked. "She made you guys uncomfortable. Hit on you. And even tried to enter your private residence. That shouldn't be allowed."

"It's already handled, rebel," Jackson admitted.

That didn't feel like enough. Now that I wasn't throwing myself a pity party, I realized how wrong it was. "Handled, how?" I needed to ensure my alphas were properly protected. Rather than just rolling over and letting someone take them, I was going to defend my pack. "Tell me."

I tried pulling out of Seb's grip, knowing Jackson had the answers I wanted. Instead, I found myself in Zeke's lap, facing Seb who was grinning like he thought my attempts to demand information were adorable.

My lips parted, about to continue my demand, when I felt a hand on my head, just gently stroking my hair. No words came out as I waited, feeling a finger part my hair before taking one of the designated sides and starting to run more fingers through the strands. I knew it was Han, he was the only one behind me, but my thoughts about everything else disappeared, especially when he used his nails to slightly scrape my scalp.

I moaned at the pleasure, my head falling backward to give Han better access.

"Before we get too distracted, there's one last thing we need to discuss."

I peeked a single eye open toward Jackson as he spoke.

"Sex. Our conversation about limits and preferences was supposed to happen before Hannah's heat."

That was when I became a mix of arousal and nerves. Jackson talked about the kind of sex we used to have, explaining in tediously sexual words about chasing me, holding me down, smacking my ass. All of which I agreed to, loving the idea of giving over to my base instincts, especially with my protective first alpha.

Sebastian described our intimacy as the time when I took charge. He let me be on top, riding him how I wanted. I was beginning to understand that his nickname for me went beyond just being cutesy.

Then it was Zeke's turn. Han stopped playing with my hair, a silent way of telling me to pay attention. "Of course, we all have our one-on-one time with you, Hannah. But Han and I... We're together."

"I knew it," I said, smiling wide with my own internal pride.

"You did?" Han asked.

I glared at the male. "I don't think I like your incredulous tone."

Zeke chuckled, turning my attention back to him. "I don't know if you remember during your heat? I knotted your mouth."

The words, any words really, disappeared from my mind. My jaw dropped open as I stared at Zeke, trying to make sense of what he said. Knotted my mouth? Was that even physically possible?

I vaguely remember sucking on Zeke, how good he tasted and how Han's presence behind me had pushed me further onto Zeke's cock. I did come out of my heat with an ache in my jaw, but I didn't realize that came from a knotting. I figured I'd just … sucked a lot of dick.

"And—" I cleared my throat "—you do that often?"

Zeke smirked. The purely sexual look on my typically relaxed mate's face had me leaning in to kiss him. When I pulled away, I watched as Han turned Zeke's face, kissing him, too.

Watching my two mates kiss had my scent blooming, my arousal heating me up from the inside. It was like watching porn, having them in front of me, and all I could do was watch.

Sebastian used everyone's distraction to pick me back up off Zeke's lap. The male immediately pulled away from Han, glaring at Seb who wasn't even looking at him.

"Did you make your hair appointment?" Seb asked.

I shook my head. "I forgot."

"That works out. I meant to tell you that you have some company's number in your phone that you really like. Where is it, I'll show you?"

"Where's what?"

"Your phone."

"Oh, yeah." I looked around, expecting it to jump out at me. It didn't. "I have no idea."

"Someone call it."

We all waited patiently, not talking so we could hear the ring or vibration. Nothing happened. In fact, the only ringing was from Han's phone making the call.

"Well, it has to be in the house," I told them.

All of my alphas started laughing, but they also started to help me look for it. It wasn't in the kitchen or the dining room. And according to Han it wasn't in his office. Jackson checked my nest.

It was then I'd remembered I'd shoved the device

between the couch cushions a few days ago that I found it, yelling at the house as I tried to turn it on. "It's dead."

"Here." Sebastian grabbed my phone, plugging it in and waiting for it to get enough juice to turn on. The cord he'd used to charge my phone was long, like ridiculously several feet long. As soon as he got the number he needed, he handed me the phone to make the call. "They're still open."

The name was Glamorous Emporium, and I couldn't help but snort as I hit the button for the call.

It rang only twice before someone picked up, their voice soft and sweet. "Hello, angel, this is Mayer. What type of service can I get you scheduled for?"

"I'm Hannah—"

"Oh, Hannah, yes, you are due to come in. Are you thinking of a touch-up or are you ready to do another color? Which did you pick last time?"

I pulled at a strand of hair as if I needed to double check the color before admitting. "Purple. But I do want to change it up."

"Wonderful, how exciting. We have an opening in about four weeks with your usual stylist."

Four weeks? How popular was this place?

I stared at Sebastian who just nodded his head like that was completely acceptable.

"Hannah?"

"Oh, yes, sorry. Four weeks. At what time?" I didn't want to wait that long at all. The restless energy inside of me had already cemented what I wanted to do, and waiting was like trying to ignore an itch. A part of me felt bad since Mayer sounded so sweet and weirdly familiar with me. But I didn't know her, and any sense of loyalty was lost with my other memories. I hadn't even considered that my memory loss would affect even my hair stylist.

When we hung up, I made up an excuse about checking that the date worked, essentially politely denying the appointment. I didn't feel like I'd accomplished anything. So, I scrolled through my contacts and called the only name I recognized.

Koda picked up almost instantly, "Hello, hello."

"Hey, Koda—"

"Hannah!"

Apparently, my voice was easily recognizable. "Yep, I was wondering if you'd be willing to help me out with something."

When I looked over at Seb, an amused and curious look on his face, I couldn't help leaning over to kiss him. Our lips broke apart when I smiled at Koda's excited tone demanding I tell her what I had planned.

Chapter Ten

I was so excited that my leg was shaking under the dining table. Every time one of my mates so much as smiled in my direction, I mock-glared at them.

I was waiting for Koda to arrive. She was finally coming over almost a week after we'd made plans, since my stitches were officially out. The back of my head still looked dramatic from the injury and subsequent surgery, but it was basically healed. At least superficially.

Originally, Zeke had planned his date to be tonight, but after I'd admitted I wanted to wait until Koda had come over, he rescheduled it. That, too, had my nerves all jumbled.

If shit went wrong tonight, it would probably ruin tomorrow's date. Not that I was going to postpone our date until I could get into a proper hair appointment. Maybe I'd actually schedule the salon if my idea didn't turn out good with Koda's help. Maybe I should've scheduled the appointment just to have a backup? Oh, well.

The beautiful chime of the doorbell had me scooting out of the chair, basically running toward the sound.

"Do not open that door, rebel," Jackson yelled.

I stopped in front of the ornate wood, bouncing on my toes. My mate kissed the top of my head before opening the door, exposing Koda and her own alpha mates.

I watched her mouth open, staring at everything like she couldn't believe what she was seeing. Her scent was the first thing I noticed—distinctly beta, although drenched in alpha scents. I worked hard to not crinkle my nose at the idea of other alpha odors invading my home. She was taller than me, especially with her boots that had an inch of platform on them. Her hair was dyed, with less than an inch of her natural roots coming in, showing it was done fairly recently.

"Hannah, oh, it's such a relief to see that you're okay." Koda immediately hugged me, squeezing me tightly.

"We've been talking on the phone," I reminded her.

Pulling away, she waved a hand in the air. "That doesn't count. I need to see you with my own eyes."

"You going to introduce us, Koda bear?" one of her alphas asked.

I watched Koda blush. "Sorry, I forgot. Hannah, these are my mates, Jenson, Aidan, and Enzo."

The males were handsome, in a commercially attractive way, but what really put me off were their scents. They lacked personality, smelling like the nest after my mates and I cleaned it, but before we'd rolled around in it.

"Hi. Do you have the stuff?" I asked Koda.

She turned to the blond male who handed her a brown paper bag. "Yep, all right here. Although Addy says we should lay some towels down."

"I'll get them for you," Seb said.

I basically dragged Koda after my mate. We were going to be using the first-floor bathroom, mostly because it was the most unused in the house, but it helped that the guest bathroom was huge.

Zeke and Han followed after us, dragging along chairs we could use from the dining table. Seb came in with a bunch of towels, helping to lay them on the floor, and then over the chairs.

"That should be good enough," Seb admitted.

"If anything truly gets stained, we'll just replace it," Han added.

It was Zeke who leaned close, kissing my cheek and whispering, "Have fun."

As soon as the door shut, Koda started taking everything out of the bag. "I've been watching videos on how to cut hair. The dying part should actually be relatively easy."

"Which do we do first?"

That question had her pause. "Dye? Maybe you'll love the color and want to keep some length?"

I nodded. "Good plan."

There wasn't much more to set up, so I positioned myself in the chair, straddling it and holding onto the chair back. I wrapped a towel over my shoulders, letting my hair fall on top of it while Koda pulled the coloring stuff out of the box. First was hair bleach.

She squeezed some into a bowl and then started to apply it.

"Thanks for doing this," I told her. "The place I apparently usually get my hair done wanted me to wait weeks to get in."

She chuckled. "I know. You're the one who recommended the place to me. It's where I got this done. I didn't even leave the place until I'd booked the next appointment."

"Smart. They did a wonderful job. And the color is adorable. Most people dye their hair to a natural shade, but I love the big statement color."

"I was already getting familiar with the stares. Now I just sort of pretend people only talk about me because of my hair."

I tried to move my head, turning around to look at her, wondering what she was talking about, but she turned my head, so I was facing forward again. "I don't want to mess it up."

"It's just bleach. I don't think that's possible."

She hmphed and I took that as her disagreeing.

"How come people stare at you?" I knew it would be something private. I was just more curious than I was polite.

"I bonded my pack. The world sees me as a beta that took the position of an omega. At a school with a lot of alphas, I'm not exactly popular."

"What about with the betas?"

My hair was officially covered in bleach. The smell was strong, attempting to burn all my nose hairs and making my eyes water.

Koda washed her hands before answering. "I've gotten a lot of support too. Probably mixed with the betas. Some think I've sold myself off to alphas, trying to be an omega while others see it as a sort of protest against omegas."

"It's obvious none of them are in a pack."

"What do you mean?"

"If they were, then they wouldn't question why you're in a pack or why alphas would bond a beta. Designations are supposed to be about biology, not social rules. They're supposed to help us understand each other, not control our actions."

I wanted to get up and pace, the conversation something I was truly passionate about. I forced myself to stay seated, as I continued. "Designations might hold facts, but I don't get why laws should be based on them. Sure, I go into heat, but it should be my choice if and when I want alphas to help me through it. It doesn't make sense to make rules on biology. We're people, with emotions, not just sex organs."

My spiel came to an anticlimactic end since it was just Koda and I, alone, in a bathroom surrounded by hair products.

"Even your memory loss didn't change your opinions and beliefs. I'm glad," Koda admitted. "You're not wrong, though. Rudimentary science has had a weird hold on social norms. The knowledge and understanding of designations were supposed to be helpful, not condemning."

"It's abuse. Not just the rules themselves that hurt people, but intelligence abuse. Like that politician guy who was talking shit about me the other week? He has easy access to the public to spread information that was blatantly wrong, knowing that no one could argue with him."

A timer went off on Koda's phone and then we very awkwardly rinsed the bleach out of my hair. It involved leaning into the shower, with the rain shower head already on. Koda stood next to me with a fresh towel trying to protect the top of my shirt from getting soaked.

We were both getting slightly splashed around the ankles, but this was the best we could do. Finally, all the bleach was out and then I had my hair wrapped up in a towel.

"Shit, I forgot a blow-dryer. Do you have one?" Koda asked.

I snorted. "I literally have no idea."

All of my mates' bathrooms had my shower and morning necessities which I've been using since I haven't slept a single night alone. Considering my room was technically my nest, I knew a dryer wasn't in there.

Koda opened the door, yelling through the small crack she made, "Does Hannah have a hairdryer?"

I heard some yelling, and then someone stomping their way up the stairs. Then someone handed a dryer to Koda who effectively shut the door in their face, earning a chuckle out of me. It took some time to get my hair dry again, the strands looking more yellow than white.

"Does this look right to you?" Koda asked when she finished. She was looking at my hair too, both of us not quite sure why it wasn't as light as we'd expected.

I shrugged. "The color will cover it anyways, right?"

She nodded. "I guess we're going to find out."

Another bowl was mixed, and a new towel was wrapped around my shoulders. Without further ado, Koda grabbed a chunk of the dye and popped it onto my hair. At least this mixture didn't smell as bad.

"How are your classes going?" Koda asked.

"Fine. I'm behind, but apparently Seb has managed to work something out with my professors. I'm trying to review everything we've already done before jumping into starting something new. Plus, I want to pick out a major."

"You're undecided."

"That's an understatement. They're so many options."

I watched in the mirror as Koda's eyebrows furrowed. I watched her bite the inside of her cheek, looking like she had something to say.

"What?" I asked.

She still wasn't looking at me, all of her intense concentration suddenly on my hair. "Did you know that I consider myself an omega? I nest, can take a knot, have a strong sense of smell, all of the omega characteristics without perfuming like one. When I first applied to the academy, I was told that they'd require a test to prove my beta status."

"Academy?"

"Braker Academy. It's where I met Jen and the others."

I felt my jaw drop. She said it so casually as if Braker Academy wasn't one of the top prestigious schools. If I remembered correctly, it had literally just opened its doors to betas.

"Obviously I submitted it. I'd hoped that whatever had stopped me from perfuming would also hide me from being diagnosed as an omega. Not forever. Just long enough to go to school. And it did. At the end of the day, when it came to picking my major, I just chose one."

She shrugged like it was no big deal. "I don't love physics, I just don't hate it either. What was important to me was that I was getting the opportunity before I decided to settle down. I wanted shit on my own timeline. I wanted everything to be my own decision."

I was nodding my head along with her words, agreeing and even feeling that need that always came right before I went to a protest, needing to feel the relief of demanding change, of doing something.

"I just hope you'll get the same possibility through your online classes," Koda finished.

"What do you mean?"

"I don't know how you're going to school right now, but I really don't know how you'll be able to get a job without some major social adjustments. Education has found a way to block the symptoms of designations, but workplaces are more blatant with their bigotry."

Her words doused all the fire inside me. The freeing feeling where it felt like if I could just get my voice heard, everyone would believe me. That I could just make a speech, march down the street, sit-in at a diner and the world would understand the need for change. My need for things to change.

The feeling of dye being applied stopped, and Koda washed her hands again before moving to crouch in front of me. "Don't lose hope, Hannah. I didn't mean to upset you. Omegas can't give up. No one else is fighting for us."

Tears burned my eyes, but I fought them back. She was right. I was Hannah motherfucking Zeal. Even if I was a little confused as to what that name meant right now, I knew it would always be a person who demanded better for omegas.

I lifted my chin. "You're right." That didn't help me make a decision on which major I would choose, only now I was determined that I was going to pick one.

We continued to talk, moving the conversation to lighter things like getting to know one another superficially. Our likes and styles and vague plans.

When it came time to wash my hair again, I was absolutely in love with the color. It was such a dramatic change from the dark purple that I almost wanted to keep my hair long. If it wasn't for that missing patch of hair over my scar, I probably would've.

"Ready?" Koda asked. She looked excited, the inspirational photo I'd sent her already on her phone that I was holding up for her to see.

"Let's do it."

"Just a reminder, I've literally never cut anyone's hair before."

I shrugged. "How hard could it be?"

****

Very hard. Cutting hair was a skill that could not be learned through osmosis visuals.

I was staring at my hair, now only a few inches long, wondering how it got this bad, this quickly.

Koda was a puddle on the floor, simultaneously laughing and crying, completely hysterical at the results. Honestly, I was starting to worry that I'd broken her.

Outside the bathroom door, I knew both my mates and Koda's were waiting patiently to see what all the ruckus was about.

"You totally should have waited for the hair appointment," Koda admitted as she tried to get herself under control.

"No way, we can totally save this."

"How?" Koda wasn't laughing anymore, genuinely wondering how I was going to save this hair. It wasn't the color, just the cut that made me realize simply cutting the hair wasn't enough.

"I have an idea. It might be crazy."

"Crazier than the initial idea that we could do this after watching a few videos?"

"Good point. I need you to ask my mates for shears."

Koda's eyes bulged, but she did as I asked, not letting the alphas push their way into the bathroom.

"Hannah, are you sure about this?" Han's voice sounded worried.

"It's her hair," Zeke said.

"I know that, but I don't want her to regret it. You can feel her emotions. Taking a day to think about it—"

"No way," I yelled at the door. "Trust me, Han. I need the shears."

It was silent for just a moment before Han said, "It's not your hair we love, Hannah. Don't feel like you have to cut it all off because it didn't turn out right."

"And if I want to shave it off?"

"Then I recommend letting Zeke do it. He's got experience doing his own hair. No offense, Koda, but it might also be the safest route."

"Okay. Just Zeke can come in."

It took a minute for Zeke to go get his clippers, as he called them, and then squeeze his way through the tiny slot Koda allowed with the open door. As soon as he saw me, his eyes warmed with sympathy.

"I love the color."

"Help me."

Zeke chuckled, pulling me into a hug that immediately had the tension leaving my body. "Don't worry. I'll fix you right up. I even have a good idea for a design, if you're interested."

I reached a hand up to touch the lines shaved into the side of his head. It was intricate and beautiful, definitely requiring a skill that couldn't be learned just by watching a few videos.

"I didn't do this one myself, but I used to do pretty basic ones," he admitted.

"Like a heart?" Koda asked.

"Sure. What do you think, Hannah?"

My excitement was back up to the level before my hair disaster. I had been going for cutesy, but maybe that just wasn't meant to be. Sweet had never really been my thing. Kind, sure. Blunt, definitely.

I sat back down in the chair and agreed. The feeling of my head being almost shaved, along with the loud buzzing sound was unsettling at first. It was louder than I anticipated since he was shaving right next to my ear, but it didn't hurt.

By the end, my hair was so short you couldn't grip it anymore. It made my face look sharper, harsher in a sexy way. It made my head look like I had a halo of color, and it further hid my scar since it wasn't obvious that I was missing a chunk of hair.

"Oh, this is so dangerous," Koda said. She was standing in front of me, tilting my chin to the side so she could take in my new haircut. "Now I'm wondering if I could pull off this look."

"Jump in the shower, rinse off those baby hairs, and I'll get you some new pajamas to change into. Then you can come out and present your new look to your mates." Zeke's declaration left no room for argument as he turned my face and pressed his lips against mine. "I also call first dibs in the nest tonight."

Just like that, he left, leaving Koda to stare at me, wide-eyed having heard that last bit. "I am totally considering this haircut now."

I laughed, smiling wide as I ran a hand over my head, feeling my new short hair.

Koda left so I could rinse off, and I took the time to enjoy it. The small amount of hair products I needed was actually blowing my mind. Even the little dollop seemed like too much. My cheeks were aching with how hard I was smiling.

Just as I turned the water off, Zeke peeked in and dropped off a little set of pajamas. I raised a single cyebrow at the very thin fabric he set on the chair.

"Koda and her alphas had to leave. Something about work and school tomorrow. She said she'd check in later."

Then he was leaving again, and I was drying off. I ran the towel over my head and then pronounced my hair as dry.

I was right in my initial view of the pajamas that they were lacy and thin. The straps were skinnier than the width of my pinky and the little tie on the shorts was purely decorative. All black, it fit tight around my breasts and ass, only slightly flaring in the midriff.

My cheeks were tinged a little red from the heat of the shower, and I wondered if I looked sexy or ridiculous. Obviously, I thought the previous.

Gripping my internal confidence with every metaphorical limb I could, I lifted my chin and made my way out of the bathroom. Could I feel the cool air on my head? Yes. Was my neck suddenly cold? Also, yes. Did all the hair on my body seem to pebble from a mix of cold and anticipation? Again, yes.

But I followed the sounds of my mates' voices into the living room. Han and Zeke were sitting on one couch together, half laying on it, so Han was leaning against the couch's arm with Zeke between his legs. They saw me first, both sitting up with looks of pure arousal on their face.

Sebastian was sitting in the center couch, and he turned around so fast that I couldn't help smiling at him. "Oh, Princess."

My attention was pulled from Seb getting up from the couch as Jackson rounded the corner from the kitchen, taking one look at me and tossing his snack back onto the island. He picked me up, holding me against him with one arm around my back and the other running a palm over my head.

I had to squeeze my legs tight around him in order to hold myself up. Seb, Han, and Zeke were following after us as Jackson carried me up the stairs toward my nest.

"Fuck, your hair looks so good, rebel," Jackson said, his scent blooming around us, becoming stronger and juicier.

"I called dibs on first fuck," Zeke called out, chasing after us.

Jackson stopped at the top of the third floor, turning to glare at my other mate. When he turned his attention to me, raising a single eyebrow in a silent demand for an answer, I had to work to keep from smiling.

"He did," I admitted.

Jackson growled, claiming my mouth right then and there, grinding his erection between my legs and heightening my arousal.

I was yanked from my mate, a whimper working

its way up my throat until I was turned to my other alpha. Out of all my mates Zeke wasn't the most classically handsome, but there was a sort of beauty that radiated from him. Even more so, there was a kindness, a gentleness, an understanding.

There was so much to learn about my alphas. These dates they were going to take me on, it would do more than comfort me about my place in this pack, it would help me fall even more in love with them—I knew it.

Zeke carried me into my nest, the others following. All the deliciously aroused scents of my mates, the comfort of my nest, I was sure that this moment was the beginning of my happily ever after. The second time.

JOSEPHINE LIGHT

Chapter Eleven

I woke up the next morning with only Seb still in my nest. He was on his phone, the glow from his screen illuminating his face since the rest of the room was still dark. My brain was still slow to conscious thoughts even as my body was trying to get closer to my mate.

We were both on our sides, facing each other, my face pressing against his bare chest. His free hand was gently rubbing along my back and a part of me wanted to continue to feign sleep so he'd keep going.

"You finally up?" Seb asked, his teasing tone had me looking up. The glow from his phone disappeared as all his attention turned to me.

"What time is it?"

"Not that late. We're all just used to getting up early."

I scrunched my nose in mock disgust. If omegas ever get enough rights in my lifetime to work, I was getting a night job. "What's the plan for today?"

"I was thinking we'd spend the day in the nest together."

My smile was huge, and I snuggled deeper into Seb's chest. I was basically giddy with the excitement that my mate wanted to spend time alone with me—and not just sexually. "Will you tell me about yourself?"

Our legs were intertwined, both of my hands crushed between our chests, and my head was lying on his bicep. He continued to rub my back as he started telling me about his life, his family. Apparently, his family's first disappointment with him was when he didn't pack bond with Aidan—one of Koda's mates.

"Our families are close," he told me. "They have

a great working relationship, and both our moms are as close to friends as they can be considering all they really do is trade gossip with one another. They had built up this grand idea in their heads about the kind of powerful pack we would be when we found an omega."

"Do you not like Aidan?"

"Aidan and I are friends. Close friends. But packs aren't between friends, it's a kinship that's hard to describe. Someone you'd trust with the love of your life. Someone whose morals and values you agree with. Someone you'd trust with your offspring. Or even consider your own. It wasn't a fully conscious decision to bond with the guys, more instinct. We're just a different type of mate."

"I love that you all have that."

"Proud of yourself a little, too, huh?"

I shrugged my shoulder. "I picked good alphas. That seemed impossible when I was living at the OC. I always figured if I was forced to find a pack, I'd spend my days hiding away in my nest, just using their cocks during my heat—"

My words were interrupted by Sebastian's growl, his scent tinged with jealousy. He turned us so I was on my back while he leaned over me, his face so close that his nose was less than an inch away from mine. "I don't like you talking about other alphas' cocks."

His legs managed to spread mine so he could fit between my thighs. Still meeting my gaze, one of his hands pulled my own away from my chest, pressing them high above my head.

Arousal was quickly pooling in my core, anticipation tingling throughout my body making me put in a lot of effort to hold myself still. Even my toes wanted to curl with excitement.

I thought he would enter me. I thought my mate

was going to thrust his already hard cock into me.

Instead, he gently kissed my nose. Then the side of my lips, just at the corner where it met my cheek. Another kiss under my chin, on my neck, my collarbone. Slowly, so very fucking slowly, he made his way down my body. He took his time at my breasts, even tracing my hard nipples with his tongue.

My chest was heaving dramatically, my body undecided between being stiff for his ministrations or trying to shift until I enticed him to just fuck me.

Seb didn't seem to pay me any attention—not beyond where his mouth was.

He kept moving downward, kissing toward my belly button, both hips, before I realized his intention was more than just about torturing me.

His shoulders settled between my thighs, spreading me so wide that I felt a slight strain in each leg. My mate continued to kiss me. At this point, he was full-on teasing me. I felt his fingers touch my core, spreading me so I was even more open for him.

I wanted to look, and I didn't. My back arched, trying to raise my hips closer to his hot breath but my mate just pressed another gentle kiss.

"Please," I begged. "Seb, I need more."

"I know you do, princess. There's just something so unbelievably sexy having you whine for me."

His lips gently pressed against my clit, the feeling of direct contact on that sensitive spot had my hips jerking. With a demand for more or less, I wasn't sure.

I was panting, breathing hard from the pleasure. I needed more. More than just one spot at a time.

"I thought princesses were in charge?" I asked.

Seb chuckled, the sound vibrating against me and ratcheting up my pleasure. "Tell me what you want then, princess. Should I suck harder on this little clit? Do you want me to press my fingers inside you and curl them just right? Or if you're feeling adventurous, I could explore this naughty hole back here."

My head was shaking. His words were too much, melting every conscious ability I had to acknowledge what he was saying, to beg for any of those things. I just needed him. More slick was pouring from me with each of his dirty questions.

I reached for him, my hands coming to the back of his head as I shoved his face back where I wanted. He obeyed, even going so far as to lick up the slick pouring from me. I barely felt his first finger pressing inside me, I was so wet. Then he pulled it out, using my slick as he touched my clit, petting it, circling it, making more slick leak from me that he lapped up.

All of my muscles were clenching down on nothing. It was nearly painful how badly I wanted to feel him inside me as he continued to play with my body.

My orgasm was close, I knew it by the way my muscles were so tense, in the fact that my eyes were scrunched tight in anticipation of something to come … I just couldn't get there until he was inside me.

I knew he felt my desperation, felt how close I was, because he started to truly devour me. His tongue pressed and licked into my opening, his finger still moving over my bundle of nerves. No matter how hard I pressed his head against me, his tongue and fingers just weren't enough.

Tears streaked down the sides of my face, the arousal and need mixing together desperately.

I was sure that I wouldn't be able to come like this, that it was just an easy way to torture me, taking what he wanted all the while knowing I was riding that edge.

One of his hands creeped up my body, playing

with my breasts before moving to the side of my ribs, almost up to my armpit and tracing something there.

Then, all of a sudden, it was like my body simply exploded with pleasure. My orgasm stole my breath as all my muscles locked down, my back arched, my toes curled, my vision became white with bliss.

I had no idea how long it took for me to come down from my own climax. But I was breathing hard, my body warm and covered in sweat, my heart still pounding hard throughout my body so I could feel the beat all the way down to my toes and reverberating up in my ears.

Seb was still down between my legs, gently lapping at my cum and slick mixture.

"You taste so good, princess," he told me, probably realizing I was finally grounded again. "I love being down here and looking up, seeing you enjoy my tongue and fingers and wearing my mark."

That's what his fingers were still absently tracing just under my armpit on my side. His claiming mark on my body.

I was pretty sure he had more to say, but my stomach growled, reminding me that I'd slept in, and had an orgasm before feeding myself. Seb smirked, immediately reaching for his phone and telling me he'd have one of the other alphas bring up something to eat.

"Don't bother, I want to stretch my legs a little. We can go down," I told him.

Rather than agree, I watched my mate stiffen slightly. "What happened to spending the day in the nest together?"

"We'll come right back up after we eat. Maybe drag one of the others up too." I knew that one-on-one time with each alpha was important, but I didn't think Seb would be opposed to the pack bonding in here.

"I can have them bring up food and stay if you

want."

He was acting weird. I knew it. I took a deep inhalation, focusing on my mate's scent. His guava scent still smelled perfectly ripe, not hinting at any dark emotions, but—I inhaled again, just to be sure. His scent was almost too perfectly calm.

My suspicion must have been reaching him because he sighed like he knew he wouldn't be able to keep holding out on me.

"Do you trust me?" he asked.

I nodded.

"Then just stay in here today. With me. Or the four of us can switch out."

"What's going on?"

"We aren't trying to keep things from you. Okay, so let me reword that. Just for today. Shit is going down outside this house and we want to give you one more day before you're forced to face it."

"I won't hide away forever. My head is healed. My life has to get back to some semblance of normal."

"I agree. Tomorrow."

I had no clue what mattered between today or tomorrow, so I agreed. Jackson brought up breakfast and I spent time with him, learning all about him. His love for working out, needing to protect me. At some point, he even chased me around the nest for a bit before gently tackling me and fucking me from behind.

After that, Jackson got into the lighter stuff, telling me about how he enjoyed the season right before winter, when it was crisp and chilly just not quite cold. He told me that he was an organized male, liking order and discipline in his work and yet he'd fallen for me— apparently an omega who never does what she's told. Near the end of our time, he drew an imaginary family tree, explaining that his family was on-their-own-business rich, not own-a-corporation rich, but he still got along decently well with Seb and Han's family because they 'admired his effort'.

That comment had me snorting at the ridiculousness, even teasing him with the sassy words, "I also admired your effort earlier," which let to him spanking my ass before taking me again.

Han and Zeke brought up dinner later, the two telling me about how they bonded with each other after already being a part of Jackson's pack. They told me all about the difficulties they had learning to be two alphas with each other. How to be okay letting one be more dominant, how they had to look at designations differently because of it.

After that heavy discussion, we moved on to them telling me some funny stories about their times together. Learning how to use lube, the different positions they could fuck each other in, and then learning how to add an omega to the mix. Between them. In a row. Countless options which just worked to turn me on and then they were demonstrating all the possibilities.

Between them. Han thrusting into Zeke who was pushed into me. Both inside me, at the same time, in the same opening, stretching me even more than a knot.

By the end of the day, when all of my mates joined me in my nest to go to sleep, I was exhausted.

Still, as I was drifting off, my thoughts wondered to what I could expect the next day. Nothing I came up with was good.

JOSEPHINE LIGHT

Chapter Twelve

There was no waiting or wondering. I woke up the next day and my mates were full of melancholy as they turned the living room TV on. It wasn't lost on me that they weren't getting themselves ready for work today.

The first news channel was talking about my 'attack'. Apparently, it was big news since more information had finally been released—specifically my name. My mates. My face from the photo taken for my OC residency card.

It was obviously me, a few years younger, which was truly freaky since that was the age my brain kept saying I was.

Someone changed the channel to another news station and this time a group of people were sitting on some uncomfortable looking couches, discussing how dangerous this beta revolution was. They were badmouthing the betas, calling them traitors and liars to their own cause since they'd 'hurt' an omega.

Another channel change, this one with a beta guest, explaining why he believed betas should get blocked out sections of civilization just for themselves. How alphas and omegas were too emotional and how the laws that affected everyone were unjust toward betas.

More flipping through the TV channels and it was like everyone was talking about me. Not specifically me, just using me in their argument like I was a prop to toss around, a weapon to wield in whatever cause they believed in.

"I have to do something. Say something." It felt impossible to tear my gaze away from the screen. "They don't understand what actually happened."

"We know," Seb said. "That's what everyone was trying to work out yesterday. What to say. Who to reach out to. But, Hannah, it's more than just the news."

"What do you mean?"

It was Jackson who spoke up next, "Alphas are demanding betas be blocked from joining packs, claiming they don't have the necessary protective gene and could harm their omegas. Betas are split, demanding packs should be a choice and wanting their own separate community away from the emotions of the other designations. There are protests, government meetings being called—it's beyond you now."

Even then, even with the spark of something in the air, no one seemed to be focusing on the real issue. Alphas and betas arguing with each other while omegas had no say. Still, we were being cast aside while change was unfolding before our eyes. We were the center of the issue and being danced around by a push and pull out of our reach.

"They're using me," I growled, pointing at the screen in case my mates weren't aware. "If I told my side of the story, they'd be forced to stop."

"No, you'd give them ammunition," Han said. "I know you want to do good, Hannah, but your heart is too much in the right place."

"What does that mean?"

"It means you don't see the potential they'll have to twist your own words."

Sebastian added, "You tell them you're an omega who goes to protests, they'll talk about how you broke a law—"

"An unjust law—"

"Not all alphas are like us," Jackson said, speaking up. "They see an omega breaking the rules and they will tighten their own hold over their omegas."

I was shaking my head, wanting to argue, but I couldn't. My anger was welling up inside me, my hands curling into fists like I was figuratively holding onto something to keep myself from exploding.

Sebastian continued, "If you admit to breaking a law, to going out by yourself, you'll be forced back to the compound, away from us, potentially forever."

My heart broke just at the words. Not only because I didn't want to be pulled from my mates, but because I didn't want to abandon my own kind to the crazed rules of alphas.

"So, I can't do anything?" Tears were falling down my cheeks and I wasn't sure if they came from my anger at doing nothing or my fear of being pulled from my mates. "Omegas will never have rights and I might have made our entire society worse?"

"No," Jackson snapped. "You didn't do anything. You have the heart of a warrior, rebel. Do not let the fact that you've lost this battle make you give up the fight."

"But there's nothing I can do."

It was Zeke who pulled me into a hug, wrapping his arms around me seconds before I broke out into tears. They came from the guilt, from the worry, from the anger of doing nothing.

When I finally managed to control my sobs, it was Zeke who spoke first, just barely whispering, although I knew the others could hear him. "Do you remember what Han and I told you yesterday? About how we had to come to terms with being two alphas together?"

"Yes." The single word was all I could muster.

"It was our love for each other that taught us designations were biological, not social. We had to unlearn everything we were taught, everything we thought we knew. Sure, we had knots, but we didn't have to use them. Yes, we're protective and possessive, but not

145

just toward an omega, toward each other."

I sniffled, grateful when a hand offered me a tissue.

"That was the catalyst for us, but also for our pack. Seb and Jackson weren't romantically involved with us, yet they had to learn the same lessons as we did. What's happening to the world outside these walls is the same thing. You're the catalyst, but everyone else has to learn how this change affects them."

"What if it's worse?" That was my fear. That I would be the cause of stricter omega rulings.

"We're not done fighting," Jackson said. I lifted my head from Zeke's chest so I could meet my first alpha's gaze. "We might never be done. But we won't stop until we're happy with the progress."

I nodded, silently agreeing. "What do we do now?"

"We stay under the radar as much as possible. There's nothing to do until someone else makes a move."

****

Breakfast had a morose vibe. I was handed around to all my mates, sitting on their laps as we ate in what I thought was an attempt to comfort me. None of them seemed to be in a rush to get into work today, and I didn't know if this was going to become a common morning routine.

At least I'd managed to get my emotions under control. I was going to try to listen to my alphas' advice and not feel guilty. Mostly because I didn't want to cry and be sad anymore. Also, because I could recognize the truth in their words.

It didn't matter that it was me that got hurt. It didn't matter how or by whom. I was just being used.

And that pissed me off. I held onto that anger with all my might, using it to help me straighten my back, to lift my chin, to stop feeling defeated.

We had just finished breakfast, and I mean, just finished to the point that no one had gotten up yet when the doorbell went off.

The alphas broke out in a mix of exasperated sighs and frustrated growls. I was currently on Han's lap, so I did my best to press my face against his throat, nuzzling his annoyance out of him. I held my tongue on asking who they all thought it was because my instincts warned against worsening the mood.

"I'll get it," Jackson said, sounding like he absolutely did not want to get it. He did move the long way around the room to leave, kissing me goodbye on my head.

"Okay, princess, show time," Seb said. "Remember, your caring alphas don't let you watch the news and we, of course, limit your screen time so you don't become anxious."

I snorted, making Han chuckle under me.

Zeke got a gleam in his eye, a look that told me he was suddenly up to something as he pulled me from Han's lap so I was awkwardly straddling him. His body took up the entire chair which meant my knees had nowhere to go, nowhere to hold myself up.

I felt him becoming harder as he wrapped his arms around me. One curling around my back, keeping me tightly pressed against his body. The other moving to my head, letting his fingers run over the short prickly hair.

When he lifted his hips, pressing his length against me, my breath caught in my throat. My emotions had been so close to the surface that the leap from frustrated to aroused was a short one.

I leaned my lips closer for a kiss. Not a hard one. Just a grazing of mouths, a moment of shared breath.

Another hand trailed down my back, the scent of pumpkin naturally mixing with Zeke's berries. Their scents complemented each other weirdly. They didn't blend so I was inhaling both pumpkin and berries simultaneously. It was more like their scents twirled around each other, always touching side by side so I would get a whiff of one, then the other. Both delicious, both mine.

"Representative from the OC is here. Same one from the hospital—Eve." Jackson's words had me freezing. I'd momentarily forgotten why Zeke was trying to distract me.

Leaning back, I glared at my mate. Thanks to him, I had to talk to the rep with the hint of arousal in my perfume. As a beta, she might not recognize the scent. I would definitely be on edge though since I could smell my mates' arousal.

"Trust me, Hannah," Zeke whispered, before kissing me one last time, then lifting me up off his lap.

My hips seemed to protest, and I took a moment to stretch them out before following after Jackson. I was trying to inhale clean air, but it seemed like my mates' arousal scent was clinging to my clothes.

Eve was sitting in the formal space. She looked uncomfortable as she sat on the edge of the hard couch. Her skirt was long enough that it covered her knees, yet her hands fiddled with the length. Despite her exposed calves, her top was much more appropriate for the winter weather with a long sleeve shirt under a vest. A short scarf, that I knew had a fancy name I couldn't remember, was around her neck as the only spot of bright color in her outfit.

I remembered her from the hospital, although she was missing the chemically sweet smell from last time.

"Hannah," she greeted, standing as I neared, a

huge smile breaking out over her face as she took me in. "You look great."

"Thank you." I wasn't really sure how to respond to that compliment, especially since she looked and sounded so surprised.

"I was hoping I could speak with you alone, if you feel comfortable here. If not, I can book us a reservation in one of the OC's designated public rooms for omegas."

I wondered if they gave the betas lessons on this type of manipulation. Turning around, I looked at my mates who were all hovering just a few feet behind me like they'd anticipated this.

"We can stay here," I told her.

"Before we go, would you like anything to drink or eat?" Sebastian asked the rep.

"I'm fine, unless you haven't had breakfast yet, Hannah?"

"I'm good," I agreed.

All of my mates came up and kissed me, Jackson on the top of my head, Seb on my forehead, Han and Zeke on either cheek.

Neither of us spoke while they left, or for a minute afterward. The rep seemed nervous again, her scent betraying the calm exterior she was failing to put forward. There was something I was missing, I could feel it like a phantom limb that I couldn't use.

"How are you, Hannah?" she finally asked. "Any luck with getting your memories back?"

"No. My mates and I have decided to move forward. Create new memories, you know?"

"That's wonderful to hear. And your doctors' appointments? Everything is going well with your physical recovery?"

I turned my head so she could see the scar. Hair

149

was refusing to grow in the immediate area inside the shaved heart, and the mark was still slightly pink, but it was mostly completely healed. "No problems. I'm all healthy."

"That's wonderful to hear. How was your heat? According to our records, yours came on earlier than usual. Was it stronger than it should be? Anything different at all?"

"Uh, no. Just a normal heat."

It was about then that I finally realized why Eve seemed different this time. She wasn't writing everything I said down. She wasn't even writing anything down.

"And adjusting to living with your mates?" she asked, flicking her gaze down the hall they left. "How has that been?"

"Normal, I guess. It hasn't really felt like any adjusting is needed. We're just … being mates together."

"What does normal look like to you? Will you walk me through a typical day?"

I felt like I was being interviewed except I wasn't allowed to decline answering or just get up and leave. Considering I wasn't allowed to admit I was taking college courses, I lied, talking a lot about my 'art project' I was working on.

"That sounds so exciting. Definitely something to keep you busy." Her attention was directly on me, her gaze meeting mine as she asked, "Can I see it? Your progress?"

My tongue felt heavy, an instantaneous reminder that my lie would take effort. "Everything's up in my nest until I've finished."

It wasn't an invitation. The opposite, actually. For all the limitations that omegas had, this wasn't one of them. Our nests were private. Even to our mates, and especially to those not part of our pack.

Nests were considered 'essential' for an omega. Not only for providing us with the necessary space, for our emotional and mental health too. At least according to the OC guidelines.

"I see," Eve said. "You're spending all your time in your nest then?"

Was this a trick question? *Yes* and I was spending time in the nest because I was scared of my mates? *No* and I wasn't in my nest so it was somehow inadequate? My head was starting to ache with the amount of tension that was filling my body. Working to keep my scent from becoming too strong, I tried to find the verbal middle line.

"In my nest, with my mate who works from home, in the kitchen. I float all around wherever I want to be."

"Have you been outside since your attack?"

"Outside?"

"Gone shopping? Out to eat? Visited a friend, even? Picked out something new for your home?"

"I mean—no. I'm more of a homebody, I guess."

She nodded, and for the first time, I felt like she didn't believe me. Sure, I'd spent a lot of time at home recently, but I'd been dealing with a lot. Memory loss and my mates and my hair and … none of that even included all the stress my mates had been dealing with over the same things.

"That's good. I think it's important that you stay home for the foreseeable future."

"What does that mean?"

"Your pack has been flagged for the potential abuse or neglect of their omega."

I was on my feet before I thought better of it. "That's not fair."

"Unfortunately, the OC has flagged multiple

accounts of you being left alone by your alphas. And with the connection of your photo and your name publicly, you're no longer an unnamed omega."

"Hold on a fucking second," a new voice said. I turned to see all of my mates looking furious.

Eve's typically low scent beta perfume bloomed with fear. She tried to step back but the couch was in her way.

"We aren't going to hurt you," Jackson growled, his words not matching his tone at all. He sat down, pulling me on top of him.

Sebastian spoke up next, "If the OC had proof of Hannah being out alone, then they'd have pulled her from this pack."

Eve nodded slowly. "True. But if the proof also showed that she was out, alone, at protests, they might just let her be. Especially if she continues to say nothing in the wake of what's going on right now."

"Is that your official advice?"

Before Eve could respond to Seb's question, I said, "Hypothetically speaking, it doesn't make sense that the OC would just let an omega break laws. Especially ones that went against what they worked to achieve."

"Do you know how many laws have been made since you perfumed as an omega?" Eve asked. "How many of those laws were designation based, specifically speaking, in regard to omegas? What exactly have you achieved?"

I glared at Eve even though her tone wasn't nearly as harsh as her blunt words. "And if I wasn't willing to sit still looking pretty?"

"Hannah," Seb warned.

"You'd find yourself back at the OC, pulled away from your mates. Most likely charges of neglect would be put forth. All of this would be in addition to the social court you'd be put through."

The alpha pheromones in the room were so strong that even Eve was getting affected. My own instincts were demanding that I start comforting my mates, which was impossible considering they were spread out.

"I think, maybe, I should go," Eve said. Her hands were back to touching her skirt, her palms sliding against the fabric like she was trying to stop them from sweating.

My alphas confirmed their agreement, and I could scent the change in Eve's mood almost immediately. Her perfume was full of sadness that I couldn't understand. Why would we be anything but upset at her thinly veiled threats. She worked for the organization that was attempting to intimidate me from speaking out against them.

It made me wonder... "Eve, are you here on official OC business?"

I watched as her eyes turned red just moments before she broke down and started crying. None of my mates were fast enough to catch me as I got off Jackson's lap and made my way around to the bawling beta. I pulled her close so that she was leaning against my shoulder and tried my best to keep my perfume calming.

"No, I'm not. I was fired." She was talking through the tears, pressing her face harder against me, but I managed to make out the words.

When I looked up at my mates, I saw the same confused looks on their face that I felt inside. If Eve wasn't here as a warning from the OC, that meant she was here trying to protect me. Protect us.

I let her cry it out, although I knew my mates were starting to get anxious for more information. Jackson, especially, was glaring at her, no doubt annoyed that he let her in the house under false pretenses.

Eventually, she managed to pull back her tears

from bawling to sniffles. Zeke came from the bar and handed her a cloth to wipe her tears and snot.

"Sorry about that," Eve said, pulling away so that she wasn't leaning against me anymore, our hips were still side-by-side. "I really thought I was going to be able to wait until later to let it out."

"Eve, will you explain what's happening?" I asked. "We're all really confused."

Her gaze flashed up to my mates', and she withered slightly under four alphas' direct attention. "I guess it all started once I left the hospital after checking on you. When I went back to work, I created a profile for you, something to help us track you in case you started to repeatedly show up in the hospital with 'injuries'."

"You thought we were abusing her?" Zeke asked. Just like Jackson, he seemed angry at Eve.

Eve looked up, biting her bottom lip as she shrugged her shoulders, whispering so quietly, "I don't know. It's my job to help protect omegas. I figured it was safer to create the profile and if she never got hurt again, no harm. But if she did, she wouldn't have to wait even longer to get a safety warrant pulling her out of the home."

Both Sebastian and Han were the only calm ones, the latter saying, "She was just trying to protect Hannah. Nothing wrong with that."

Seb agreed, asking, "What happened next?"

"Well," Eve started, "this part gets a little technical."

"Just do your best," Han said.

"So, before I'd even made a profile for Hannah, there was already one made. It just didn't include her name or anything, it was a profile missing key information. And when I created hers, adding in that new information, it was technically everything missing from the original profile, and the two were somehow merged."

Han nodded like this all made sense to him.

"At the time, I had no idea about the circumstances of your injury except what you told me. Then I went home and saw the news."

"How did that lead to you getting fired?"

"Well, I might have gone back to the compound, logging in to the server, and meaning to update your profile. That's when I'd learned about the merging profiles and the protests you'd been involved in before and, yeah, I figured you were out protesting and something went wrong so I deleted the account."

"When was this?"

"Days after I visited you in the hospital. That's why I have no idea how the news got access to your name, Hannah."

"How high is your access, Eve?" Han asked, leaning forward even more like he didn't want to miss her answer.

"There are no levels. Once you're employed you get access to the whole database. It's a high honor that takes years of training."

"Someone still had to have access."

"My guess would be that someone leaked it on purpose," Seb said.

Eve immediately shook her head. "No way. The compound is all about protecting omegas, this broke so many protocols. What I did was already unheard of. But deliberately hurting an omega?"

"The only other option would be that your main server was hacked. But if that was true, I highly doubt the only information they took would be Hannah's name."

"Maybe. Or maybe the consequences of whatever else they took haven't appeared yet."

"Possibly." The way Seb agreed with that single

word made me believe that he didn't actually think it was possible.

At least both Jackson and Zeke had calmed down slightly. I imagined that they were picking up the same vibe from Eve that I was—a beta raised and trained to see omegas as better than them. It was ... sad really. No designation was better or worse, they were just different, required unique ways through life.

Unfortunately, Eve was a product of being raised a beta, taught all her life how wonderful and amazing it was to be an omega, and that she might even get a spark of that joy, that remarkable life, if she dedicated hers to helping them.

The difference between Eve and the OC? She actually believed that her designation was meant to help omegas. To protect us because we're so weak, so consumed by emotions, so reliant on alphas who might overstep their boundaries. She wanted to help, to care for others. She's fucking kind and the OC took advantage of that.

"Someone had enough skill to figure out who deleted the profile," Han pointed out.

Eve really started to fiddle then. Interlocking her fingers, readjusting her legs so one was on top than the other, scrunching her nose and shaking her head like she couldn't even understand herself. "Well…"

"Eve? Tell us please," Seb said. "This is all about the safety of Hannah which we need to take very seriously. That means knowing everything."

Eve nodded, flexing her hands over her thighs to stop fidgeting. "I was called into a meeting this morning. They started by asking about the omegas under my care, specifically the newer ones. I tried to play it off normal, showing them my notes and everything, but then they started asking why I'd deleted the account. I lied, said I didn't. They argued that I either did it on purpose, or failed to originally create one, since the profile for Hannah didn't exist. Either way, it was a fire-able offense."

I did my best to comfort Eve, but since I wasn't *her* omega, my perfume didn't do much for her.

"You know, I started volunteering there when I was thirteen. In the laundry room at first, then I made my way to a part-time assistant position. I'd been with the OC for years before I even tried for a representative position."

"Why'd you do it then?" Jackson asked. "Why risk your job by deleting Hannah's profile? You couldn't have been sure that your assumption about Hannah was right."

"I think, for now, I'd prefer not to answer that. It's personal." None of my mates argued despite clearly wanting to. "There's nothing more I can think of, so I should be getting home. I need to find a new job."

It was painful watching Eve get up, making her way to the door. She was awkward and obviously upset.

"Wait." I ran into the living room, looking around for my phone. I couldn't remember the last place I'd had it. When Zeke came into the living room wondering what I was looking for, I told him, "my phone. I can never find the damn thing."

"Where's the last place you remember having it?"

The look I gave Zeke was equal parts asking him if he thought I was an idiot and telling him he was one.

"Right, sorry. Well, you spent all yesterday in the nest, but the day before Koda came over—"

"The dining room." I did my best impersonation of a sprint considering my socks on the floor were potentially life-threatening devices. My phone was on the table, and I grabbed it before heading back to Eve who was standing self-consciously by the door still. "Here. Put your number in it so we can keep in touch."

Eve's eyes went wide like she was in shock. That look remained on her face even as she accepted the phone and added her number.

Then she left, and I turned back to all of my mates asking, "Now what?"

Chapter Thirteen

Despite all the new information Eve told us, there was nothing to be done. It didn't change the fact that I still shouldn't contact the press. If I was being honest, I had my doubts about staying quiet.

If the OC was willing to overlook all the rules I'd broken, just to keep me quiet, I was certain that meant my voice would have an effect. My mates disagreed.

Rather than continuing to argue, Zeke had declared that he was calling in his date night with me. Which led to me looking at every piece of clothing I had, trying to figure out what to wear. Zeke said something comfortable and easy.

I had originally picked out some tights with a thin, spiderweb-esque skirt, and then a top with long sleeves that came off just one shoulder. Then I showed Zeke, and he recommended something 'loose'.

The new top was a heavy sweater that had been cut to just below my breasts. A string was at the bottom which allowed me to pull the hem tight around my rib cage only. It was the bottoms that I couldn't figure out. Sweats? Something loose off my hips?

My phone was telling me the temperature outside might need more coverage than having my whole stomach exposed.

I found a long skirt, one that would be tight along my thighs but both sides had a slit going up it, making it flowy and was pretty accessible to my legs.

What I wanted to do was get large safety pins, like comically large ones, and pin the slit together to give it more of my style. I just didn't have any, so I was out of luck. Not that it stopped me from making a note on my phone to get some ordered for later.

I stomped my way down the stairs, platformed boots in hand, only to stop on the bottom step while all four alphas stared at me. Jackson growled, the sound tempting my slick to leak which was very dangerous considering I wasn't wearing anything underneath my skirt.

"Nah uh," Zeke said, stepping between me and Jackson when the alpha tried to get closer. "No fucking before the date or else we'll never leave."

I sat down on the stairs, lifting my leg and working to get my boots on.

Seb's low growl caught everyone's attention. Through gritted teeth he said, "You're not wearing any underwear, princess."

Zeke's head turned around to look at me so quickly that I wondered if he had hurt his neck. His gaze immediately went to my legs. A smirk pulled at his lips, lifting up one side of his smile. "Atta girl."

He held a hand out to me to help me up and then pulled me so my back was against his front while my other mates said goodbye. Whenever a kiss went too long, he shoved at their shoulder, demanding distance. My arousal was just barely perfuming in my scent as we left.

Each of the alphas had their own vehicles, all large enough to drive every member of the pack at once. Zeke's had a weird, folded table in the back that he explained was a travel tattoo station.

"I thought you worked at a studio?" I asked as Zeke started driving.

He tapped a little button on the roof of the car and pulled out a pair of sunglasses he put on. Then he pointed to the little handle in front of my legs. I found a large pair of heart shaped glasses for myself.

"I do," he agreed. "Sometimes people pay more for a house visit. Some people even pay for us to be at events."

"Where are we going?"

"It's a surprise."

"Yeah, and when you tell me, I'll be surprised."

Zeke chuckled. "Nice try. I thought you wanted to get to know your mates better."

"I do."

"So, ask me something."

I knew it was a distraction, but it was such an enticing offer that I couldn't refuse. The questions came out without any thoughts, wanting to know how he grew up, what his favorite memory was with me, his favorite color.

How did he become a tattoo artist? Did he have a favorite piece he's done? When was his birthday?

We talked for so long that I didn't even notice when he'd parked at our destination until he turned the car off. I immediately looked out the window, trying to figure out where we were. The parking lot was just a designated lot of dirt with a path off to the side and arrows directing to the 'entrance'.

I was basically skipping as Zeke led me down the path. The building was a dark black color, which was shocking. A little fence surrounded it, also black, and it looked like dead vines were intertwined on it for decoration. Little rocks on the ground were a mix of dark reds and burnt oranges and some that looked purple depending on the angle.

"What is this place?" I asked, my voice just a whisper.

"It's a garden." I turned my attention away from the gloomy colors to stare at him in shock. "Full of poisons, actually."

Then my jaw actually dropped open. "No way."

That explained the dark vibe of the place and made me even more excited for this date.

Inside, the same dark floral decorations lined the wall. Hanging from the ceiling was a giant chandelier, the fake flames radiating a warm orange glow which added to the eerie ambiance. There was an older couple inside, looking through all the potential souvenirs off to the side while another female stood behind the desk where the signs all pointed to start the tour.

When we got directly in front of her, she didn't so much as glance up from her book. Her naturally curly hair was pulled back into a messy bun, although a portion of the back that was meant to go up had been missed so it was still dangling. Even the little brown baby hairs around her forehead were tight curls. The glasses she wore weren't cute, the lenses making her eyes so big that it meant her eyesight must be really, really bad.

The book she wasn't looking up from was a literal textbook. By the looks of it, she was probably halfway through, the single image, a diagram on the bottom corner of the page, several hexagonal shapes all linked together with random letters around it. The rest of the page was filled with tiny, printed words, making it obvious why her face was literal inches from it.

And yet, the most shocking thing about the woman was that she was obviously an omega. Her floral scent was distinct enough that it didn't blend in with the rest of the nearby garden.

Zeke cleared his throat, trying to get her attention politely. When that didn't work, he said, "Good afternoon." Still, nothing. "Is this where we start the tour?"

A different voice, a male voice from behind us, said, "Yes."

That got the omega behind the desk to look up, her gaze immediately finding the male who spoke before her eyes widened as she realized we had been talking to her. She blinked her owlish eyes as she apologized.

"Rosy, will you get them some maps and a mask?" the male asked. He obviously worked there, not only from the way he spoke with the omega—Rosy—but the dark green apron tied around his neck and covering most of his body was a dead giveaway. A tool belt went around the apron, and a heavy-duty mask was dangling around his neck.

"Of course," Rosy said, shuffling around a lot of things to find what the male asked for. "I'm sorry about that. This chapter was just so interesting, and I got caught up in the dissection of the C18 Carbon. Just a single component and yet it determines the subdivision of a toxin. Amazing, right?"

I nodded, more amazed by her than actually understanding her words.

The male behind us chuckled too.

Rosy opened the map and leaned her face only inches from it as she started to draw on it with a dark marker. "You're going to start here on your self-paced tour, since we unfortunately are done with our guided ones today. Just follow the path. Remember, don't lean closer to smell any of the flora and funga. And if it's in a wire cage, definitely don't squeeze your fingers through to touch it."

Next, she underlined a few of the letter and number combinations on the drawn path before flipping the map booklet to the next page. "Here is how you know what you're looking at. Most plants have a little placard with a description, but the map has all their names."

"How come the names aren't out there?" I asked.

"Sometimes people get it into their head that a

certain name of a plant might not be toxic, or that it's harmful in a different way than they think. If you have to read the description first, it's easier to resist the urge to touch or sniff."

She was smart. It was a weird thought, but one I could barely get past. This omega worked, she was intelligent, she was literally actively learning.

"We do ask that you keep your masks on the entire time." The male walked around to the back of the desk, grabbing a water bottle out of a little cooler that must be back there. This close, I could scent his alpha designation, and the fact that he was clearly mated to the omega here.

Zeke and I both declined even though I was tempted to buy one just so I could keep talking to Rosy. An omega with a job? How was that even possible? I had so many questions.

Picking up the map and masks, then handing me mine, Zeke paid, and we made our way to the door with a final warning above the frame about the deadly and harmful plants in the garden.

I was basically bouncing with energy and excitement as Zeke and I put on the matching black masks. They were pretty thin, still breathable, but I figured it was more of a reminder to not lean over and sniff than anything.

As soon as we were outside, I squeezed Zeke's arm, wondering if he'd noticed she was an omega.

"I did," he agreed. "The only thing I can think of is that she's not considered an actual employee. She's probably not getting paid. But they're also not having to pay another receptionist. Ingenious, really. Now, put all thoughts of the other omega out of your head. This is our date, yeah?"

I went on my tippy toes to kiss him—realized I

couldn't. Tried to touch our noses, which were also covered. Then, in probably a world record timing for breaking the rules, considered taking my mask off.

Zeke laughed, leaning down to touch his forehead to mine.

With our hands clasped, we started our tour. The cobblestone pathway had been dyed a black color and the walls of the garden were made of stone, making the whole place feel like it was centuries old.

There was a lot more green than I'd anticipated, not only because I just assumed the plants would continue with the dark vibe, but also because it was still winter. Some areas had a solar warmer, others had missing leaves where the elements did finally have an effect. The flowers, though, were beautiful. Colorful and harmful, I was aspiring to be like them.

We took our time through the garden, reading all the plaques, looking up their names, talking about which one was our favorite, laughing at the uniquely harmful consequences of some. Our words were slightly muffled by the masks, but not enough that it made it too hard to understand each other.

A lot of the names were new to me, but some were so infamous that they had a second plaque explaining the history of use.

The garden's grounds were huge. A tour was only part of the location because in the very back there was an 'event area' which gave me all sorts of ideas. We saw a few employees working—one hosing down large gardening equipment, another lying down on their back taking pictures of a flower that was slightly drooping, and even one sweeping the walkway with a broom that looked like it was meant more for flying than cleaning.

When we came to the end of the tour, arriving back at the welcome center, I couldn't help saying, "This was the best date ever."

Zeke smiled widely, not the cocky kind that came with confidence, one that showed I'd made him happy. It was a cycle of happiness between us, reminding me that this was why I refused to go to the media and explain my side. This wasn't something I wanted to risk.

"We're not done yet," he admitted.

We left the garden, and Zeke started the long drive back toward the city. He stopped for a quick meal which we ate in the car, enjoying the greasy, filling deliciousness.

As soon as I finished, though, I asked, "Now where are we going?"

"It's another surprise."

I groaned, the sound long and loud and put-out.

Zeke chuckled. "I thought you enjoyed your first surprise."

"I did."

"You'll enjoy this one, too."

I grumbled under my breath about bossy, demanding alphas, which only made my mate smile. The drive brought us back into familiar territory, or at least, somewhat familiar. Most everything was the same, except a few restaurants or shops that we'd pass weren't the ones I remembered. It didn't feel too much like a big deal, stores closed down all the time randomly, or moved to a new location.

At least, that was what I told myself.

Zeke parked in a surprisingly empty public lot that had shade coverage, not that we needed it with how cold it was. The shops we passed didn't give a hint as to where we were going since they were all different. A vibrant shop that sold large cookies, a deco store that was a mix between a coffee shop and a place to play games, a bar that was only for betas.

I was led into a shop whose name I missed, but their selling point was immediately clear once I managed to blink through the blindingly white lights. It was a tattoo shop. The desk in front was decorated in artist drawings, the walls also covered in them. Different styles from bubble art to drawings that looked like a photograph to artwork so colorful and cartoonish that it was amazing to me that someone actually drew it.

A few people were waiting on the bench that we passed, Zeke pulling me further into the room. Six stations in total, the building was longer than it was wide, fitting each station against the wall with a thin aisle to walk down. All the artists gave Zeke a quick greeting, none of them bothering to question what he was doing there or with me.

Three artists were working. Two on large pieces, another on a small design around a bellybutton. Zeke took me to a station that was obviously his by the comfortability he had with it, patting the large chair for me to sit on.

The workplace had a little printer, which I thought was odd until he picked up a tablet and turned that on. There were also more familiar parts for a tattooist like the cart with the needle and machine, box of tight gloves, and towelettes. His desk drawers were labeled for the colors like, 'bright', 'pastel', and 'dark'.

"What are we doing here?" I asked, whispering so I didn't interrupt the concentration of the other tattooists. Technically music was playing in the background, but I didn't know if interrupting the song would bother anyone.

"You don't need to whisper," Zeke said, also whispering.

I glared at him.

"Let me get everything set up."

"Am I getting a tattoo?"

"Do you want one?"

I thought about it. I had no idea what I'd get, but it sounded like fun. Maybe something small and cute, just a random design. I could even get something around my wrist or ankle like faux jewelry.

"Let's do this first, and if you want something after, I'll do it for you," Zeke said.

I wanted to ask what 'this' was, but I was also conscious of the other people in the building. Alphas and betas. No omegas here.

It took a while for Zeke to do everything. Printing something out, then cutting it down to shape before setting it on the cart. Then he started pulling out ink and pouring little drops into tiny cups.

All of this seemed normal until he had me get off the chair and switch spots.

"Uh…" the sound I made was purely hesitant.

When he tried taking off his sweater, which was also his shirt, my instincts panicked. I grabbed his hands, stopping him from exposing himself in front of others. A growl started in the back of my throat, a warning that I wasn't happy.

"Okay, not all the way off," he agreed. Instead, he worked just one arm out, and I did my best to keep his stomach and chest covered to any prying gazes. With his shoulder exposed, I saw that the back of his arm had a blank space that he was prepping.

"Are you able to tattoo yourself?"

"Kinda. But this spot is too hard for me to reach."

I looked over at the other artists. None of them looked ready to stop what they were doing to help Zeke. Maybe the one doing the bellybutton piece, although my guess was that the others in the lobby were waiting. The idea that came to mind seemed ridiculous, yet I couldn't help asking, "Am I going to do it?"

"Yep. Here, take this and place it where you think looks good. Then just peel back the paper and the outline should still be there. Don't worry if you don't like the positioning, we can clean the area and try again."

This was an absolutely crazy, and potentially terrible idea. I refused to say either of that out loud though because I didn't want him to change his mind.

I did as I was told, setting up the paper so the image was placed in the perfect spot and then slowly revealing it. For now, it was all one color, but it should be easy enough to trace over with the proper needle. At least, I was giddy enough to think it would be easy.

"The reference is on the tablet if you want to take a look," Zeke said.

It was beautiful. And familiar. We'd just seen one of these flowers in the garden, admired its dangerous, threatening colors.

A buzzing sound demanded I pay attention as Zeke went through the process of explaining how to tattoo. It was probably the world's quickest explanation for what I needed to do and then the buzzing sound was in my hand, vibrating against my fingers.

As much as I was worried that I would hurt him, I was also excited. Not only was this going to be fun, but the amount of trust my mate had in me was like an aphrodisiac.

I took my time. The piece itself was probably just as big as my palm, with a lot of lines that were definitely not as straight as they could be. Still, I put all of my concentration into it.

By the time I finished, my hand was cramping from how hard I was holding the needle, my neck ached from my dramatic lean to make sure I was doing it right, but I was in love with my artwork. And maybe even a little with my alpha too.

Zeke walked me through cleaning it and putting a clear bandage on it then cleaned up his station. The moment he finished, and he was about to tell me he was ready to go, I jumped on him. I didn't care that we were in public, I needed to show him how much I appreciated him, how much fun I'd had, how happy I was with him.

My hands came to the back of his head, keeping him close as I kissed him. His hands wrapped around my thighs, holding me up, and probably helped to keep my bare ass from showing considering the split in my skirt was raised dangerously high.

"Zeke, man," someone called out.

My alpha pulled his mouth away from mine, earning a whimper that made him growl, baring his teeth at the other alphas in the space. Then he was carrying me out, my face nuzzling into his neck as I inhaled his scent. I couldn't help myself, licking up the column of his throat, tasting the mix of sweat and berries together, humming at the taste.

"Fuck, Hannah. Do that again, please."

Begging from my alpha had slick leaking from my core, no doubt creating a wet spot from where I was pressed tightly against him.

I licked his throat again, before gently biting down, maybe even squeezing a little too hard and leaving a slight red mark from my teeth. Both of our perfumes bloomed, mixing together in a scent of lavender-berries that I was desperate for more of.

I bit down harder, sucking along my mate's skin and leaving a bruise that felt like a claim.

It was already dark out, but the occasional passing lamp allowed me to see my work as I continued to mark my mate's skin. My hips had started to move, grinding against him as I worked for my own pleasure.

My back made contact with something cold and hard, making me gasp at the shock. Zeke used the moment to take charge, readjusting his grip so his hands were under each cheek, the tips of his fingers incredibly close to my core. His mouth found mine, his tongue immediately meeting mine, tasting my gasp.

I needed more than kissing and my hands seemed to work of their own accord, trailing down his neck and chest and reaching between our bodies until I found the top of his sweats, trying to push them down.

"Shit, Hannah." He tried to pull away, but I clung tighter to him, squeezing my thighs around him and wrapping my arms around his neck again.

Then I found myself in the back of the car, still straddling Zeke as he sat down and worked to get his sweats low enough to expose his gorgeous cock.

I didn't need any more incentive, I dropped down his entire length in one stroke, groaning at the way he filled me up so completely. Hands came around on my hips to help me move up and down on him and we were already so close to the edge that my mate was telling me to come, demanding it.

"You better come, Hannah, or I'm going to knot your mouth next time," he told me, continuing to thrust into me at the same time. "You won't get to feel my cum inside you, I'll knot so far inside your mouth that you won't get to taste me either."

I whimpered, my arousal somehow increasing with his dirty words.

"You were desperate for me. Jumping on me at my place of work so that all those other alphas got a tease of what they could never have. Why's that? Huh, Hannah? Why can't they have you?"

"Because I'm yours."

"Because you're mine."

I slammed my mouth over his, clashing with him almost violently as my orgasm forced its way through my body. More slick and cum leaked from me, the liquids spilling down my thighs since my mate didn't knot me.

"Why?" I asked, panting from the exertion of my climax.

"I'm going to take you home and knot you properly, omega."

With how excited my body got at his words, it was like my first orgasm hadn't even happened. I climbed off my mate, making my way to the front seat and ignoring the stain of cum and slick on my skirt. Zeke got behind the wheel and drove us home where he made good on his promise to knot me in my nest.

It was the perfect ending to a perfect date.

Chapter Fourteen

The next week was all about finding a new normal. Jackson was officially working from home now, making himself my designated security. Both Seb and Zeke were still at their normal jobs, although I'd learned that Zeke had a little security camera on his desk that was connected to Jackson's phone. Seb's job apparently had enough security that Jackson wasn't too worried.

According to the television, the only thing that the public could agree on was the demand for change.

Alphas wanted more protection for their omegas. They wanted betas gone because they claimed the other designation didn't have the right instincts to care for their mates. On top of that, the extreme loudmouths agreed with that disgusting representative, Adam Whatever, that omegas should be forced to take mates after a certain age. For their protection, of course.

I was really starting to hate that word. Protection. It was becoming synonymous for weak. It meant that alphas were shifting the responsibility, the blame, to omegas for not being as strong as them rather than holding other alphas responsible for their actions.

According to them, alpha instincts were too strong to ignore. Those protective urges demanded the alpha to protect their mate and pack but to also claim an unmated omega if they scented one.

It was amazing how the same logic meant to boost their designation, defiled mine.

According to them, I was also too emotional. That meant I had to be locked away. Rather than being rescued by princes, omegas were being locked away by them.

Alpha instincts forced them into a rut the same

way mine pulled me into a heat, both of us unable to partake in society during that time. Yet, I was the one too unstable to work and alphas weren't. The logic wasn't logical.

The worst part was my mates agreed with me. So even when I went on a raging speech about how illogical these asshole alphas were, they just nodded their heads agreeing. I didn't change any minds as I paced in the living room with my eloquent words thrown at the TV.

I had no idea where the alphas opposing these ridiculous extremists were—except in hiding. My alphas suggested they were keeping quiet, scared that their omegas would be taken from them, or even targeted to prove a point. Of course, there were also the few rare alphas who didn't want omegas because of the 'emotional manipulation' so they probably weren't bothering speaking up either.

The issue with a loud minority was that it made it seem like their idea was more popular than it was. That meant people like representative Adam had a better chance of convincing his colleagues to vote with him since his extreme ideas were parading around like they were socially accepted.

What I could say for the zealous alphas, at least, was that they were in agreement about the kind of change they wanted. The protesting betas were having a different problem.

Some betas were simply protesting against the alphas' demands to kick them out of packs and society. They argued that betas served a purpose in packs, to help comfort an omega during the day, to be a nonhormonal fuck for the alpha outside of a heat, to be a level of stability in a home.

These betas wanted to be part of packs. They claimed that there were three designations for a reason, and a perfect pack would have at least one of each member.

Then there were the other betas. In some ways, they agreed with the alphas. These betas didn't want to be a substitute for omegas. They argued that the hormones of the other designations didn't affect them, so they should have their own part of society where they could live without having to bend to the whims of the more emotional members.

No one was agreeing with each other, not between the designations or even in them. Yet, through all of this, omegas still weren't shouting out our own opinions. At least, not publicly. I had done plenty of shouting.

I spent the last week pouring myself into my online classes—when I wasn't yelling at the TV. I had a point to prove, and I was going to do it by graduating. I still had to wait to choose a major, and I was claiming that as the reason I was undecided about which one to pick. Koda spoke the truth when she pointed out I'd never be able to work in whatever degree I picked. But that wasn't my fault.

Alphas claimed we didn't want to work while also saying we weren't allowed to. Am I destined for a job? Maybe not. But there were omegas out there like Rosy, who so obviously had a passion and wanted to be immersed in it.

I was at the point of even bringing my laptop into my nest so I could look at my classes as soon as I woke up. Sure, I took a few sex breaks throughout the day, and my mates ensured I ate.

It was late into the night, leading into the weekend so all my mates were up and relaxing while I was still on my laptop. Every time someone moved, my gaze flicked up to them, like when Jackson started a fire, or when Han got up for a book, and even when Seb simply got up to stretch his body.

I had finally finished reviewing everything and now I was to the point of actually completing assignments. My stress was perfuming around me as I looked through the quiz, again, determined that my first real grade would be a good one.

I was stalling, I knew that.

With my laptop on the kitchen island, I had the perfect view of all my mates, sitting on the couch, feigning watching TV as they took turns glancing back at me, wanting to comfort me yet giving me the space I asked for to do my quiz.

When Seb stood up from the couch, I was already shaking my head. "Let me just look it over one more time, and then I'll be done."

"Princess, you finished this quiz almost half an hour ago. It's one grade. I promise, whether you do bad or good, it won't make too much of a difference."

I ran my hand over my head, only slightly wishing I had hair long enough to pull on. "I have to do well. I need good grades if I'm going to graduate."

"Look at your grades before. They were all good. You've never taken these classes for granted. You need to trust yourself. And more importantly, this was supposed to be an opportunity for you. Not a punishment. Don't stress yourself out."

Seb continued to walk around the island as he spoke, coming closer, and pulling me into a hug so that my gaze was forced away from the screen. I heard my laptop make a small clicking sound that had me gasping.

"Did you just—"

"Look at that. A perfect score. Congrats, princess."

Seb's words got the rest of my alphas jumping up, celebrating and distracting me from the espionage of submitting my quiz literally behind my back.

"Time for a break now, rebel," Jackson said, pulling me back to the living room and setting me on his lap.

"Just for a little," I agreed.

"You don't want to burn yourself out," Seb said, coming to sit next to Jackson, pulling my feet onto his lap and starting to rub them. "Trust me. I did years of schooling. A little bit everyday keeps you consistent and makes sure you don't get mindless on accident."

I groaned when I felt the deep pressure against my foot's arch.

A blanket was laid over me, the slight scratchy texture of the sarape on my cheek was perfect. The weave meant tiny holes so I wouldn't overheat which was why I usually hated the extra soft, fluffy blankets.

"I just feel like…" I trailed off for a moment, trying to find the right words. "I guess I'm worried that something will happen, and I won't be able to take the classes anymore. I want to get them done before I'm kicked out."

"You won't," Seb said. "I know it's hard to fully understand since all you know is being an omega, but betas are simply allowed to attend college. Your student account is set. Hannah Baumgartner exists, regardless of what happens to you as an omega."

"But what if it's the schools that change? You saw that protest the other day on the news. Betas are getting tired of being treated as less than alphas and omegas. And they're so infuriated about it that they want to have their own parts of the city. Their own schools and malls and places of work and neighborhoods."

"Even if it did happen, it would take years. You have time, princess. I promise."

I snuggled deeper against Jackson. His chest was

vibrating gently, not enough to make any noise, but strong enough to make all my muscles relax. The three of us were silent for a while, even the TV had been muted, the only sounds from the crackling fire.

"Where are Han and Zeke?" I wanted all my mates to come cuddle with me.

"Getting dinner."

I wished they'd said a temporary goodbye, but I didn't think much about it. For the next few minutes, the three of us just relaxed together. It was a temporary solace that I was basking in.

When Han and Zeke came home, smelling of arousal and delicious food, our lighthearted mood continued into the night.

Even into the weekend.

We kept the TV off, mostly stayed off our phones—both Jackson and Seb struggled with that portion—and had a lazy, safe weekend.

As we were getting ready for bed, my mates grumbling about needing to get back to the 'real world' the next day, the doorbell went off. I had been in the bathroom with Jackson, just finishing brushing my teeth as my alpha was doing the same.

My curiosity had me quickly rinsing my mouth, ignoring the shouts from Jackson telling me to wait, but I couldn't. Strangers at the house, especially in a neighborhood like ours, weren't solicitors. And I lived for drama.

Zeke beat me down the stairs, and rather than continuing with me to the door, he wrapped his arms around me and kept me off to the side, letting Jackson pass us by, smirking the whole time. "Nice try, rebel."

"Who is it?" I asked.

Han and Seb made their way down the stairs too, yet none of my alphas had an answer for me.

I watched Jackson check who it was, his mood immediately plummeting, his scent blooming with frustration.

"Take Hannah upstairs."

Zeke didn't ask questions, just started walking, his arm around my stomach automatically taking me with him.

"No, wait, who is it?" I did my best to claw at the walls and corner to keep Zeke from being able to make any progress.

"Reporter," Jackson said, making the other alphas stiffen.

"How did they get our address?" Seb asked.

Han shook his head like he understood Seb's unspoken question. "The OC wouldn't put an omega in danger like that. Especially one that, for all intents and purposes, is obeying their rules."

Did that mean Seb thought the person outside was here to ask about me? Would I be able to tell my side of the story?

The excitement and nerves mixed together in my body. I knew I shouldn't, but I wanted to talk to someone about what had truly happened to me. My mates worried about what speaking out would mean for our pack, but some decisions were bigger than just the five of us. Right?

Or maybe acting as the type of pack that the asshole alphas were trying to destroy was its own act of defiance. Was that enough? To live in secret and keep our voice hidden behind voting and money passing hands?

My internal debate distracted me from trying to stop Zeke as he pulled me up the stairs. To my surprise, and delight, he stopped high enough up that no one would be able to see us, but we could still hear. Didn't stop him from covering my mouth with his hand and keeping his arm banded tightly around my stomach. It was a compromise I was willing to accept.

Paying attention to the discussion downstairs I heard Seb say, "Let me handle this. I have the best experience with the media."

"You'll also be the most recognizable," Han said. "Jackson should do it. Especially since he's first alpha."

I was getting nervous that the person at the door would leave. If the reason they were there was because of me, I wanted to be a part of the conversation.

Finally, Jackson opened the door, greeting whoever was there gruffly.

I was just barely able to hear the person outside, asking Jackson if they heard about some supposed fight between two alpha packs nearby. When he said no, they continued to give him information, claiming it happened just a few houses down, that an omega was involved.

"Do you have an omega?" the reporter asked. "How would you feel about a dominance battle over them? Should they be allowed?"

Jackson didn't answer, simply shutting the door in the person's face. A few minutes later, he said, "All clear. Hannah, come on down here."

Zeke chuckled against my ear before he whispered, "good luck."

I slowly made my way back down the stairs. Both Han and Seb were trying, and failing, to hide their smirks as Jackson glared at me.

"I didn't actually open the door," I reminded him, immediately stating my case.

"Because you know you shouldn't or because Zeke caught you in time?"

I stuck up my nose. "Does it matter?"

Jackson sighed, opening his arms. My body didn't even hesitate, running the few steps toward him and jumping into his grasp. "I need to keep you safe, rebel."

With my legs still around him, I leaned back slightly so I could meet his gaze. "What about the other omegas who need to be safe? If that reporter had been here for me, maybe I could have told my side of the story. Omegas need someone to stand up for them."

"I agree. But some random reporter was not the best option for that. You have no idea if they would've cut your segment, using your words out of context. Or maybe they were simply a test from the OC to see if you'd talk if given the chance."

"You think they'd do that?"

"I wouldn't put anything past them right now. They're a business, first and foremost. And you're a direct threat to their profits."

Jackson was right—as usual, I was learning. Some random reporter wasn't the solution for designation rights. If I wanted to play the political game, I had to do it right, not just whenever the mood hit that I needed to do something.

I kissed him. First his forehead and then dropping little kisses down his nose until I met his mouth. "You're right."

Jackson groaned. "Sexiest words you could ever say, rebel."

The other alphas laughed as I pulled back and pretended to glare at him.

Rather than set me down, Jackson carried me upstairs to the nest. I did my best to block out the internal voice in my head that was saying I wasn't doing enough for my designation. Telling me that simply living in defiance wasn't helping anyone. It was harder than it should have been to ignore that voice—and I knew that it wouldn't be the last time I heard from it.

JOSEPHINE LIGHT

Chapter Fifteen

It was the middle of the week, and the middle of the day, as I flipped through the electronic textbook on my laptop. Han was working at his desk, the two of us in an easy, comfortable silence.

That was when the door slammed open. I screamed, the sound loud and short as I recognized the blond alpha in the doorway.

Han jerked up from his seat, the chair sliding back and slamming into the wall at the sudden intrusion. "Holy shit, Seb. Ever heard of knocking? Or entering the room like a normal person without threatening to break my door off the hinges?"

It was weird to hear my posh alpha cuss, and I had to work to hide my smile. Seb had definitely startled Han, and the alpha was not taking it well.

I moved next to him, wrapping my arms around him and tucking my face against his chest. The tension seemed to drain out of him as he wrapped his arms around me.

"I think it's time for a break," Han said, his words muffled as he spoke them against the top of my head.

"It definitely is because Hannah and I have a date."

My head jerked up, barely missing Han's face, as I turned to look at my blond alpha. "A date?"

"Yep."

"What about work?"

"Done for the day. Any more questions?"

"Where are we going?" All sorts of ideas came to mind, and I tried to remember if Seb had hinted at anything in particular these last few days.

"Get changed. We're getting all dressed up."

I ran out of the room, racing up the stairs to find something to wear. Dressed up. Like dolled up. Fancy. Definitely a dress then. It was the afternoon which made me wonder if maybe there was a formal limit, but then again, if we were planning to drive a few hours to get there, maybe not.

Pulling out several outfits, I mixed and matched shoes and tights and dresses. I wasn't sure whether the tights should blend in, just providing warmth, or if I wanted them to be a statement piece.

When none of the outfits fit my mood, I pulled out a dress I'd overlooked because it was long. To my surprise, the length was more of an illusion. All black, the bottom part was sheer, great for showing off my legs. The top was a one-piece bodysuit, the heart-shaped neckline continued down the stomach, the sides cut out to truly accentuate the heart, and coming together between my legs. It had thin straps that I could have probably tucked in and gone strapless, but I liked them out.

I made sure to put some of the special jelly on my thighs since they were going to be rubbing together with each step. It had a slight smell to it that made me wrinkle my nose, but it wasn't an option unless I wanted to chafe.

I grabbed my boots and then made my way down the stairs, feeling an extra bounce in my step. Dressing up was fun. It might be unusual for my outfit to lack any fun colors, but the sexy cute style more than made up for it— especially after I'd added a studded choker.

Standing up, I bent over to hide the laces in the boots, wanting a sleeker look, only to hear, "Goddamn, princess," from behind me.

Just for fun, I shook my hips, knowing my ass looked good in the outfit. My cheeks might have been covered, but only barely in the one-piece dress, and the sheer outer layer wasn't hiding anything.

Warm hands cupped my ass, the scent of fresh guava, like the kind you just cut open, mixed with the sea salt hint from his arousal surrounded me. The thickness of his member was obvious too, creating a flurry of excitement in my lower stomach.

"You're lucky we have a reservation, or we'd never leave the house."

I laughed, standing up and only slightly swaying from all the blood that rushed to my head. Seb chuckled, grabbing onto my biceps to help steady me. I flashed him a smile as thanks and he leaned down to kiss me, taking his time, slowly exploring my mouth.

His hand tightly wrapped around mine, he pulled me to his car. Just as large as Zeke's, yet missing a huge table in the back taking up space, Seb's car was slightly fancier. The seats a nicer fabric, the center console more elegant, and even the ride seemed smoother.

"What made you decide on today?" I asked.

"I booked this date a while ago actually. I just figured you'd rather it be a short surprise."

I nodded, "You assumed right."

My leg was already bouncing in anticipation of where we were heading. I tried to distract myself by asking about my mate. He told me all about how he was raised, with etiquette lessons in sitting and dining and greeting people. Despite how much he admitted breaking away from that harsh mold his parents cast him in, I could still see some of it in him.

His perfect posture even while driving, the way he spoke, his words never mumbled or unclear. Even compared with Han, there was something just … formal about Sebastian.

"Did you ever like it?" I asked him.

"Like what?"

185

"The formal attire. The fancy dining and being waited on hand and foot."

"It has its perks. I never grew up worried about food on the table or whether I'd get gifts for the holidays. But I also wasn't allowed to talk to other kids my mother saw as 'beneath us'. I wasn't just encouraged to be proper, I was punished if I wasn't. When it's a choice, I have no issue occasionally making it. But my life was dictated too closely, I never felt like I was free … like I had a choice in anything."

I felt the frustration at his past in his words. Or maybe it was my own understanding that helped me to relate to him. "Do you feel like you have plenty of choices now? Enough freedom?"

"I do. I remember when we first started courting you, back when you were still living at the OC and hiding your involvement with the designation movement. It was the first time that I wished I was back to getting everything I wanted."

"What do you mean?"

He shook his head, a smile pulling at his lips like he was thinking of a fond memory. My mate was absolutely gorgeous, even from the side profile as he drove. I had never really been interested in cars, or got the appeal of men driving them, but seeing Seb's face, his long fingers on the wheel, completely relaxed and in control, yeah, there was something incredibly sexy about the image.

"We weren't particularly interested in finding an omega, but my mother had arranged for us to get our scents documented for the OC. At the time, it was better to just let her think she was getting her way since we never figured we'd actually court anyone."

Omegas at the OC were required to go through all the scents of potential alphas to find the right pack.

Technically, we weren't forced to pick one. Even so, the betas watched as we sniffed at the swatches covered in alpha scents, and if we had a particularly strong reaction, the omega would find themselves with a date.

I didn't remember scenting my pack, but considering how much I loved their scents, and remembering how much I hated smelling the swatches, I could imagine being shocked at the scents for this pack. I imagined being caught unaware of how much I enjoyed their combined smell that the beta watching me would have run off with excitement at the chance to pack me up.

"As soon as we met you, I think we all knew we wanted you," Seb continued. "You, princess, were not as immediately convinced. You liked our scents well enough, but I remember you telling us that if you were ever in a freak accident, and you lost your nose, you'd still want to love your pack."

"Would losing a nose stop your sense of smell?" I asked. "Like, if your nostrils were flat on your face, would your sense of smell be the same?"

"That's a complicated answer. Technically your nose does have some olfactory senses, although the majority of your ability to smell comes from the direct connection of the smell receptors in the nose reaching up to the brain."

The answer didn't really answer the question for me, but I nodded anyways.

"Anyways, we courted you for a while. Obviously, our charms worked in the end." He glanced over at me quickly, winking in a way that had me rolling my eyes at him.

"Will you tell me more about your job?"

Even though I already knew it, hearing Seb describe his work was unavoidable proof that my mate was incredibly smart. When he said he did years of schooling, I realized then that he wasn't exaggerating. I figured that he went into a scientific discipline because he wanted to prove to himself that he was enough. After all, he needed more than money to get into his current field.

I was proud, and slightly envious that he was able to break free of his gilded cage. That was what I wanted for myself.

When Seb finally parked the car, I still didn't have a clue where we were. The building was huge, and even the car port was fancy with several people in tailored suits waving cars in, opening doors, and even acting as guides.

I half-jumped when my door was opened by someone not Sebastian. The female smiled at me, offering me her hand to help me out of the car. Her suit was obviously tailored to her body and considering how good she looked, it made me think that I might've wanted to start wearing suits. Not the shirt part underneath, just the pants and coat combo would be perfect.

"How are you doing today?" the beta asked. Her eyes flared when she caught my scent, quickly dropping my hand and taking a half-step away.

"Just dandy," I told her. My mate came around the car to pull me close to him.

"If you'll follow me." She led us to an elevator, even getting in to press the button for us which I thought was kind of funny. The small space was just as elegant as the garage, which was making me even more curious about what we were doing.

Was this an event or a restaurant? Because I was hoping food would be there. Even if it was little samples or something.

I probably should have told Seb that Han and I had worked right through lunch. My excitement about the date had distracted me from my hunger, but it was now nudging my stomach with its little reminders.

The elevator ride was dramatically long.

When the doors opened, the beta held her arm out in front to stop the doors from closing on us and said, "Enjoy the show."

Show. That caught my attention.

Sebastian chuckled softly, pulling me further into the room. It was crowded, although not in a need to push anyone out of the way. Along the floor was a literal red carpet that was meant to act as a walkway. Along both sides of it, people and couples conversed, standing around in nice clothes that no one else accidentally matched.

The ceiling was high, showing off that this level was more like two floors rather than one. I could see there was a sort of balcony along the wall with some chairs and tables already set up. Dangling from the ceiling was probably the world's largest golden chandelier with enough arms and flame-shaped bulbs that I'd hate to be the person who was in charge of keeping that clean.

We continued following the red carpet, even going up the stairs toward the balcony. I wanted to lean down and pull at the carpet to see if it was glued down to the stairs. It was so perfectly folded over each lip that I was impressed and curious as to how they cleaned it.

"What is this show?" I asked, whispering as Seb helped me into a seat.

The table was small, the light golden cloth laid over it bare of any food. Seb sat on one side of the table and me on the other, the railing in front of us teasing me to lean over it and see just how high we were.

A loud screeching sound pulled my attention back over to Seb who was dragging the table off to the side and moving his chair closer to me. I smiled widely, loving how dramatic and disruptive it was yet he didn't even care that people were glaring, scoffing at us under their breath.

"That's better," Seb said once his chair was so close his thigh pressed against mine.

"What is this exactly?"

"You'll see."

I groaned, but then someone behind us cleared their throat to get our attention.

"I'll be your waiter for the day," the male said. He was young, and his suit was less security and more server. The back of his coat had a weird flair, and the white undershirt had a stiff collar that was flicked up around his neck. "Are there any allergies the chef needs to be alerted to?"

"None," Seb said.

The waiter nodded and left and then Seb leaned in, whispering, "This food is going to be fancy, which is code for tiny yet overpriced. If you're still hungry later, we'll get a snack on the drive home."

"How fancy is fancy?"

"Think potatoes, whipped so they're a puree on top of the most delicious bite of steak. You'll want more, but that'll be the entire course until the next tiny portion comes along."

My mouth was already watering at Seb's talk of food.

His hand landed on my thigh, the heat from him easily penetrating through the thin sheer fabric over my legs. Each finger slowly started squeezing, his pinky dangerously close to my core.

Leaning closer to me, so close that his lips bumped the shell of my ear with each word, he said, "Spread your legs just a little, princess."

I obeyed, and his hand moved higher up my thigh,

and then settled. Every finger seemed to have a direct line to my arousal, and each slight movement, each simple twitch was a tease. My perfume was only barely tainting the air, and I hoped since we were mostly around betas that they wouldn't notice even that much.

Eventually, the waiter came back with drinks for us in gold glasses. The first sip of my drink was bitter. I did my best to hide my distaste as the waiter left and I balanced the glass on my knee.

"Here, try mine," Seb said, plucking my drink from my grip and shoving his own in my hand before I could argue. His drink was a slightly darker color than mine had been, and I was hesitant to take a sip. But when I did, the flavors burst on my tongue. I almost moaned at the taste, and I had to force myself to lower my hand so I didn't chug it all. "Better?"

"Much," I agreed.

The lights on the chandelier finally dimmed, and the audience became hushed. Below the railing, on the ground level, I could see a beautifully decorated floor mosaic. Small tile pieces were part of the ground, growing and spiraling into flowers, so long as those flowers were golden. It was an elegant beauty, the kind of beauty you knew was created for the space, not the kind that was so beautifully done that the location just had to include it.

With the quiet pressing down on everyone, the sounds of steps and something else were clearly audible. I watched as several chairs were set up in the center of the floor, along with a giant sleek golden piano. Several people were pushing it, and then bending down to mess with the legs. Finally, someone came out and set a bench down in front of the piano and then everyone left again.

The anticipation was killing me. My foot was bouncing, unable to hold still in these teasing moments before the surprise truly began. I felt like I wasn't breathing enough, trying to stay quiet with the rest of the audience. I was even leaning forward, closer to the railing, blatantly ignoring my mate as I waited to see what would happen.

More footsteps.

This time, people came out in elegant clothes, more than just the black outfits that forced employees into the background. They held instruments—all but one who made their way to the bench in front of the piano.

The audience seemed to settle. The quiet was no longer dramatic but patient.

As they settled into their seats, I admired the way they caressed their instruments. Every movement seemed purposeful. They looked like they'd been created for this exact thing, their muscles formed simply to hold up whatever instrument they needed. Their straight backs, crossed ankles, all of it was second nature to playing.

And then they started.

Slow and soft. Not startling anyone with a dramatic piece.

They played and I was sucked in.

Music wasn't something I ever really thought about. It existed and I liked it, but this was completely different to the everyday songs I listened to or heard. Without words, yet I could feel the story. The sounds weren't telling, merely pushing and pulling and swinging the narrative along.

So ingrained in their minds, there were no stands for reading the notes. Everything they played, they had memorized, and that somehow made everything even more beautiful.

As the first piece died down, I started clapping. My hands were the only noise echoing throughout the room. I didn't care.

Beside me, Seb chuckled, and when I finally stopped, he grabbed my hands, pulling them to his lips to kiss.

The next song started and at some point, the waiter started dropping off the courses. Seb was right when he said they were tiny. Some were only two bites, although we did get a few bigger ones which took maybe four bites.

Seb was also right that they were delicious. Everything was perfectly cooked. Every bite had me wishing for more, yet there were only the tiny portions before our plates were yanked away and the next was appearing.

I wondered if the point of the small portions was to keep the distractions minimal while we listened to the music. The few bites of food were enough to keep us sidetracked from our hunger without pulling too much of our attention toward our plates.

When we finally reached the dessert portion, I had tears in my eyes, and I was trying to be subtle and quiet about how clogged my nose was from trying to stop myself from bawling.

I'd never read ... listened to ... experienced a story that didn't end happily. In this one, there was only sadness and despair and longing. It broke my heart. A part of me was angry that this story didn't end in a positive light, and yet, I understood that it only made it more real.

They finished without a flair, ending on notes so low that I knew the story would never fully be as happy as it was in the beginning. The lights came on, and the musicians stood, bowing to the very calm clapping of the audience.

I didn't bother with the polite tapping of hands, I banged mine together, ensuring everyone knew that I fucking loved the show.

The woman with the cello glanced up, her gaze somehow managing to find mine almost instantly.

I blushed, wondering if she too thought I was callous and loud like literally everyone else in the building. I didn't care, though. I absolutely loved the performance, and I was going to show my love the way normal people did, not the fancy people who considered this their due because they paid. Well, I didn't pay for shit.

Once the musicians left the floor, the audience began talking again. They weren't loud like a mall or public space, however, it was more than obvious that a lot of personal conversations were happening.

"What did you think?" Seb asked, handing me a swatch of fabric from his jacket pocket.

I dabbed the cloth under my eyes, wanting to blow my nose in it but figuring that would be rude. "It was amazing. So sad, yet amazing."

"Pardon the interruption." Seb and I both turned to see our waiter again, empty handed to my disappointment. "Olivia Grace has requested to meet you both."

Was that the cellist I'd made eye contact with? Or were we in trouble because I'd clapped too loud? Could you be in trouble for that?

Sebastian didn't seem worried, so I let him pull me up from the chair, wrapping my arm around his elbow as we followed the waiter. If I was honest, I was still feeling slightly hungry. Not starving, although I knew I'd need a snack before bed.

We went down the stairs and then veered off the red carpet in the direction that the instruments were carried off in.

The doors we passed through blended in with the walls, sliding to the side as they opened like a secret passageway. Immediately, the high-class vibe of the room disappeared. The hall was still clean, but it lacked the golden touches, the over-the-top decorations that no one seemed to compliment because they simply expected it to exist.

My eyes ached with how bright the hall was, and I relied on Seb's nearness to guide me where I needed to be as I fought with my eyelids to open against the onslaught of potential blinding. Omegas were said to be sensitive to bright lights, that's why we required dim and dark in our nest. Most alphas considered this a weakness, as proof that we weren't meant to be out in public.

I always thought it simply showed weakness on the betas and alphas. They enjoyed the brighter lights because they needed them to see. Omega eyesight was superior enough to be satisfied by the low settings.

All of my thoughts about designations disappeared as the waiter opened a random door, letting us step through. Fortunately, the lights were softer here, more normal for a room. Along one wall was a couch, a few thin blankets tossed randomly along the arms and back. The opposite wall had two racks. One with normal clothes and the other with fancier pieces. Against the back wall was a beauty station. A desk that held a mirror, lights all around it, and a lot of makeup and hair products. Sitting on the little round seat in front of it was Olivia Grace. She looked almost the same except her hair was now up, the long locks exposing a claiming mark on her neck.

I knew she was an alpha, her honey scent filled the space and forced my nose to inhale it.

"Thank you for coming," she said. Her voice was sweet and filled with an accent that made it painfully obvious she was bilingual.

"You were amazing," I told her.

She smiled, dimples forming on her cheeks. "Thank you. It is rare that we get such a standing ovation for our performance. I'm glad you enjoyed it."

My mate was behind me, my back to his front, and I leaned against him. He was holding me while I tried my best to keep all my questions to myself because I had so many, and I didn't want to annoy her, but I also didn't know what else to say.

Glancing down at a dainty watch hanging from a lightbulb around the mirror, Olivia Grace said, "I have some time before my interviews. Would you like to talk some more?"

"I have so many questions," I admitted.

Olivia Grace gestured to the couch for Seb and me to sit down. I was barely on the edge of my seat before I demanded, "When did you start playing?" She was patient with me, explaining everything I wanted to know about who created the pieces they played, why she picked the cello, how she met her orchestra mates.

I wasn't sure how long we actually talked, but eventually, a knock came on her door before someone opened it, not even waiting for a response. I recognized the male as another member of the group as he leaned his head in to say something. His words caught in his throat as he stared at us on the couch.

"It is time?" Olivia Grace asked.

The male agreed with an accent similar to Olivia Grace's.

Seb and I stood, and I thanked Olivia Grace again for meeting with us. We all walked back down the hallway together, the other members of the group apparently at the interview already. Now my stomach was officially grumbling for dinner. I wanted something big and filling.

Back where the performers had played, the

interview was being held. A bunch of people were standing around, cameras at the ready, and little recording devices in their hands.

Murmurs started at our appearance, and I wondered if Olivia Grace was going to get in trouble for being late. I had no idea if we went past the time or not.

As we headed toward the elevator, I heard someone yell out my name.

It didn't occur to me that it was one of the reporters. I didn't question whether or not the voice was male or female, with or without an accent, or even if I'd given Olivia Grace my name at all.

I turned around, looking for whoever called my name.

Flashes started, and immediately people started moving closer to me, talking over one another as they demanded answers to questions that I wanted to answer but no one would stop talking long enough to let me. Seb was pulling me toward the elevator, and I stumbled over my own feet, still facing the reporters as I walked backward.

My bravado was failing at all the lights, the voices, the nearness of strangers. Why were they yelling? The questions were becoming meaner, more demanding. They weren't asking me questions—they were trying to set me up. I knew that much, and my heart was breaking with each vulgar insistence.

My mates were right. They didn't want my answer, they didn't want to hear my side. They wanted confirmation for what they already believed was true.

That I was attacked by betas.

That I supported representative Adam's claims that omegas needed to be more heavily protected.

That I was hiding away because I was scared to leave the house after what happened.

That the attack almost killed me.

I was shaking my head—it was all I could do to argue. Every time I opened my mouth to say something, no one heard, or maybe nothing was coming out, I didn't know.

Seb pulled me back into the elevator, the reporters refusing to stop following. I was pushed behind my mate, and I grabbed onto the back of his coat, terrified that he'd leave me. Terrified that he'd step away from me and I would be swarmed again.

I never would have thought this would be scary. They were just people, just cameras. I wasn't sure why I was feeling overwhelmed.

This was exactly what I'd wanted, the opportunity to tell my story.

Yet it was also exactly like my mates had expected.

I watched as the alphas from the orchestra helped push the reporters back. They weren't acting like people then. Like I was a person. Their desperation for the story was more than curiosity and interest. They were dangerous. Yet, reporters.

My mind was in a panic, tears were blurring my vision until finally, the doors had enough space to close. Immediately my mate turned to me, pulling me in so he was holding me tight. His scent was all wrong, like an expired guava, telling me he was equally as distressed about what happened as I was.

I wanted to say something, to ask what the hell had just happened, only I didn't want to break the silent seal around us. Everything felt like too much. I was overwhelmed, and honestly, hurt.

It felt like I'd been betrayed by the people I'd thought would help me. They were this last chance I was holding onto in my mind, playing out scenarios of what could be, and all of those dreams just broke.

Seb held me tight, and the tears I felt for sure would come didn't. I was just being held, and then the doors dinged open, and I was being dragged along. The parking area was empty of people. All the news vans were parked where the guests had been before.

As soon as I was sitting in the seat, my door still open with Seb beside me, I burst into tears.

"Oh, princess," Seb pulled me to the side, so I was leaning against his chest again. "You're breaking my heart. But we have to go, okay? I don't trust those assholes not to come back down and chase after you."

I didn't want to let my mate go. He pulled my hands off his shirt and then slammed the door shut behind him.

I hated that I was crying, that I had gotten spooked over something that I couldn't even properly explain. What was scary about a bunch of people that wanted to interview me? Was it the way they'd all talked over each other, pushing at each other to get closer to me as if their cameras wouldn't have been able to zoom in from several feet away? Was it the way their scents mixed together until my own senses were overwhelmed?

The driver's door pulled open and I startled before realizing it was my mate.

A loud ringing sound came through the car like a song and my mate pushed a button on the center console screen.

I missed whatever the person said because Seb was leaving the parking area, and my attention was on the little mirror, watching as the elevators opened again and a bunch of people rushed out, their cameras immediately catching us as we drove away.

My heart broke, realizing my back-up plan, my last hope, was nonexistent. And I started crying again.

****

At some point on the drive home from my date with Seb, I'd stopped crying. My eyes were shut, but I wasn't sleeping. I felt completely drained, my cheeks raw from crying, but it was my body that felt weird. Like it was too heavy.

When my door opened, it took all of my energy to turn my head and blink open my eyes.

"I'm so sorry, princess," Seb said.

I shook my head, trying to tell him that it wasn't his fault. None of it was, especially not my broken hope. He'd tried to warn me. Over and over again he told me that the media wasn't my friend, and I nodded my head along, not believing him.

Now I did.

He pulled me out of the car, holding me as he walked into the house. I kept my face tucked against his neck, my arms and legs tight around him as I held on.

On top of all my crazy emotions, I felt guilt. Guilty for ruining this amazing date with Sebastian.

"I'm sorry," I told him, whispering the words against his neck. "I'm sorry."

I knew my other mates were close, but I didn't want Sebastian to let me go. I was only vaguely aware of him taking the steps up to my nest. Even with my eyes closed, I knew the dimmed lights and scents of my nest once we arrived.

Seb carefully lowered us both down and then I felt Jackson at my back, two of my alphas squeezing me between them. I didn't have any tears left, but I was freezing. When Jackson rolled away, a whimper came out. The sound quickly cut off when he came back, pressing himself tightly against me and throwing a blanket over all of us.

"What are you thinking, rebel?" Jackson asked.

"Talk to us."

"Where's Han and Zeke?"

"They're making you some dinner."

I didn't want to eat even as I felt how hungry my stomach was. I just wanted my mates close, but there was also no more of me to be shared, so I guessed it worked out.

"I don't know why I'm crying so much," I admitted. I wished I could somehow get closer to both alphas, wanting their bodies pressed tighter against me despite already feeling their warmth on my front and back.

"They were verbally attacking you, princess," Seb said. Behind me, Jackson growled, but Seb continued like he hadn't even heard the first alpha. "Not even press conferences are that bad because usually someone maintains some type of order. Celebrities are used to the flashing cameras and questions but they're usually walking or, again, have some type of security."

"Did you hear what they asked?"

I looked up, needing to see Seb's face when he responded. He looked so sad, heartbroken just like me when he nodded.

"I feel like we lost. I kept thinking that no matter how bad things got, I could still tell everyone my side of the story and then they'd magically believe me. I'd do an interview or something and then I could clear everything up. But those people, they'd already decided who I was. Now what can I do?"

Hopeless.

That was what I was feeling. In my heart, my body, even my soul.

JOSEPHINE LIGHT

Chapter Sixteen

When I woke up the next day, I still felt exhausted. My mouth felt gross since I hadn't brushed my teeth after dinner, and I hated the smell of food tainting my nest. Wrinkling my nose, I made a mental note that I was going to clean out my nest as soon as possible.

I knew that Seb was still in the nest with me, my other alphas already gone. Considering my mate should have been at work, I already knew something was wrong. If it was a normal day, Seb would have left the nest to put on his faux-suit pajamas rather than stripping down to his boxers last night and calling it good enough. If we were just taking a pack day, all of my mates would be with me.

"Is it bad?" I asked, my voice croaking at the first use in a few hours.

Seb dropped his phone, turning to face me. He didn't respond right away, leaning down to kiss my face. My forehead and cheeks and nose and chin and eyelids and then finally my lips.

"I'll take that as a yes," I mumbled.

"You have all of us, you know that right?" Seb asked.

I nodded, feeling just a little bit of the tension leaving my body. He was right, I did know that my mates would support me. If I was being honest, that felt like the only thing I was sure of.

My mates had warned me, and I didn't listen. I wasn't going to make that mistake again.

"A part of me wished I could just convince you to stay up here in this nest until everything passed," Seb admitted.

"I'm not hiding away in here." That had me sitting up, glaring down at my mate. "I might have freaked out yesterday, but I can handle it today. Yesterday was an emotional fluke. I was already sensitive because of how the concert ended."

"Of course, princess." Seb kissed my forehead, but I could feel that his lips were fighting against the pull of a smile.

"I'm serious."

"I believe you."

I glared at my mate who just smiled at me. His pride was more than obvious in his smile and his scent. Getting up, I huffed and changed into a comfy set of pajamas before bracing myself to leave my nest.

I ignored the fear of whatever I was going to see downstairs. Ignored the embarrassment for how I'd reacted last night.

Grabbing my mate's hand, I pretended I wasn't squeezing it harder than normal, and we made our way downstairs.

Almost immediately after leaving my nest, I heard noises coming from the first floor. No one was yelling, but multiple conversations were happening, the news was on TV, and all of my mates were pacing, the scent of stress filling the room and making my nose wrinkle.

Jackson was on the phone, his hand pressing the device so hard against his ear that I wondered if it hurt. Han, too, was on the phone, pacing, walking back and forth as he listened to whatever the person on the other line was saying. Zeke was making breakfast, all the while glaring at the TV. He had a notepad on the counter, and I watched as his gaze barely flicked down to whatever was in his pan, his attention fully on the screen as he wrote something down with his free hand.

My instincts went into overload. I needed to

comfort my mates, calm them down, reassure them.

I went to my first alpha, hoping that calming him down would help with the rest of the pack dynamic. He was still holding the phone to his ear when I wrapped my arms around him, pressing our bodies close. I felt his muscles relax under my grip, his large frame curling over mine in an awkward, yet sweet hug. His apple scent surrounded me, the frustration making his usually crisp, fresh scent come across as sour.

Inside my chest, I felt a purr start. My mate had done so much to comfort me since I woke up in the hospital. Helping me through my heat, pack meetings to ensure I was feeling safe and happy, staying home to protect me, carrying me like I wasn't a burden when I needed to be as close as possible to him. His presence was always near, just around the corner, ready to help me with whatever I needed or wanted.

Once he was calm, I raised onto my tip toes and kissed him. I loved his thick lips. I loved his muscular body and his dominant temperament that meant even in this kiss he took charge. His mouth pressed harder against mine, demanding my lips part for him as his tongue made its way between my lips, tasting me.

My hands roamed over his body, simply holding on as my mate took what he needed from me. As he pulled away, still so close that our lips were touching, I stared at his face. His eyes were closed, his scent quickly losing some of its sour edge.

"I'm going to fix this for you, rebel."

I kissed the tip of his nose. "I know you will."

Reluctantly, he let me go, and I made my way to Han. He was on the phone still, no longer pacing, watching me as I neared him. Pressing the phone between his head and shoulder, he opened his arms for me.

I collided with him so hard that he had to take a

step back. This close, I could hear someone on the other end of his conversation talking. It didn't sound like he was talking to Han, more like the phone was simply catching the other male's side of a conversation.

"How are you feeling?" Han asked, talking quietly, probably so he wouldn't catch the attention of whoever was on the other line.

"Better than last night."

"That's not saying much."

I shrugged. "Who are you talking to?"

"Our pack's lawyer. He's reading up about publication rights. The problem is that most laws have been formed to protect reporters and media sources, not prohibit them from abusing their connections and public appearances."

"I thought it was best to stay away from the media as much as possible. Let them just run their course."

The look on Han's face told me I was missing something.

"That's not an option anymore. Go get some breakfast. I'm going to tell him to call me when he actually finds a solution."

I nodded, finding both Seb and Zeke in the kitchen already, the former having taken over writing on the pad. Before I dove into the seriousness of the situation, I wrapped myself around Zeke's back, careful that my hands didn't accidentally bump or hit anything hot or edible.

"Morning," I told him.

"Morning. I've made a strong savory breakfast today. Figured we'd need all our strength and energy to handle all this shit."

"It smells delicious."

My mouth was literally watering with how good it smelled. He had definitely cooked up a breakfast feast, which was saying something considering we always had a lot of food needing to feed five of us.

I wanted to stay in that moment. Wrapped around my mate as he finished cooking. But the temporary solace was broken when I heard my name—except not in any of my mate's voices.

An image of me from last night was on the TV, taken from such a side angle that you could see Seb standing in front of me, blocking the other reporters from getting too close. Then the image started to move, and I watched me.

I watched as Seb pushed me into the elevator as the camera continued to get closer. It zoomed in on my face, my eyes wide, my head shaking back and forth. My lips were forming the same word over and over again, but you couldn't actually hear me.

As the clip ended, two alphas appeared on the screen, both of them behind a desk and only slightly facing each other.

"It was more than obvious just in that few second clip how terrified the little omega was," the first male said.

The female nodded, her lips pursed in disgust. "If my omega had been essentially attacked like that, you can bet I wouldn't have handled it as well as this alpha."

"Again, we're seeing this pattern occurring of betas attacking omegas."

Someone changed the channel as the female alpha went to agree. This new station had four people sitting around on a couch, as if they were trying to appear like they were conversing in a living room and not having a scripted debate on TV.

"It was more than obvious that she was disagreeing with everything being asked," one of the males said. A little banner appeared on the bottom of the screen with his name and designation—Spencer O'Neil, Beta. "Look at her head shaking, her mouth clearly saying the word 'no' over and over again."

"You're telling me that you look at that video and see an omega answering questions, not one being needlessly bullied?" a different male asked, his tag claiming he was Elijah Flynn, Alpha. "She wasn't claiming her disagreement, she was clearly afraid."

"So what, if someone is scared, they can't answer questions?"

"That's called coercion."

"That's called bravery."

Another channel, this one with just one person behind a desk, facing the camera. An image of a male I was pretty sure I should recognize was in the top corner. "Representative Adam has put forth a temporary bill to limit omega movement outside the Omega Compound and their respective pack homes until a vote can take place at the end of next month to solidify the rules of movement for omegas."

She kept talking. I knew that by the way her voice was still heard, by the way her lips kept moving, yet I wasn't understanding her words. I hadn't fully deciphered the first thing she said. It was like I suddenly lost the ability to comprehend my own language.

"They can't actually do that, can they?" I wasn't sure who I was asking, but all of my mates were nearby, and I was hoping someone would answer. Anyone. "They can't force me to stay in the house. That's apocalyptic shit. It has to be illegal."

"Someone has offered up a similar proposal every year, it's never had enough votes before," Seb admitted.

"So, it won't go through?"

"I don't know, princess. Right now, both alphas and betas are blaming omegas for the problems between the designations. They might agree to this temporary ban just to settle everyone down."

He must have seen how angry those words made me because he pulled me close. "I'm not of agreement, princess. Just telling you what I think will happen."

"Maybe it'll be a good thing for omegas," Zeke said, earning my immediate glare. "No, think about it. Right now, the other designations are blaming omegas for all their problems. We can see how ridiculous that is, but they think this is an actual solution. When it doesn't work, the next vote to make it permanent will fail."

"Feels like a risk," I said.

"There's no other choice. I've already left a message for our district representative on behalf of our pack, but I don't know how useful that'll be or if they've already made up their mind."

"C'mon," Jackson said, "let's have breakfast first. Then we'll try to talk everything out."

That was what we did. I pushed all thoughts about everything happening outside of the home from my head and focused on a pack meal. There was nothing more to be done at the moment and everything was out of my control. But I was doing my best to be strong. It was easier than last night since all of my mates were present, and my instincts helped me to keep them calm.

I ate all of my serving and then snuck bites from all of my mates' plates as I moved around to sit on each of their laps.

When I finished, I found myself on Jackson's lap, leaning back against him. My hand was rubbing around on his chest and shoulders, just enjoying the feel of my mate.

We were all slow to get up. Slow to clean the dining room, to clean the dishes. Eventually, we had no other choice but to sit our asses down in the living room for a pack meeting.

The TV was still on, the words muted as we'd tried enjoying these last few minutes of peace from it. We all watched the video being played, a banner along the bottom of the screen reminding the viewers that the content may be graphic.

Alphas fought each other in one clip, the destruction they brought down on everything around them almost seemed faked since they were in front of a large, beautiful home with a tended lawn and even a white picket fence. The next clip were protestors, their faces covered in masks, holes cut out just for their eyes and mouth, and they were chanting something about cutting off the noses of alphas for equality. Signs depicting bloody faces were waving around and it suddenly made sense why their masks didn't have nose holes.

"When is the vote?" I asked.

I never looked away from the TV, watching more and more protests, so many kinds flitting across the screen. Then the channel changed to something that appeared infinitely calmer but had my anxiety immediately heighten.

It was the view of whatever chamber the representatives worked in, all of them sitting, one by one voting yes or no. A little box in the bottom corner showed the number for each vote, keeping tally.

It was close. Too close.

"What happens if omegas have appointments? Doctors or emergencies? Childcare?" I hated looking at the group that determined my life. Had they consulted with any omegas to make their decisions or simply did what they did best?

"I pulled up the proposed bill," Seb said. "It has hourly restrictions, meaning omegas won't be allowed to make appointments before 7:00 in the morning and after 7:00 at night. Beyond scheduled appointments, omegas aren't allowed out during that block, even with a chaperone."

That got me up off the couch, pacing. "This is fucking ridiculous. All of this is crazy. How many of these dimwitted representatives even have an omega pack member? How can they possibly make a choice like this for an entire designation?"

"Representative Adam doesn't have one," Han said. There was an intrigued tone in his voice that had me momentarily glancing away from the screen. "Obviously even the omegas he's courted have rejected him, that's why he wants to remove the decision from the omegas' hands."

I was back to watching the little counter that would determine my fate. All omegas' fates.

"There has to be something we can do." Then an idea came to me. "Where's my phone?"

We all searched for it, the device somehow appearing from Han's office. I opened the masquerading social media platform, hoping the password that I remembered using was the same, and then punched the air when I was logged in.

"What are you doing?" Zeke asked. His face was over my shoulder, watching.

"I'm looking on here to see how I can help. I'm not going to sit around just moaning about how unfair all of this is." I shook my head, my frustration with myself tainting my scent. "Obviously, holding onto hope that the media would be on my side was a bad plan. But actually taking action, that would definitely help."

"What kind of action?" Jackson asked.

"I don't know. Something. I'm more than healed now. And even when I'm not doing anything, I'm still being used, so I might as well do something."

The phone was plucked out of my hand, earning a growl from my chest. I stood up, using the couch cushions as leverage, attempting to go chest to chest with Jackson despite my smaller height.

"Give it back," I demanded, my hand out for my phone, never breaking eye contact with my mate.

"Start talking shit through and I will."

"I just want to do something, is that so bad? I want to make a difference—to stand up for my designation."

"I get that, rebel. I promise, I do. But doing whatever feels right isn't always the answer."

"What does that mean?"

"Remember what we told you about our connections?" Seb asked, standing next to Jackson so he could meet my gaze and hold my attention. "Sometimes it's better to work behind the curtains."

"Like how?"

"Your classes for one. If you finish those, you'll have a solid argument to make about omega capabilities in education. Before that, anyone can argue that you didn't finish college."

I felt the frustration slowly start to leak out of me, but my mate wasn't done.

"Plenty of those representatives that voted no are people we know or have some sort of connection with. We have people on our side, but they aren't going to keep associating with us if we're causing too many problems."

I pointed at the TV. It was still on the current count for the vote, but my mate understood the gesture.

"Right now, your image isn't associated with a single side. Despite how they're using it. But if you were at a protest or made a statement, that all might change."

"I do nothing, then?"

Jackson reached out, pulling me closer, and I wrapped my legs around him. "I'm not saying that. Just that whatever you do needs to be a pack decision. The same way we all talk about what we're going to do and say publicly. We need to be on the same page. You're a part of this pack, Hannah."

Despite the slight admonishing tone, I smiled at his words. I was a part of this pack. This new version of me was accepted by all my mates. That meant I had to do more than focus on myself and my own needs, I had to keep my pack together.

And as happy as that made me, I couldn't ignore the kernel in the back of my mind that reminded me of the other omegas. The ones trapped at the OC. Trapped in packs that didn't treat them as anything more than a baby maker.

"We'll come up with a plan together, rebel. Trust us."

Jackson's words soothed me, and I nodded against his neck. I would trust my mates. They'd never done anything but protect me.

Setting me back down on the couch, both Han and Zeke took up the seats on either side of me. Zeke whispered about helping me find the perfect way to fight back which had Han leaning closer to whisper, asking what we were whispering about.

"Hannah is right on one front," Jackson started.

"Just one?" I asked.

He continued like I hadn't spoken after a quick glare in my direction. "We can't do nothing. I think we should lay everything on the table. All of our connections, what we can do, and then we'll create a plan. Who we can talk to, whose hands money needs to go into, everything."

I nodded my head so hard that a slight headache

started on my forehead.

Hope was a distraction that I clung to, excitement filling my veins as all my mates got comfortable, Zeke even bringing the notepad and pen to the living room.

Before we could even start, I heard clapping.

No, that wouldn't make any sense. My gaze went to the TV for a moment. I was riding the high of my pack, my happiness clouding my prediction on what I was about to see.

Two. That was how many votes the No's were behind. Two. Less than the members in my pack.

The temporary movement ban was in order. We had forty-five days until the vote for permanency occurred.

Chapter Seventeen

The first week after the ban was implemented, I refused to slow down. We had pack meetings each night, for hours, talking about what we could do.

Money donations and phone calls. We were looking into companies that made donations we approved of, literally shifting to a new soap brand because they were supporters of a representative that was adamant about not restricting omegas so harshly.

Seb and Zeke were forced to go back to work, and while they were gone, I worked on my classes.

Since I wasn't allowed to leave the house during certain hours, even with my alphas, it made me want to leave all the more. To be petty and go on a walk. To demand my alphas take me on a date in a blatant 'fuck you'.

Instead, I was being mature. And patient. That meant doing everything covertly.

My mates kept me informed on everything that was being done and I think they knew that I was feeling a little left out. Seb was going out and talking with board members and Jackson was working on our pack's contingency plan and Han was using his cyber skills to shut down propaganda sites in support of the ban and Zeke was keeping track of every possible mention of me in the media to find public allies.

Me? I was searching the app, trying to find out what everyone else in the world was doing. The issue was that the app was made up of mostly betas, the omegas hiding under anonymous names, and the betas were focused on their own battle for rights against the alpha designation.

One night, I told my alphas my plan to create an omega only mod. Like a discussion board within the app, proclaiming myself as an omega and wanting others to join in so we could finally figure out our voice.

It was a risk.

My alphas had been thinking about it, discussing it, and all the while I kept making notes for how I'd set it up, desperately hoping that they'd understand this was something I needed to do.

All of that led us to a pack meeting in the living room. I was sitting on the floor, my back leaning against the bottom part of the couch, between Zeke's legs as he kept his hands over my eyes for a surprise. Apparently, I wasn't to be trusted to keep my own eyes closed, which had made me roll my eyes since I refused to admit they had a point about my potential for looking.

I heard my alphas shuffling around and tried to get comfortable. The hard floor on my ass wasn't great for long term.

"No peeking," Zeke chided.

"I wasn't."

"Sure. Let me guess. The floor is hard?"

"It is!"

"Hannah, you've been sitting there for a minute. Maybe two."

Something was set down on the short table in front of me, a soft noise that meant they were trying to hide it but couldn't quite achieve it. I rubbed my hands on my thighs, telling myself that they might've enjoyed the joke of me peeking, but they'd be actually upset if I had. Right?

"Okay, Zeke—"

The rest of Jackson's words were lost as I shoved Zeke's hands away from my face. In front of me was a laptop, a new one. It was already out of the box and unwrapped which meant the alphas had already set it up for me.

Before I could even get my thanks out, Han said, "This is a special laptop. I've rewritten the rules of the gateways to make it seem like the access is coming from a different location."

I stared at him, waiting for him to explain everything he just said in a way that actually made sense.

"When you use this laptop, no one will be able to trace it back to you."

I nodded, understanding that bit now. "Why do I need that?"

"You're going to set up that mod," Jackson said, "using that computer only. The site might keep you anonymous among its members, but we're worried about infiltrators. This way, if anyone breaks through the site's protective layers, you'll still have the laptop's anonymity."

"Will I need to create a new profile?"

"Definitely. Don't follow your old account. And anything you might have admitted about yourself as that account, try to change slightly."

I was so excited, I was nodding along, hoping my agreement would get me closer to actually being allowed to start. My hands were sliding across the closed laptop, almost petting the smooth surface as I waited.

I was finally going to be able to do something. My fingers felt like they were actually tingling with the anticipation of typing. I already knew which profiles I wanted to reach out to that might be willing to help. Higher, more trafficked accounts could put their weight behind an authentic solution.

A lot of these chats were places for people to vent without getting in trouble. Some of them actually created plans. In order for people to join and attend, they'd want a recognizable name and profile in support of the event to prove they weren't walking into a trap.

I knew there had to be more omegas on the site than just me. I might have outwardly rebelled, but there were other omegas who complied maliciously. They would make outrageous demands, using the full force of the omega needs bullshit to get whatever they wanted. Others feigned compliance just to buy themselves some time. Pretending they were simply searching for the perfect pack and just not quite finding the right one yet. And I thought of Koda who was able to hide her omega designation in plain sight. She couldn't be the only one.

If I had been smarter back then, I would have befriended those omegas. At the time, I hated that they weren't rebelling like I was. I thought the only way forward was to publicly beat against the laws built.

"What kind of mod am I creating?" I asked. I had grand plans for an omega only mod, my imagination showing how amazing it would be if omegas could save themselves. But no matter how much I envisioned leading an omega-charge, I had no idea how to actually plan an event.

"Something to get everyone working together," Jackson said. "All the causes are spread out and it's only lowering the full force of numbers. Alphas, betas, omegas, most are on our side, but they're all fighting individual causes rather than one big umbrella issue."

"We need to get everyone who opposes the ban to realize that it's the real deal. Doing nothing, just assuming it won't pass because it's so outrageous, is putting everyone in danger," Zeke added.

"I know there are other omegas who won't be happy about this," I told my mates. "I just wish I had a way to get in contact with them too."

"I can download an encrypted messaging app,"

Han said. "You could find them on social, maybe reach out and get a private number then suggest they get the app too. It would be a risk, though. The messages might keep out anyone trying to intercept them, but if they willingly reveal their phone, you'd be outed."

I shook my head. "They wouldn't."

"It's too big a risk, rebel," Jackson said.

I stood up, needing to show my mates how serious I was about my words. "Think about what would happen if the omegas revolted. We just agreed that all the designations need to work together—that means omegas. It's a bigger risk with a bigger reward."

"Even if the omegas stood up, they have no voting power," Sebastian reminded me. "We need to get the betas and alphas on our side, working together. That's our focus with this app. If you can't get enough followers, then we can go to picking out specific omegas for help."

My frustration was tainting my perfume, and I knew my mates could sense my annoyance down the bond. Any big speech would be a waste of breath because I knew my mates were right. No matter how much I wanted to dramatically change the world, to bring omegas into equal rights with the other designations, this wasn't that kind of fight. This was all about stopping that permanent movement ban. Just like the betas and alphas needed to focus on one issue, so did I.

I agreed, albeit reluctantly. My disappointment was quickly washed away when Han sat down next to me and watched as I finally got to login on the secret laptop. Zeke was still behind me, his hands going back and forth between my neck and Han's shoulders.

The three of us sat together as I created my profile and then set up my page. I looked up accounts that I had memorized as being big names to add some credibility to my own, sending them a message through the app. Not all of them would respond, but maybe one would. Especially with the new note on my profile. Something so rare, even in this app, that I was hoping it would catch attention. Omega.

I was a strange mix of excitement and nerves. For all my bravado, it was easier to claim I wanted to shout my demands from the rooftop than actually made the proverbial climb up the ladder. It was the same feeling I got when I snuck into omega rights rallies. I always had nerves in my stomach to the point that I wondered if it would cause literal damage.

The first event I had gone to, I had to leave early because I was perfuming too much. Hiding my emotions was never possible, but after enough events, and not getting caught, my fear was replaced by excitement, and that was much easier to blend in with the betas.

Working on the computer, so close to my mates like a physical form of protection, it was a near perfect moment. I was surrounded by love, acting in the best interests of my designation, and in comfortable clothes. The trifecta of a perfect day.

Then one of my mates' phones went off, except no one moved to answer it. My brain was slow to notice the specific ringtone that meant Koda was calling. But when I did, I stood up quickly, ignoring the ache in my knees and the slight tingling of my ass as my nerves decompressed from being sat on for so long.

I got to my phone just as the ringing stopped, but I immediately called Koda back.

She answered halfway through the first ring, "Hannah."

"Koda? What's wrong?"

"I'm so angry." She didn't sound angry. It sounded like she was crying, especially as she sniffled again. "Do you have time to talk?"

"Of course." My mates were all watching me as I stood frozen, worry for Koda making me hold still while she spoke to ensure I didn't miss a single word. "What's going on?"

"Have you seen the protests going on? Alphas against betas. Betas against packs. It's been causing a lot of trouble at Braker with the two designations mixed all the time, which, in case you were wondering, has been hell on my instincts."

I nodded even though she couldn't see me.

"We got a school email basically saying that protests and political arguments needed to stay off campus. That caused an uproar, because of course it did. We're not talking about tax increases, we're talking about the rights of designations. I have no idea what Chancellor Kelly was thinking with that declaration. The man has a beta assistant, so he isn't completely opposed to betas."

"Didn't he try to kick you out when you joined a pack, though?"

"Eh, that was complicated. Jenson was my professor, too. Although I do remember him saying something about the only reason there wasn't a rule that alphas and betas at the school shouldn't bond was because no one thought it would be needed."

"See?"

"But he also wasn't … I don't know … mean. I guess, if I was being honest, and if I was giving him the benefit of the doubt, I could see that we'd sort of backed him into a proverbial corner."

"There were a lot of stipulations in that."

She sighed. "I know. I just keep associating the fact that I didn't get kicked out of the academy with him. He could have sent the reporters away, but he created a whole interview session where he basically said he supported me staying simply by not refusing to kick me out."

"He let reporters on campus then but isn't letting the students stand up for their designations now?"

"Right? It's so confusing."

Zeke grabbed my free hand, pulling me back toward the couch since I'd been stuck standing as I spoke with Koda. I pointed to a blanket on the other end of the couch, silently asking for it. He obliged, covering it over me and him as he sat down next to me, pulling my feet onto his lap.

"How's the temperament of the school right now?" I asked.

"Toxic. I walk into a classroom and there's a literal line between where the alphas and betas are sitting. The air on campus is thick with tension. And of course, there are the professors who are hoping this whole thing will lead to Braker going back to being an alpha only academy. That's sort of why I'm calling you."

That had me sitting up. I thought she was just calling to vent.

"I had a meeting with Chancellor Kelly today. He gave me the option to switch my classes to remote."

"What does that mean?"

"Apparently, the professors will create physical copies of the lessons and send them home with Jen for me."

"Ah, no offense, Koda, but that seems like a lot of work for one student."

"Right? That's why I can't figure out if I should do it or not. My mates are worried for my safety on campus, but I keep thinking that if I let myself be run out of Braker, then there wasn't a point to me attending in the first place. There was a reason I chose BA."

"It's just an option, right? You don't *have* to go remote?"

"Yeah, just an option. Aidan recommended that I talk to you since you do classes from home."

"I do…"

"But?"

"Honestly? I wish I could attend a real school. That I had the option. I wish that I was outwardly proving that our designation was capable of learning and sitting in a classroom just like everyone else. It's one of the reasons that I take the classes now even though I fucking hate having homework."

"I know. I feel the same way."

"That being said, you aren't much good to any movement if you end up outed as an omega and kicked from the academy because of all the alpha tension on campus."

She groaned, the sound filled with frustration. "I know. I can't decide. Several outlets have already tried reaching out to me for an opinion piece, but I don't know if it's better to tell them I'm staying at the academy or to admit the tensions are high and I'm scared. Will I get critics or sympathy?"

I knew what I wanted to say. I knew that I wanted to tell her to stay at the academy and hold her head high. To represent everyone who was a pack member that wasn't an alpha but still able to have a life outside the home. She could've been the face of the designation rights movement if she wanted.

Yet, she wasn't truly a part of the movement. In spirit, absolutely. Koda was a perfect example of wanting more than the limits of your designation and managing to achieve it. Except she wasn't trying to break designation barriers, she simply wanted to live her life.

I tried to focus on that, on the solution she was asking for and not the one that I wanted. The problem was, I only knew bits and pieces about Koda's life at

Braker.

"How did everyone react when the news broke that you bonded into a pack?" I asked.

"Uh, the news loved it. And the betas mostly did too. A few alphas grumbled about how I would get tossed aside for an omega, and some just believed we'd eventually add an omega in anyways, so it wasn't a big deal."

Support. Sympathy.

I sat up straighter, my excitement at that information making me temporarily biased in my answer. I physically pulled the phone from my ear, knowing if I said anything in that moment, it would have been all about the movement and not about Koda herself.

Having a friend was new, and I was determined not to mess it up. Just like my mates put me before the omega movement, I would put Koda before it as well.

"Hello? Hannah? You still there?"

"Yeah, sorry, I was just thinking," I told her.

"I think I want to stay. To keep going on as normal."

"Really?"

"If I was willing to switch schools, I would have done that back when it made my mates' lives easier. I just hate all the attention. And I know agreeing would have made Aidan's relationship with his mom better."

"Uh." I wasn't sure about that last part, but Koda was going strong, so I was switching from an advisory friend role to a completely supportive one. "Okay. I like that plan."

"You don't think it's dumb? Like I should just do the classes at home and make it easier on everyone?"

"I don't think that's easier for anyone. Maybe for your mates since they'll know you're safe all the time. Would you be happy being at home all day, every day?

How strong are your nesting instincts?"

"Even if I went remote, I wouldn't stay home. I'd go to a shop or a library or something."

"It's probably better that you stay at Braker, then. At least you'll have the safety of being on campus. Something."

Despite her verbal commitment, I heard her groan, obviously still conflicted on what to do.

"Do you have to make a decision now?" I asked.

"No. It was an open-ended offer. I just wanted to make it now. I didn't want this option hanging over my head like mistletoe at a stranger's party."

I chuckled at that comment. "If only major life decisions could be simple."

"I know, right?"

For the next few minutes Koda and I talked about lighter topics. Some of which I didn't understand at all since she was complaining about an assignment on exoplanets and how she wanted her focus to be on blackholes. I knew about the latter, but the former was like gibberish to me. We jumped around from topic to topic, catching up, commenting on each other's stories.

The whole time, Zeke stayed on the couch with me, his head leaning against the back cushion with his eyes closed. Under the blanket, his hands continued to run over my feet and ankles, so I knew he wasn't asleep.

At some point, all of my other mates had kissed my head, forehead, and cheek before disappearing. It was over an hour later that Koda and I finally hung up. My mouth was weirdly dry from all the talking and when I got up to drink some water, I drank the whole glass without stopping before refilling it and finally feeling better.

Koda's predicament at BA was more proof that the omega and beta struggles were intertwined. My mates were right in saying we needed the designations to come together. At the minimum, we could all agree that no new pack laws should be created. None barring betas from packs or limiting omega whereabouts.

What the next step would be, I didn't know. I wanted to help betas maintain their rights, but was it better to lift up the betas to equal status of alphas and then work on omegas, or start with omegas since we were so far behind and bring us up to the level of betas?

I was going around in circles. This but that. That then this. This and that.

Representative Adam was a bad alpha, a designation elitist, and an overall manipulative asshole. But he saw his opportunity and took it. He created a plan and we somehow fell right into it. We just needed to figure out how to climb the hell out.

Chapter Eighteen

One week later

My laptop was suddenly closed, my head jerking up to see Han standing above me, a secret smile on his face. I had already finished my homework for the day and Han had left to get us a snack as I switched to my secret laptop.

For better or worse, my mod was getting a lot of attention. I was trying to explain to all the commenters that I didn't want betas to stop fighting for their rights, just that I wanted the omegas and betas to join together.

We had a month left until the permanent movement vote and I was still struggling to get the betas on this forum to ban together. I was going into chats where betas were planning protests demanding a separate area for themselves and reminding them that they were leaving the omegas behind. Omegas that would side with their proper inclusion in packs and society. I was posting on my own page, asking omegas to reach out to me, to give me a chance to provide them with a voice. Despite all the traction, I didn't have any messages from omegas.

It wasn't all a loss. I had a small following of betas, even a few alphas, that were wanting to help. The group was small, though. We could form an event with good numbers, but the goal wasn't just to promote omega rights. Getting everyone to work together was feeling impossible.

"It's time for a date night," Han said.

My immediate reaction was to argue. I'd hurried through my classes so I could focus on this specifically, but my mate's smile had me keeping the words to myself. He looked so excited, and I wasn't going to be the reason he lost that happy vibe.

Setting my secret laptop on top of my school one, Han handed me a drink and I realized he had gone out and gotten us smoothies for a snack. My tastebuds immediately watered in anticipation, and I didn't hesitate to take a sip.

Like last time, I could see the flecks of the authentic vanilla bean flavor, only when I took a sip, I almost choked on the drink. It didn't taste nearly as good as the last one and I had no idea why. I struggled to even swallow the sip I'd taken.

"Thank you," I told him, holding my drink although not taking another sip.

Han laughed, then offered me his drink which he hadn't even tried yet. I felt bad taking it, especially since I figured he'd picked out a flavor for himself that he liked, but he started sipping mine, so I tried his. Immediately the mix of peanut butter and coffee hit my tongue. It was so good. I was pretty sure this one would be my favorite of all time.

"Come on. You can take your drink with you."

I accepted Han's hand, letting him pull me along, up the stairs, to his bedroom. The space was soaked in the scents of him, Zeke, and me. It should have been a weird concoction of pumpkin, berries, and lavender. Instead, it just reminded me of my mates, of comfort and safety … and sex.

Han's space wasn't usually this clean. I wasn't sure if it was because he was raised in a family that had a maid, or if it was because he worked from home and never really needed to worry about his appearance, but Han was the messiest of all my alphas. Not dirty, just messy. Clean shirts that he'd tried on, then decided to change out of were never put away. He liked having all his shoe options on display. He usually kept his closet door open, and he had the kind of decoration style that liked everything he owned to be on display.

For our date, he'd done more than put his shoes and clothes in their proper spot. He set up one of his laptops on the edge of the bed, stacked on top of folded blankets making it slightly elevated. Little fairy lights had been added to the walls, just barely lighting up the place, creating a romantic atmosphere.

Setting my drink on the nightstand so I didn't accidentally spill any, I crossed my legs and turned to face my mate. "Are we going to watch a movie?" The question was mostly rhetorical since I could see the beginning of the movie paused on the laptop.

"That's just for the background. I picked one of your favorites in case what we're going to do is utterly unsuccessful and you hate it."

I laughed at that. "And what are we doing?"

Lifting the laptop, he set all the folded blankets in my lap, placing the screen back on the comforter and angling it properly. This close, I saw that there were only two blankets. They were thick and fluffy, which wasn't my favorite, but they each had their own cute design on it. One was black with pink skulls while the other was a light green with little all-white hummingbirds on it.

"Are these what you ordered?" I asked.

Han nodded. "I know you typically don't like soft blankets, but all the reviews said this type was the simplest to start with."

He threw a couple more items on the bed before joining me. With his back against the headboard, and his legs extended out long, he somehow managed to look sophisticated as he grabbed the black and pink blanket.

"The idea," he started, "is that we do each other's, and then combine at the end. We'll cut strips along the edges, all the way around, and then tie the two blankets together. Some people even add decorative strings or stones or whatever."

Spreading out the blanket, I ran my hands over the soft texture. It was a thick fabric, not something I would particularly like to sleep in, but that didn't mean I didn't absolutely love this idea. I was getting to create something, to finally be an artist without the frustration of failing or feeling like I was an idiot. This was simple and I could see how much thought went into it.

I leaned over and started the movie, then moved so I was sitting next to Han, my shoulder touching his bicep, both of us positioning the blankets over our laps so we could start cutting them.

Rather than handing me a single pair of scissors, he offered me several, their handles all different colors and the blades all funky shapes. I grabbed the one that made a half-square shape and Han grabbed one that was half-circles.

To my surprise, I already knew this movie. It was weird to think that even in the years that I'd lost, my favorite movie was still the same. Then again, this movie was fucking hysterical, so how could anything top it?

"How come you picked hummingbirds?" I asked him.

"Honestly? I was staring at the website to order the blankets and I froze. They're custom pieces only, so it wasn't like they had options to choose from. I kept trying to think of something that represented me."

"I'm a skull?" I teased.

I watched as Han blushed, his cheeks turning pink, the color spreading to the tips of his ears and down his neck. I chased that color with my lips, kissing his cheek, the cusp of his ear, his jaw, and down the column of his throat.

"Anyways," Han continued, "I was trying a lot of

different things at first. Like a computer and a necktie and even the fucking sun. I wanted something that represented me, not just one aspect of my life like my job or my clothes."

I nodded, slowing down on my cuts to the blanket since I was basically racing through. We had time and I wanted to use it.

"It's kind of cheesy, and a lot convoluted now that I'm saying it out loud. But I kept thinking that one of the best parts about my life is that we spend our days together, working close to each other. And I knew a random interesting fact about hummingbirds and how they have to constantly work for their food because they're so fast and their wings beat so hard. Wait, I think I could explain that better. So, when I was looking up—"

"I get it, Han. Truly. And I like it. I'll always see hummingbirds and think of you now." Somehow, I managed to get even closer to my mate, the outer part of my leg pressed against his. It made our arms slightly awkward as we cut, but neither of us complained.

When I finished my blanket, Han still had his last side to go. I looked over at his, then did a double take. "Uh, how long were we supposed to cut the strips?"

"Just a few inches, I think."

Holding up one of the edges of my blanket, I started laughing, the sound bubbling out of me dramatically as I let him take in my work. I'd literally cut maybe an inch of fabric, my cuts close together compared to his, which were more artfully placed apart.

I was laughing so hard that my stomach was starting to hurt, and my volume had definitely reached its max. Simultaneously, I felt like I was going to die from laughter and also like I was never going to be able to stop.

My artistic ability was so bad that I managed to

repel the simplest of activities. I totally should have asked more questions or looked at an example. Zeke had given me fake confidence that I'd be able to do artsy stuff after our date. Apparently, I'd forgotten that he'd done literally all the prep work, making my only job tracing the outline of the tattoo.

When I was finally able to catch my breath, my stomach felt like I'd laughed a six-pack into existence. "I'm going to go back around and make some of these longer."

"They need to be long enough that we can make a knot with the fabric."

"Do you think yours are too short?"

"Let's see. Cut just one strip longer and I'll try tying them together."

I did and Han was right, his lengths were long enough. It was cute with the little knot and tails sticking out. Undoing it, I resettled the blanket over my lap. It was probably harder than it should've been to reline my decorative scissors up with the already made cuts and extending them.

"I'm glad I didn't say fuck it and go with the higher difficulty fabric that I figured you'd like better," Han said.

I playfully glared at him as if he wasn't completely correct in that assumption.

This time around, I was somehow slower. Looking down at the blanket made my neck ache but lifting the blanket up to cut in front of my face made me realize how weak my arms were. Despite how much my body seemed to be rebelling at any sort of artwork, I was having fun.

Finishing with the cuts, I set the blanket and scissors down for a little hand break. Han had already finished, patiently waiting for me, his focus on the movie with his free hand resting on my leg.

Taking my hand in his, he started massaging my fingers, my open palm, and even my wrist. Every bit of pressure felt amazing, and I couldn't explain in enough words how a hand massage was turning me on. It was, though.

I felt his hands start to work their way up my arm to my shoulder, then to my neck. I wasn't even pretending to not enjoy the attention, fully curved forward so my mate would have all the access he was willing to give. As his fingers pressed against my nape and then stretched up to the back of my head, I groaned, loving the feeling.

I felt a tug at the hem of my shirt, a silent question about whether I wanted to take it off, and I didn't hesitate to pull it over my head and toss it far away. Moving so I was between his legs, giving him the best access, I wiggled my shoulders in a silent request for more.

Han obliged, moving his hands all over my back, tracing down my spine, making the most delicious circles around my shoulders, and running his thumbs down the sides of my neck, earning another moan from my throat.

Then his hands started to roam forward.

First, it was just over the front of my shoulders, then down to my collarbone. He even caressed the front of my neck, not with a lot of pressure, but feeling his touch in a tender place was teasing me closer to the blissful edge.

The first touch of his hands on my breasts and I wanted more. Harder or faster or something. Han was taking his time, kneading my breasts, tracing my nipples before pinching them, lavishing my chest with attention. He worked his fingers back up to my neck again and I couldn't even complain because everything he did felt so good.

His hands continued down my back, toward my hips, his fingers moving around toward my front again. I leaned back toward him, wanting to give him as much access as he wanted, my legs parting so he could reach the area I desperately wanted him to touch.

Rather than take the hint, his fingers continued down my thighs, pushing my shorts and underwear down, reaching as far as his long arms allowed before circling back up to my hips.

Arousal was forming between my legs, and my nipples were hard from all his playing with them. His chin was resting on my shoulder so he could look down at my body as he played with me.

"Do you know where my mark is?" Han asked. His words almost didn't make sense at first, my head so full from the fog of arousal. "Hannah?"

"Yes. On my ass."

Han kissed my neck, a small prize for answering his question. "I'm going to make you come on my fingers, and then I'm going to have you present. I want your ass in the air so I can hold onto my mark as I take you there. If you're a good girl and come with just my cock inside you, I'll let you pet your little clit for a proper orgasm after."

Slick was leaking from my core just from Han's words. His hands were touching me, caressing my sides, moving down my stomach so that his fingertips were simply teasing the distance to my core.

"Please, Han," I begged.

"Is this what you want?" His fingers finally moved down to my clit, just barely circling it despite my hips chasing his touch. He gently swirled his fingers at the bundle of nerves, and I felt all my inner stomach muscles tense, but it wasn't enough.

"More."

His fingers pushed further down, entering me easily with how slick I already was. My designation had a reputation for being easily and quickly aroused, and at this moment, I didn't care that I was meeting that. I was glad for my slick, glad that anytime my mates wanted me, my body was prepared. And damn—it always felt good.

Two fingers didn't make me feel full, still, there was something intimate about having him inside me. In and out, he moved his fingers, so they touched every inch inside me, his free hand continuing to touch my body, playing with my increasing arousal.

There was no hiding how wet I was. Han used my own slick to wet his fingers and then started on my clit again. With his fingers inside me, the pleasure on my clit, and his other hand playing with my breasts, I came.

My orgasm was short and weak, a blissful tease that didn't make me satisfied, only needing more. Even with his fingers inside me, I felt empty, needing more pressure and thickness.

"Very good, omega. Now present for me."

I scrambled away from my mate, shoving my bottoms off my ankles, going onto my knees, and pressing my chest to the bed. Spreading my thighs so my mate had a perfect view, I gripped the bed sheets in my hands, already anticipating what I wanted.

My alpha's body heat radiated from him, raising my anticipation as I felt him behind me. His pants were still on and despite the laughter coming from the laptop, I could hear his zipper lower. I spread my knees even further, ignoring the feeling in my thighs that told me I was stretching myself to my limit.

Han's hand started at my neck, ensuring my top half was pressed down on the bed how he wanted. Then he slid his hand down my spine, admiring the curve that came with how hard I angled my hips. When he traced his fingers around the edge of his claiming mark on my ass cheek, I whimpered.

Mating bonds had a sort of intrinsic arousal wherever they formed and that added to my excitement.

I felt his cock as he pressed it against me, not pushing inside, just sliding along my slick.

"Han," I whimpered, grabbing the sheets harder in my fists.

His hand came down, smacking my mating mark at the same time that he thrusted into me. My hips had tried to move away but his hands held me in place, ensuring I felt both movements to their fullness.

My mate's cock was perfect inside me. Better than his fingers, pressing against my inner walls. We started moving then. I bounced back as he thrusted forward, each hit of our thighs loud in the room.

He felt so good inside me, and my body was already primed from my last orgasm. I was so close, my body sensitive to each drag of his cock as he pulled out, to each flex of his fingers as he held me in place.

And his scent—his pumpkin alpha scent tinted with spice from his arousal surrounded me. I wanted to lick him, to taste his sweat from his chest and bite him again.

But my mate wasn't letting me up. He was forcing my body to endure the pleasure, his hips thrusting faster than I could push back. Just as I was getting close, he pulled out, his breaths heaving like it had taken more effort to stop.

"No, please, I was so close."

Again, he smacked his hand down over his mark on my ass, the slight burn only teasing me more. I felt his fingers dip inside me again, collecting my slick before he pressed his arousal-coated fingers to my puckered hole.

"I'd like to take you here, Hannah. What do you

say? Want to be a good omega for your alpha?"

My eyes rolled to the back of my head at his words, more slick spilling down my thighs. My body answered his question before I could even utter the single syllable agreement.

He was slow, yet unrelenting as he pressed deeper into my ass. His hand on my ass cheek tightened, connecting us in both ways.

Once he was seated fully inside, we were both breathing hard, the tension between us about to snap. He pulled out slowly, all the way so that I was left feeling empty, then pressing back in. My omega body conformed to what my mate wanted, yet that bite of pain from his thick head pushing in and out past my tight ring of muscles was a delicious sensation.

Again and again, he moved, slowly picking up speed as he pulled all the way out and slammed back in. Eventually, my body relaxed enough to let him enter me without any resistance, and then my mate truly started to fuck my ass.

I felt the sensations throughout my whole body as if the pleasure nerves in my ass were connected to every inch of me. My fingers tingled from how tightly I was clutching the sheets, my thighs ached from being spread so far apart and holding up my weight. Sweat began to form on my back with all my effort to maintain my posturing while simultaneously shoving my hips back harder onto my mate's cock.

I wanted to ache after this. I wanted to feel him everywhere, in every tight spot from my shoulder to my knees—it would be a reminder of this moment.

My second orgasm was approaching, just out of reach. I had no idea if I would be able to come with just his cock in my ass, although I desperately wanted to.

"Come on, Hannah, I can feel how close you are

to coming. I want to feel you tighten around my dick, milking all of my cum from me."

It was his words that finally pushed me over, the orgasm tightening every muscle in my body, squeezing my lungs as I endured the serotonin being released to every part of me. My fingers and toes and thighs and back and head, it was all pleasure.

Han fucked me through my orgasm, reaching around to touch my clit while I was still coming. I was too sensitive, but too weak to move away. His fingers were covered in the slick that was streaming down my thighs, making the pads of his fingers easily glide over my bundle of nerves.

I wasn't sure if it was a second orgasm, or just an extension of the first, my vision went black, and I screamed, somehow forcing my lungs to work simply to use my voice. He knotted inside me, stretching me and coming, each pump of his cum making me shiver.

My body collapsed, and Han fell on top of me, still mostly dressed. I was slightly crushed until Han rolled onto his side, pulling me with him. The movement tugged at where he was locked inside me, my body threatening another orgasm that I wasn't sure I could handle.

I felt oversensitive and yet needed to be held. My body was hot and my skin cold. Despite the tiredness of my body, my mind was in a panic.

Then Han draped his arm over my body, his leg too, basically cocooning me. A purr started from his chest, instinctually calming me. My eyes were closed, and I felt a weight inside my body as if all of my muscles and tendons and bones were relaxing. I was still awake, just resting, enjoying the feeling of being so heavy I wasn't even able to twitch a finger.

Knots took a long time to deflate so we cuddled

the whole time. Eventually, the movie ended, and Han reached up, starting it over. I tilted my head wanting to be able to see the screen, thankful we'd fucked facing the end of the bed so we could watch.

About a quarter of the way through the movie, Han's knot deflated, not that he pulled it out of my ass. We continued to lay together, intertwined and cuddling. At least until I started to sweat from the soft fabric underneath me. As much as I wanted to keep lying with my mate, I couldn't stand the feel of my sweaty under-boob against the fluffy fabric.

Han reached for a small washcloth he had piles of in the nightstand, helping to separate us without leaking cum everywhere. I sat up, wincing at the tender feeling on my ass.

"Sore?" Han asked.

"Yeah, but I like it."

"Let me know if you want any pain relief."

I shook my head. My body would probably be fine by the time I woke up tomorrow, omegas were made for sex after all, so I wanted to keep the soreness for as long as possible.

Han stripped down to his boxers and I just watched him, enjoying the show. He tossed me my clothes to put back on, which I did without standing up because I was lazy. Then he awkwardly pulled the sheets off the bed so he could wash them. They weren't covered in cum, just drenched in the smells of sweat and sex. I almost asked for them to be put in my nest, but I was distracted by Han bounding onto the bed.

"Ready to finish this project?" he asked.

"Definitely. Cutting had to be the hard part, right?"

We matched up the two square blankets and then got to work tying them together. The movie finished as we did as if we'd timed it perfectly. Han stood holding the two corners so I could see it—and all its crooked glory.

My head dropped backward so I was looking at the ceiling as I said, "I think when we turned the blankets to do the second sides, we forgot to check that it was still lined up properly." We had both just assumed we rotated the fabric enough.

Making a 'gimme gesture' I grabbed the blanket, starting to undo the knots on the first side we messed up. Considering we'd tightened the knots so they wouldn't easily come undone, it was harder than it should've been to undo them.

By the end, my fingertips were slightly raw, nevertheless the blanket was officially put together. My side had extra fringes along all the edges from my first time cutting all the way around, but I liked to think that it just added to the personality.

I was beaming, my smile burning my cheeks as Han held up the blanket. It was weird to feel proud of myself for a date art project, but I did. I wanted to take all this positive energy and try my art project down in the living room, except I wasn't that delusional. Han had helped me with this project, and I'd almost fucked it up still. Better to get more practice before I restarted the 'beginner' project downstairs. Maybe I would even ask Zeke for help.

"I love it," I admitted.

"I'd offer to let you keep it in your nest, but I know how you feel about the texture. I was thinking we'd keep it in here."

I sighed, a soft dreamy sound. "That sounds perfect."

The skulls and hummingbirds were so different, the colors not matching at all, yet they somehow complimented each other. Reaching toward my mate, he tried to offer me the blanket and I just took it, setting it on the bed so I could grab Han. I was on my knees, the bed sinking under my weight meaning Han was still taller than me.

Understanding what I wanted, he leaned his head down, kissing me. We hadn't kissed during our entire fuck session, and I melted even further against him. I was riding the high from my accomplishment, my ass was sore, and my mate was radiating love.

It was a perfect date.

JOSEPHINE LIGHT

Chapter Nineteen

One week later
I gripped the sides of my laptop. My fingers were digging in too hard to the screen, yet I couldn't let it go.

It was good news, and I didn't want to believe it. No—I wanted to believe it, but I was scared.

One of the representatives that voted in agreement to the temporary ban had been pulled from office. Their constituents had voted for an emergency election, and they lost their seat. I wasn't even aware that was something that could be done, and despite the representative's claims that it wasn't fair, it was legal. The other representatives were getting nervous.

Alphas might have liked pretending they were better than betas, but they still needed beta votes, especially since betas make up most of the population. Despite alphas being in most of the leadership positions, they only succeed by pandering to betas.

Apparently, the alphas forgot about that.

"Hannah?"

I looked up from my screen to see Han had turned around in his chair, giving me a curious look. "Did you see this?"

He came over to look since I'd forgotten to turn the laptop around and I watched his eyes widen.

"This is good news, right?" I asked. "Maybe Representative Adam will be next."

"I doubt it, unfortunately. He's so extreme his followers almost worship him for his political views. It does mean that he might lose the votes on the permanency, though. This could be enough to spook the representatives who were on the fence. The temporary ban barely passed as it was."

"What do we do now?" Someone had left that information on my page last night, so I figured it wasn't public news yet. Or at least, not news that was being broadcast, most likely in an attempt to keep what happened quiet. "Is there a way we can secretly broadcast this?"

"What do you mean? Like send this to a news channel?"

I tensed. Just the thought of working with reporters bothered me. I didn't trust them with this. Before, I'd believed because they were on TV, because they claimed roles as journalists, that they had some humanity for their audience. I've learned the truth. "I don't think they'll report on it. And even if they did, I don't trust them to not twist it. I want the story to break out around them leaving them scrambling to report it."

Han nodded his head, not so much like he was agreeing, more like he was thinking. "I could break into some websites and change the entire face to just be this information. That will take some time, but I can do it. Although, it will be a little harder without any links to reputable news sites."

I scoffed. "Reputable."

"I know, Hannah. But a lot of people still only get their information from those types of media outlets." He went back to his desk, and I followed, hovering around him, holding my laptop in case he wanted to reference the information sent to me.

The comforting silence that usually surrounded us in Han's office was missing as Han looked up sites, opening several tabs on each of his screens, and started breaking through their protective firewalls to post what we wanted.

I was barely able to hold still as I watched him.

He typed so fast without even glancing down at the keyboard like it was as easy as talking. In a way, he sort of was communicating with the technology.

Jackson must have felt the change in my emotions because his scent was suddenly permeating through the office. "What's going on?"

I glanced up at my mate quickly, doing a double take when I realized he was leaning against the doorframe, shirtless, covered in sweat, and slightly heaving. No wonder his scent was so strong, he'd been working out and I was amazed to see that even his bulky muscles had a pump from whatever he'd been doing.

It felt impossible to look away from Jackson even as my brain tried to remind me that I was watching something important.

Han was the one who spoke up, saying, "One of the representatives just got booted from office. We're trying to leak the information."

My perfume was starting to bloom just looking at Jackson. It didn't help that my emotions were already high. The giddy excitement I felt over this information was making it even harder to not run to my mate. I wanted to celebrate, I wanted this to be the piece of information that meant the world was finally righting itself.

Even I knew that would be too premature.

Jackson came closer, stepping into the room to watch as Han continued working. His apple scent slammed into me making me groan.

I was bouncing on my toes, fighting the need to fuck my mate and be here while Han worked on this. It didn't help that my arousal was making Han's scent bloom as well. He didn't slow down as he typed despite his pumpkin scent growing stronger.

There was something incredibly sexy about

watching Han work, knowing he was aroused, yet not so much as looking up from his multiple screens. It was hard to keep up with what he was doing, especially as I watched his side profile, his serious features.

A chime went through the house, taking all of our attention away from the screens toward the office door, as if that's where the random person was actually waiting.

Jackson growled, "Han, what the hell did you do?"

"That's not about this. It has to be a coincidence. Even if I had fucked up, which I didn't, but if I had, they wouldn't have gotten here this fast. Also, I didn't fuck up."

I was reassured, although I only made it one step toward the door before Jackson grabbed me. "Nice try, rebel. You stay up here with Han."

Looking back at my mate who was already staring at his screens, I agreed. I planned to sneak down the stairs anyway—

"Han," Jackson demanded. "Keep Hannah up here."

That got my mate to look up from his computers. I didn't even have time to argue before Jackson started making his way out of the room and down the stairs. He was stomping each step, but I couldn't follow because Han wrapped an arm around my waist, pulling me back so I was actually sitting on his lap.

"Han—" I tried to struggle out of his lap. He kept one arm bound around me as he started closing everything on the screens. "Wait, what are you doing?"

"I don't have a good feeling about this."

"What do you mean?"

"We rarely get visitors, especially ones that don't reach out before coming. And someone shows up on the same day that you get a leaked message about the vote?

Shit's going down."

The only thing I felt at his words was panic. My mate was down there. Was Jackson in danger? I needed to protect him.

I was desperately trying to push out of Han's hold, a sort of haze covering my mind with my only thoughts about Jackson and the potential danger for him downstairs.

"Shit, fuck, Hannah, I didn't mean it like that."

Han was trying to turn my waist and I was getting nowhere in my attempts to separate us. His grip around me tightened moments before he started purring, my body physically relaxing, slumping against his chest.

"Jackson is fine," Han said. "I promise. I meant I was worried about you, not him."

"Me?"

Han didn't get time to answer. The same stomping steps made their way back up the stairs. That time, when I tried to scramble from Han's lap, he let me.

I climbed my mate, wrapping my arms and legs around him as best I could the moment I saw him. He was wearing a thin tank top he must have put on to answer the door, although his sweat had soaked into the fabric. I took a deep inhale, needing his scent to calm me, to tell me that he wasn't injured. Instead, I was hit with a strong sense of anger. Considering he was holding me tightly, I knew it wasn't directed at me.

"What's wrong?" I asked, my face so close to his neck that my words came out mumbled against him.

"That was an assistant to Representative Adam." Each word seemed to be pulled from him, his grip becoming impossibly tighter around me. "He would like to meet with us tonight."

"Why?" Han's voice was right behind me, his hand rubbing up and down on my back.

"Apparently, he wishes to speak with Hannah's alphas about a mutually beneficial agreement."

"Zeke is in a session right now. It's a multi-hour piece, he won't be home for a few more hours."

"I know. I explained all this. The prick isn't showing up until after dinner."

Lifting my head, I turned to look at Han, admitting, "You were right."

****

Dinner had been a strangely loud and hectic affair. My mates were going over every possible topic that could be brought up at the meeting about to happen. What we should say, how we should respond, reminders about what specifically not to say.

A lot of it was not so subtly aimed in my direction.

Neither Zeke nor Seb was happy that we hadn't called them right away to tell them, but the decision was Jackson's to make as first alpha. He also made the decisions about who would take the lead in the upcoming conversation.

My job was to be a perfect little omega. I was told I wasn't allowed to demand why Adam was an insecure asshole who asserted his power and dominance over the other designations. Or point out that his beliefs were so obviously wrong that it was why he didn't have a pack omega. Neither was I allowed to admit my true reasoning for being at his restaurant nor my opinions on anything he said about my presence there.

Only Zeke wasn't dressed up for Adam's appearance. My other mates had a form of social obligation to look nice for the male, and even I'd been encouraged by Jackson to wear something semi-formal to keep up appearances.

I was sitting between Zeke's legs, his hands

drawing aimlessly around my thighs and up my stomach carelessly. My scent was a mix of annoyance and arousal, the latter thanks to how close to my core Zeke's fingers were getting.

"I still think we should refuse," I told my alphas.

Zeke and I were in Han's bedroom as the alpha finished getting fancy. The door was open, though, ensuring both Seb and Jackson could hear me. Sebastian peeked his head around the door to give me an unimpressed look.

"You're telling me that if we cancelled right now, you wouldn't be desperate to know what he wanted?"

That earned a glare from me. "Maybe. It might be worth the killing curiosity to keep his scent from my home."

Seb snorted, the sound so uncharacteristic from him that I knew how blatant my lie truly was. I wanted Adam to come. I had grand imaginary plans for what I'd say to him. How I'd yell at him and get him to change his mind. Not that I would—I'd learned my lesson about grand proclamations from the reporters. I was meant to be behind the scenes, blending in with crowds, a voice unidentifiable but raising the volume of others.

I stuck my tongue out, ignoring the heated look Seb gave me before he disappeared to finish getting ready.

Jackson came to the doorway, not entering Han's private space. He was dressed in a nice pair of black slacks and a black shirt that he'd left unbuttoned at the top. The look was serious and sexy. On anyone else, the outfit would make him seem like he was trying to blend in, but there was no hiding Jackson, and his clothes were a testament that he demanded attention no matter what fabric was covering him.

"You going to be a good girl, rebel?" Jackson

asked.

I couldn't even pretend to glare at him, simply taking him in. If any good came out of this meeting, it would be seeing my mates looking this good. "I'll be good so long as he is."

That was the best he was going to get, and he knew it.

Just in time, the doorbell rang, the chime spiking my adrenaline. This was it. It felt like I was moving slowly as I scooted off the bed, waiting on Zeke. I would have sworn that my blood felt thicker, struggling to push its way through my veins to all my extremities. Even my ears felt heavy—did blood even go to ears?

All of a sudden, I was in the formal greeting space, and I realized I needed my mates.

"Hannah, what's wrong?"

I felt my lips part, felt the words on the tip of my tongue, but they disappeared when someone knocked on the door. This was really happening. The alpha that was trying to socially break my designation was about to come into my house and I realized for the first time that I *hated* that idea.

"Hannah, look at me." The alpha bark had my brain focusing, every instinct telling me to appease my alpha over everything else. Jackson was cupping my face, his nose so close to mine that I was forced to only see his dark brown irises. "Tell me you can't handle this, and I'll send him away."

I shook my head. I had no idea what was wrong with me, why my emotions were freaking out, but I did know that I didn't want to send Adam-the-asshole away. Sebastian was right, I wanted to know what Adam had to say.

"I need to get the door, rebel," Jackson said, "But I'm not leaving you until you calm down. I felt your panic earlier, and your heart is beating too fast for my liking. If you can't settle your heart rate, I'm taking you to the emergency care."

"I can't go outside. It's too late."

Jackson growled, the sound doing more to settle me than his words. It was a blatant reminder of how fierce my alpha was. A protector. He wouldn't let Adam hurt me. I looked at how strong he was, and my heart finally stopped threatening to overwork itself.

I was safe.

My shoulders rolled back, and my chin lifted. No more panic, or fear, or emotional bullshit. I could handle this with my mates. I trusted them.

Jackson stood to his full height, looking down at me with a smirk over his lips. "Atta girl, rebel."

As soon as he stepped away, my other alphas came in to surround me. Zeke behind me, his arms around my stomach and keeping me pressed against his front. Sebastian and Han on either side of me, so close that my shoulders touched their arms.

I took in a deep breath, and then Jackson opened the door.

JOSEPHINE LIGHT

Chapter Twenty

Representative Adam came with his pack. Two other alphas, not including his alpha assistant.

They looked completely at home as Jackson settled them onto the guest couch. I watched one of Adam's packmate's nose wrinkle slightly, and I wondered if he was overwhelmed with my scent in the house or if he could detect Eve's scent when she sat there a few weeks ago.

Adam and his pack sat on the couch, the assistant standing behind them looking more like a security guard than an administrator of any kind. All the alphas smelled terrible, like black pepper, salt water, and some kind of strong alcohol.

I curled myself into my mate, attempting to subtly inhale his berry perfume or risk seriously offending Adam's pack—something I wasn't completely opposed to doing.

"Here you go." Seb carried all three drinks from the bar like he was a professional waiter, handing them out directly to the alphas.

I was sitting on the couch opposite our 'guests' with Zeke by my side. His body was so close to mine that we were touching at every possible point of contact, the heat from him radiating even through his comfy clothes. With his hand on my thigh, squeezing semi-tightly, he was the designated alpha in charge of ensuring I didn't act on any potential negative emotions this conversation was most definitely going to bring.

Han was half standing on my other side, leaning against the couch's arm, his ankles crossed like he was having a leisurely conversation. Jackson was behind me, standing tall, no doubt with his arms crossed because regardless of the fact that he'd been telling me all day I'd need to behave, I knew those same words were haunting him now. Sebastian was the only one sitting slightly away from me, taking up a single seater couch off to the side.

"I guess you're probably wondering why we're here," Adam said. He gave a sort of self-deprecating laugh as if the whole situation was crazy. "Firstly, we figured it was about time that we came and checked in on you all. A member of your pack was severely injured at one of the businesses that I own, and I didn't want you all to think that we abandon our patrons. Omegas are so important to our society, and even one injured is a gross negligence."

It was Sebastian that spoke up first, easily taking the lead. "Hannah's already been cleared by the doctor. We are back to our regularly scheduled programming, thankfully."

That comment got a few chuckles from Adam's pack.

One of the alphas whose name I didn't bother remembering leaned forward, asking, "But the attack, that must have left some emotional scars."

"Hannah's head trauma has unfortunately caused her memory to lapse. She doesn't remember the incident."

Again, the words came from Sebastian, leading the conversation rather than Jackson. My posh mate had literal training in deciphering and speaking formal ambiguity. It was easy to admit that Seb took conversing with Adam naturally, still, I wondered if Adam took it as an insult that Seb was speaking with him rather than my pack's first alpha or if Seb's name was truly that powerful.

"A blessing of sorts," Adam said, earning nods

from his packmates. "I couldn't imagine how tough it's been dealing with an omega going through such a traumatic time."

I stiffened at those words, hating being referred to as if I wasn't fucking present. Sure, Adam was turned slightly so he was looking directly at Sebastian. That didn't mean he should just exclude me. Also, who worries more about how other people handle someone else's trauma? Not only did it ignore the very real fear that my mates had for my safety and health, but it was degrading as shit to what happened to me.

Zeke's hand on my knee squeezed tighter, and he shifted in his seat, inconspicuously adjusting so he was slightly leaning against me rather than simply touching me. A hand touched my shoulder, the gentle weight of Jackson's presence reminding me of his pleas that I be a good omega for this meeting.

"Hannah's strong," Sebastian said, his chest puffing up. "We're just happy that she's here, with us, and healing."

Those words filled me with pride, calming the tirade of emotions I hadn't even recognized growing inside me.

"Of course," Adam agreed. "There's been a lot of speculation surrounding your omega and how she's doing. She's become quite recognizable, actually. Lots of people are worried about her."

There was something ... odd in his tone. I couldn't place it and my alphas didn't stop speaking to give me a minute to think about it.

"We've ensured all of our families understand that Hannah is fine," Han said, speaking up for the first time. I had no idea if what Han said was true or not considering the only conversation my mates had about their families was that we all didn't get along.

Adam waved a hand in the air like Han's comment was obvious, "Of course. I was meaning the public. Unfortunately, the world has been watching this pack since the incident. Lots of people feel like they know someone once they see them on the screen, especially those that make a reoccurrence in such a dramatic fashion."

"We've noticed," Seb said, nodding solemnly like he was agreeing to something terrible. "Unfortunately, there's nothing we can do about everyone talking about Hannah."

"I actually had an idea about that. A way to help protect your omega. It's the second reason we're here, now that we know she's okay."

Behind me, my mate's growl was loud enough that I knew everyone could hear it. His hand was still on my shoulder, his fingers digging in like he was trying to anchor himself to me, taking comfort from me rather than offering it. I turned my head as best I could and kissed his hand, reaching up with my own fingers to reassure him. My instincts screamed at me, demanding I do more to help my alpha, to wrap myself around him or maybe even get on my knees to thank him for his protection.

Just as I was about to crawl over the back of the couch to my mate, Jackson's growl softened.

Despite his scent having bloomed with anger, I could scent the bitterness of the other alphas. I doubted my mates could scent the slight change in their shift since my designation had the best sense of smell. That didn't stop the smug smile from pulling at my lips no matter how much I knew I shouldn't allow it.

On top of that, I wouldn't have thought Jackson would have been the first one to break civility, but I appreciated that it wasn't me. Looking over my shoulder, I smirked at Jackson who didn't find me nearly as amusing as I found myself in that moment.

"We didn't mean any offense," Adam said, the apology barely existent. "You're protecting your omega as best you can. Sometimes it helps to have friends in high places, though."

Was he supposed to be the friend? And why did his apology have a 'we' when he was the idiot that insulted my alpha?

"What do you suggest?" Sebastian asked. He was leaning forward now, looking intrigued, and bringing all the attention back to him.

"An interview. Something calmer than being attacked by the press. As easy as this sit-down, just talking, explaining what happened and how she's doing now."

"It would be a short interview considering Hannah lost years of her memory," Han joked.

One of Adam's pack members spoke up, the one that smelled like salty water, saying, "Memory loss is technically a medical diagnosis. She wouldn't have to admit that in any interview. That would be a violation of privacy."

"If I was being honest," Sebastian started, "I would admit that I'm not particularly trusting of reporters at the moment. You'll recall the last time I took Hannah out and the unfortunate events that transpired. Putting her back into that position doesn't particularly appeal to any of us."

Adam turned his gaze to me, temporarily, a look on his face like he was seeing a dying dog, not a person. "Understandable. But I do have some expertise with reporters and the public. I can tell you that scrutiny will continue to follow you until the public feels like it's gotten the answers to their questions."

It took me longer than I'd like to admit to

understand Adam's suggestion. A few weeks ago, I would have jumped at this opportunity. Except now I knew what the reporters were like. How they pushed into your private space, all huddled together with bright flashing lights, demanding to be heard over one another. They'd stared at me, yelling questions that had to be tongue twisters to get out, and shoving devices into my face, unrelenting in their pursuit.

Then there was the fact that the offer came from Adam. I had seen the way the female reporter had set him up for success in that one-on-one interview, and I knew any help he offered would be with the same vibe, the same set-up that aligned with his vile propaganda.

Han shook his head back and forth, not adamantly, but softly. "Hannah doesn't have the experience you do with talking to reporters. I've seen the footage that was recorded the night she and Sebastian were overwhelmed. The flashing lights and yelled questions weren't a safe space. Right, Hannah?"

I almost didn't answer, so used to the alphas talking about me like I wasn't here. The silence in the room was deafening, the words finally coming together in my brain, making me realize I needed to actually say something.

"Right. My mates have been telling me that the best option is to stay out of the public's attention, and I agree with that."

"Your mates are wise," Adam said, speaking to me for the first time.

I groaned internally, hating what I'd said. To anyone else, my words would have just shown that I was in agreement with my alphas, except I knew that what Adam actually heard was that my mates made the decision since it was their idea. I could have just said that *I thought* it was best to stay out of the public's eyes. I could have stopped after agreeing with Han or maybe even demanded to know how I was supposed to conduct any interview when I couldn't fucking leave my home anymore. Damn, that would've been so good!

"My suggestion was for an intimate interview, not with a news station but an actual journalist. One with integrity and an omega of their own. You'd sit down, in a particularly comfortable seat if I say so myself, talking about your recent experiences. No pressure, a single camera, nothing overwhelming."

I felt my eyebrows pull together, my confusion more than obvious in my features and my scent. Hopefully, Adam would believe that the emotion came from not understanding the type of interview rather than my absolute curiosity at his intentions. After all, he thought I was a dumb omega.

"I'm not sure—"

Seb's words were cut off by Adam. "I'm talking about the long-term effects of protecting your omega. Right now, whether you like it or not, she's a public figure. Her name, her designation, her injuries, it's all being addressed by morning shows and talk segments. There's nothing you can do about that, no hiding her, only ensuring that she isn't used as a tool by people who hadn't even bothered to check in with how she's healing."

That was fucking laughable. The chuckle almost made it past my lips, getting caught in my throat.

Pressing my face against Zeke's shoulder to hide the sound, I cleared my throat as quietly as possible.

"Who exactly were you thinking of?" Seb asked.

"Presley Abject. She's someone I would have my own personal interviews with if we hadn't been friends for years and I knew she'd take it easy on me."

"Oh, yes, Presley. My mother knows her omega's parents ... a friend of a friend. How is mating treating them all?"

"Wonderfully. Like any good alpha, Presley is still focused on her career, aware she needs to provide long-term, and I know she wouldn't mind if I set up a meeting."

"Did she take off time for her mating? We wouldn't want to pull her from bonding with her omega. It's important for the pack health as well as the health of her omega that mates stay close together, especially so close to leaving marks."

I wondered if it was as obvious to Adam as it was to me that Seb was trying to turn down this offer. And I wondered if it didn't matter how subtly Sebastian changed the topic. If Adam would continue to lead us back to where he wanted because his offer was more a demand.

"Presley is never truly off the clock." Adam's words were losing their careful teasing, their lightheartedness. "And even if she did take off time, I know this issue would be close to her heart."

For a moment, none of my alphas responded. Adam took a slow sip of his dark liquor, the look on his face so cocky, it was obvious that he thought he'd won.

Won what, though?

Was he trying to slip me up in the interview, forcing me to admit that I am an omega who was at the sit-in protest of his diner? Would that actually help him keep my designation under lock and key? Or was I supposed to lie, supposed to further his narrative that I was a victim to the betas?

I wished that I remembered what happened. Not knowing felt as if I was missing a piece of this puzzle—the single piece that would help me to understand Adam better. Help me play the game better.

"Doing an interview, any interview as a member

of this pack, requires a conversation with our families," Seb finally said.

It sounded like a last-ditch effort, and Adam's smile said he knew it too.

"By all means. Call them. Have a discussion. I'm not unfamiliar with the names in this pack, and I'm more than sure all our values and goals align. Protecting omegas is always at the top of my agenda—it controls almost everything I do. In the meantime, I'll go ahead and book the interview with Presley. It'll take about three weeks to book the studio and set up lighting, makeup, all that jazz. Plenty of time to speak with your families."

Adam finished his drink in a huge gulp, setting the glass down harder than he probably should've. Then he was standing, buttoning his jacket again and reaching a hand toward my alphas. Everyone stood except Zeke and me.

I didn't care if I looked like a bad omega for not saying proper goodbyes. As far as I was concerned, they weren't true guests in this house. I crossed one leg over the other, playing with the fabric covering my knee as I waited for my alphas to shut the door and come back to me.

Nothing about this suggestion felt like a good idea. The fact that it came from Adam was warning number one. Number two was that he essentially didn't let us refuse. Then, there was the Presley issue, number three, which was mostly just on the basis that I didn't trust anyone that Adam would speak fondly of. Finally, the last concern was the timeline. Three weeks? That would be just days before the permanency vote for the omega movement proposition. That couldn't be a coincidence.

I refused to be used as a weapon for Adam to wield. My attack, my silence, all of it had already been used against my best intentions. Still, I'd managed to justify that to myself because it was out of my control. They were using videos and pictures and comments that were taken out of context.

Sitting down and lying—or even dancing around the answer like I was a professional ballerina—was me changing sides. Even if I didn't lie, if my truth was twisted for the wrong audience, that would all be on me. My fault.

"Hannah."

My name pulled me out of my spiraling thoughts. Jackson was crouched in front of me, hands on either side of me like he hadn't wanted to touch me and risk startling me. His scent was bitter, no doubt he'd held back his emotions as best he could while Adam was here, which is why Sebastian had taken the lead. Now that we were all alone again, he wasn't holding back.

"We can get you out of this if you want."

If I wanted? Why did his words sound weird? I looked up at Han and Seb, both males standing off to the sides of Jackson, watching me intently, both with mirror looks of worry on their faces.

"I can't do an interview that makes things worse for my designation." I needed them to understand that. I understood that they didn't want to piss Adam off, but I wasn't going to be used to hurt other omegas.

"We know, rebel. We never thought you would. The question is whether you think you can handle the interview setting?"

"What do you mean?"

"Could you sit down, in front of a camera, and be interviewed?"

"What do you mean?"

A headache was forming between my eyes. He said he understood that I wouldn't do an interview that hurt my designation, yet he wanted to know if the act of being interviewed would freak me out? Did he think I could somehow talk my way around an actual answer to a professional social investigator? Or was he planning on my memory loss to be effective in not answering questions?

"Do you trust me, rebel?"

I nodded, slowly. I did trust my mates. Not just instinctively. It was a lesson I was learning over and over again. "Yes."

"Good. Let's get you to bed. I'm taking you out on a date tomorrow."

Jackson lifted me from the couch, carrying me up the stairs with ease as my other alphas followed. With the way I was wrapped around him, I watched my mates climb the stairs after us. The scents of nerves and frustration and relief were swirling around us in a mayhem of mixed uncontrollable emotions.

We undressed, my mates keeping their boxers on while I slept completely naked. Usually, I preferred pajamas. If I was honest, I was too distracted to put them on. My mind was buzzing with nothing, jumping from topics so quickly that I couldn't have honestly answered the question of what I was thinking about.

It wasn't just me that was distracted either.

I wanted to comfort all my mates, wanted to grow myself or multiply so I could wrap them all up in my arms and scent. Instead, I had to settle for a puppy pile. Jackson on the bottom with me laying on top of him. Sebastian on one side so I could reach out and touch him while Han and Zeke cuddled on Jackson's other side. Han was closer, but Zeke reached an arm out to hold my hand.

In the dark silence of the space, I couldn't help asking, "What's the plan?"

"Don't worry, rebel. We have three weeks to get

you prepared. I'll explain everything tomorrow, you'll need your sleep."

Despite my internal protests, I did fall asleep almost instantly.

Chapter Twenty-One

Jackson woke me up so early that I wondered if I actually got any sleep. I was moving so slowly as I got ready, unable to even muster a thank you to Jackson who laid out the clothes he wanted me to wear.

I wanted to ask what kind of date demanded that we get up before the fucking sun, only I couldn't seem to convince my tongue to move.

We weren't the only ones who got up, though. Sebastian was mysteriously missing from the nest and as soon as I woke up more, I planned on finding the energy to worry about that.

My head was resting against the cold counter of the island, the position weirdly comfortable, although that might have simply been because of how tired I was. Jackson was packing up our bags with snacks and water bottles and different sprays that I didn't bother investigating to their actual use.

Something was set on my head, and it took a lot of effort on my part to raise my hand, feeling the fabric of a hat. Apparently, we were going outside.

"What time is it?" I managed to croak out.

"A little after 4:00," Jackson said, sounding as awake as if he'd said noon.

"In the morning?"

My mate was lucky that I was too tired to even complain about wanting more sleep or I couldn't guarantee this date would happen. I knew Jackson woke up early to work out, but I never knew he woke up this early. How did he even function the rest of the day?

Closing my eyes felt so good, as if keeping them open was an exercise in itself.

Something loud slammed down beside me, and I jumped, the momentary shot of adrenaline in my system making me feel awake.

"Drink up, princess." Sebastian handed me a cup, the clear plastic with a simple logo of a muscular bicep, before kissing my temple.

I wasn't particularly hungry, but a smoothie wasn't really food, so I took a sip. The fruit flavor was fine, but it had a weird chalk aftertaste that clung to my tongue.

"Let me try." Jackson grabbed the drink from me before I could warn him about the lingering aftertaste, and he handed me the drink Sebastian had handed him. "This is good. Try mine, rebel, we need to be heading out."

Jackson's drink was a mix of chocolate and coffee, and it was delicious. I swore that I could almost feel the energy from the drink seeping into my veins and waking me up.

"Good, time to go," Jackson said, grabbing both backpacks and his drink.

I hugged Sebastian, who yawned and then told me to be safe, before I followed Jackson out to the car. As soon as I was seated, he started the car and took off, his hand on my knee in a casual touch.

"Where are we going?"

"There's a hiking path about two hours away that should be hidden enough for us to have a chat, work out some plans, without crossing paths with anyone."

It was still dark outside, and I was pretty sure that even two hours wasn't enough time for the sun to wake up, but I had the seat heater on, and my delicious smelling crisp apple mate, along with a thick smoothie to chug down. I was perfectly content on the long ass drive.

Reaching down, I untied my shoes and pulled my

feet up to rest on the seat. "Am I technically allowed to be out this early?"

"Nope. But all our cars have tinted windows, and I don't break any driving laws, so we'll be fine."

"It's the dumbest rule," I tell him, although he already knows. "It doesn't even consider kids who haven't fallen into their designation yet. Are children not allowed outside anymore? And what's the punishment if an omega is even caught outside? A fine? Jail time?"

That last option made me snort. It was hard to have legal recourse for omegas when no one deemed us as smart enough, strong enough, or capable of anything.

"Do you think there's ever been an omega murderer?" I asked my mate.

Jackson laughed. Loud and boisterous to the point that I was mildly worried he would forget he was driving. "Thinking of becoming a murderess, rebel?"

I shrugged. "I was just wondering what sort of legal punishments omegas actually face."

"Usually, the recoil lands on their alphas. For negligence, endangering the public, bullshit names that take humanity away from omegas."

"But that's only if the omega was bonded. What if they weren't?"

"It's a good question."

It was also one I would never get an answer to.

For the rest of the drive, we talked about random things. I was definitely awake, just not functioning at full capacity yet. By the time we arrived at the dirt parking lot, the sun was just starting to rise, although we would definitely be needing flashlights and jackets for this beginning portion.

Jackson's backpack was significantly fuller than mine. The straps over his shoulders made his arms and chest look wider. Stronger. Like he could still pick me up and carry me with ease as he hiked.

For the first few minutes, we walked in silence, getting our bearings with the flashlights and warming up our bodies against the chill. Me probably more than him.

Eventually, Jackson broke our comfortable silence. "You want to talk about this interview?"

"What is there to talk about?"

"I think you should do it."

I had no idea what I expected Jackson to say, but that wasn't it. My feet literally stumbled over each other before I caught myself.

"What? Why?"

"Isn't this what you wanted? You were so adamant before about wanting to go to the reporters and tell them your side. This is a perfect opportunity to do that."

"I don't trust whoever Adam trusts."

"That's why it's actually beneficial we have a few weeks to prepare you."

Prepare me? For what? I was only getting more confused from this conversation. "I thought you wanted me to stay out of the public's attention. What happened to us being behind the scenes?"

"We'd love it if everyone outside of our pack stopped showing your image and using your name. Unfortunately, that just isn't happening. On the most basic of levels, Adam was right. Until the public feels like they've wrung out all the information they can from you, they're going to keep using you."

"Then maybe we should do an interview on our own, without Adam's guiding hand. Tell him that it's an excellent idea and that we're going to refuse his offer but take up his idea."

"We could. Sebastian certainly has enough social ego to wield as justification."

"But?" I asked, because I could sense it even if he didn't say it.

"But, if you're going to do this, I think it would have a stronger effect if it was preluded by Adam's hand pushing you to speak. I was thinking about what Eve said, how the OC is keeping tabs on you but holding back on pressing charges against us..."

I sucked in a breath. I had completely forgotten about that. I'd been so busy dealing with the actual ramifications of my forced publicity that I'd forgotten the worst hadn't come yet, that it was still hanging over my head like a hat you get so used to wearing you forget that it's blocking the sun until you take it off. Then you're fucking blinded by the brightness.

"We can't do the interview," I told him. "I'm not risking the OC pulling up charges against you."

No way. Absolutely no way. I couldn't even believe that Jackson was considering going through with this when my mates could wind up in jail for a decision I made. I was almost angry at him for being so willing to face the charges. But I was not going to be letting that happen.

"You don't want to hear my plan?" he asked.

"What plan?"

"The one I made last night when Adam focused all his attention on Seb."

"A plan that's completely new and hasn't been run by any of the others?"

"That's the one."

I wasn't going to agree to it, I already knew that. Still, I figured agreeing to hear would be fine. Then I could point out all the plot holes. Except, rather than a loosely thrown together timeline of events, I realized why Jackson felt comfortable suggesting this path.

I couldn't stop myself from interrupting with

questions. "Is Eve even willing to work with us?"

"We won't know until we ask, but I think so. She did come to warn you, that has to count for something."

"And what happens if it all goes to shit? If the OC does press charges and Adam gets his votes and the public turns against me?"

"We leave."

"Just like that?"

My breathing became heavier as the trail turned more into a hike than a walk. It was hard to think when I was doing my best to get my lungs to keep expanding and ignoring the dry scratch in my throat. No matter how much I drank, it was like my throat simply wasn't getting any of the liquid goodness.

"Sometimes, you have to save yourself," Jackson said.

I wanted to argue. Omegas weren't rare, we were just hidden, forced into shadows and nooks and crannies. They needed someone to stand up for them, to be their voice, and demand to be seen. I'd always thought that was me—yet I've hated being in the limelight.

I could admit, even just to myself, that part of my resistance to not doing Adam's interview came from the memory of the reporters surrounding me. My mate protected me then, but it felt like without him, I would have been trampled. They would have simply watched me crawl into a corner and freak out without offering a helping hand. It was strange to look at strangers and realize they didn't care.

Maybe that's where Jackson's insistence on being behind the scenes truly came from. Another version of protecting me, even from myself.

For so long, I wanted to be the person that made the difference, and here I was, rejecting that offer.

"If I did the interview, what's to stop Adam from

refusing to release it?" I asked, almost panting between each word.

"He won't have a choice. It'll be live."

Needing to think, I stopped walking, my mate easily staying with me. Despite the chilly air, I was sweating, and a good portion of my first water bottle was already gone. I'd been so distracted with our discussion that I'd barely taken in the view beyond watching where I was stepping.

It was beautiful, the way nature always was. Personally, I preferred to see the beauty of trees and animals and whatnot from my airconditioned home without the sweat and bugs.

Jackson swung his backpack around and pulled out a healthy bar for us to snack on while we enjoyed the temporary break in silence. Just this slight pause and I felt like my brain was working properly again.

"If I did this interview, what do you think will happen?" I stared at my mate, not so much as glancing away from his gaze. "Not what you hope will happen, what do you think will happen?"

"I think … Adam will lose the vote. I think every time an issue comes up for omegas, you'll be expected to play politics. I think you're going to lose a lot of your private life. Your followers will be as plentiful as your opponents. I worry how you'll take the stress if you do this, and I worry how you'll handle the guilt if you don't. I also think that you'll probably drop your classes."

"What? Why?" That seemed like the opposite of helping my designation. Except, once the initial shock of his words settled, I realized, he was probably right. I only took classes because I wanted to prove an omega could complete them. Yet my little non-major courses were nothing compared to Koda's high-level degree. She was doing something impressive, and I could do something equally so, if I chose this new plan.

He shrugged, readjusting his backpack, getting ready to start walking again. I followed his lead, and we continued on.

"You've had two major traumatic instances in the last few months. And both of them have changed you. The first made you braver. You forgot all the times you've fought and lost. You forgot how long it had been between your protests and you were ready to get back out there. Then your date with Seb happened. It crushed your hope, hearing petty questions from people who wouldn't have spit on you if you were on fire."

"Gross."

"You know what I mean. I need you to want it, either way. Sebastian and Han can help you with doubletalk, so you don't get manipulated in interviews. And I'm going to help you train."

"Train for what?"

"To be stronger. Faster. How to balance. I've always said I would be around to protect you, and then I wasn't. If something like that ever happens again, I want you to get away. I was also thinking about getting you a gun."

That last part had me choking on air.

"Better safe than sorry, rebel. Don't worry, though. I'll be taking you to the range, so you'll be an expert by the time you actually start carrying. Plus, I coated it in pink."

He was bribing me with a pink gun … and it was working. I could already imagine the blurry face racing after me, before I turned around, whipping out my tiny pink weapon. They'd laugh, and it would be the last thing they'd ever do.

I didn't ask if it was legal for me to carry a weapon, because I already knew the answer. I also didn't ask how Jackson managed to procure one for me. Or make it pink.

My hand ran over my head, feeling the pricks from my hair ends. Zeke was the one keeping up with my haircuts since it was growing crazy quickly this short. That also meant dying it a lot, although we were able to reuse containers considering how little dye was actually needed for each touch-up. I had no plans to grow it out yet, especially since my mate was still keeping a shaved heart around my scar.

As my thoughts went back to our conversation, I felt myself on a precipice. To help the other omegas or ensure my pack stayed together. What was I willing to risk? Either way, it felt like a lot.

The trail we were on led us to a gorgeous view of a lake. Despite the whole trail being quiet, there was something extra serene about this area. Maybe it was because we weren't walking anymore so I wasn't panting out each breath, disturbing nature with my need to breathe.

Then, disturbing the beautiful peace, was a soft alarm coming from Jackson.

He had a thick watch on his wrist which was making the noise. A quick tap of a button made it stop.

It definitely wasn't a wake-up alarm considering that it took a few hours to get here and then even more to hike to this spot. Maybe it was for him to actually start work?

"What time is it?" I asked.

"7:00."

I felt my whole face frown. My lips pulling down, my eyebrows coming together, even the slight scrunch in my nose.

"Omegas can officially leave their home with supervision."

A growl started in my chest, my annoyance and frustration and anger all perfuming around me in a toxic cloud. I stared out at the still water, trying to distract myself with the calm I had somehow found before.

Off to the side was a little wooden sign. Stomping my way over to it, I read the faded words thanking someone for caring enough to protect this natural water landmark.

The kind words only had me growling more.

Of course someone would have had to put in effort to save this place—because apparently morals meant nothing. Right and wrong simply didn't exist. You had to work for everything in life. Like saving a plot of water. Stopping omegas from being systemically abused.

"When we get back, let's call Eve," I told my mate. "If she's willing to help, then I'm all in."

I'd always hated that the other omegas didn't blatantly fight back. In the beginning, it had come too easy to me. I had nothing to lose and everything to gain. For this next round, I had everything to lose, and everything to gain.

And I wanted everything so bad. I wanted the freedom and my pack. I wanted the social acceptance and the legal change.

I thought about Koda, how all she wanted was to be able to learn like everyone else. I thought about Eve and how everyone had forced her into believing she was somehow less. I thought of old Hannah, who'd been reckless and brave and desperate.

The Omega Compound was threatening us. Adam was attempting to back us into a corner. This was the time to fight back or cower. To play their game or forfeit.

Jackson grabbed my hand and pulled me away from the lake and back on the trail. I was a mix of anger and confidence, feeling like I could have set the world on fire. Like I could literally kick ass if needed.

Speaking of which. "Earlier? When you said train me? What does that mean?"

"That means cardio several times a week. Weight training, too. Stretching every night and as many hikes we can fit in for overall body strength. Hearty foods, protein in your smoothies. On the weekends, weapons so you know how to load and unload and clean and fire."

I groaned, hating all of those ideas. I wanted a bed, a nest, and an unscheduled mealtime. Fucking alpha extremist assholes making me have to work out.

"Ready to start now?" Jackson asked.

There was something in his voice that pulled my attention away from my internal tantrum. He sounded excited, definitely too excited for me to simply workout.

"I thought we already had. We're literally on a hike."

"We're walking, not running."

My eyes went wide as I stared at him. Running this path? I was already huffing and puffing just from the speed we were going. Any faster and I was pretty sure my body would give out.

"I'll even give you a few second lead. Start running now, and when I catch you, I'm going to fuck you."

Arousal. That was the emotion I'd detected. I was so tired that I hadn't even considered trying to identify that scent.

I was paying attention now. His words excited something primal inside me, wanting him to chase me, dominate me.

"Just run?" I asked.

"Run, rebel. Don't worry, I'll find you quickly."

I was already breathing hard as I looked around, trying to figure out which direction I wanted to run in, then I took off. I wasn't feeling tired anymore—I felt alive. Like I could've run forever.

Rather than head back down the trail, or toward the water, I went off in the opposite direction. It was open, which meant he'd easily be able to see me, but hiding wasn't truly the point. The point was the arousal currently flooding my system. The pleasure and excitement and even slight anxiety that came from trying to hide.

Eventually, the flat land began to rise and fall, just subtly enough that I could feel it in my calves. I started turning, aiming in the direction I thought was further away from the parking lot, although I had no clue if I was even correct in my directional assumption.

A few skinny trees appeared randomly, spread out like they sucked out all the water in the surrounding area forcing nothing else to exist nearby. They made me think of weeds, really tall weeds that just managed to push their way to the surface to survive.

I heard him first. The sound of his boots slamming against the earth.

A burst of energy helped me sprint, but I was sucking in as much air as I could. My backpack was bouncing against my back, my legs starting to slow down even as I tried to make them move faster.

All of a sudden, I wasn't running anymore. Arms wrapped around me as I fell, my knees and hands scraping against the dirt. Most likely, I'd scratched up my body, but I didn't care. The slight biting pain mixed with my excitement, adding to my pleasure.

"Caught you," he said, the words heavy in my ears.

Behind me, I felt him press his hand between my shoulder blades, pushing me into the position he wanted. My chest wasn't all the way on the ground because I was breathing so hard, and I didn't want to inhale dirt. Arching my back, I shook my hips, wishing I had something to grab onto like bed sheets.

His apple scent was strong with his arousal, my own lavender tainted arousal blooming too. I was nervous about being in public, not that I wanted to stop.

I still had my pants on, and Jackson had his, yet I could feel the pressure of his hard cock pressing between my legs, teasing me. My core was already wet, already ready for my mate to thrust inside me whenever he stopped playing with me.

His hand cupped between my legs, over my clothes and feeling my center, as he groaned. "You're soaking wet for me, rebel."

A whimper came from my throat.

Jackson pulled my pants down to my knees before shoving my legs together. He took a moment to unzip himself and then he thrusted inside me without hesitation.

In this position, with my thighs pressed together, on all fours, he felt huge inside me. His hands wrapped around my waist, yanking me back with each of his thrusts, slamming into me hard enough that I wondered if his thighs would leave bruises against mine.

This was fast and hard, brutal and efficient.

The anticipation from my run, the feel of his cock hitting that perfect spot, had me already close to my orgasm. Then one of his hands went to my nape, the spot where he'd claimed me, his fingers tightening around his mark. His other hand wrapped around my front, seeking out my clit to rub gentle circles on the nub.

"Fuck yourself on my cock, Hannah," Jackson told me. "I want you to make me come, beg me to knot you here."

My body instantly obeyed, moving myself back and forth over his cock, forcing my already exhausted muscles to ignore the burn, ignore the shake. I needed my orgasm more than I needed rest. Needed his knot more than I needed water.

"Please knot me, Jackson. Fucking, please. I want to feel the pressure from your knot. I want to come, please, alpha."

He groaned, both of his hands tightening, working harder to drive me crazy. I was moving as best as I could, caught between his hands, using my pussy to jerk him off. So close, my orgasm was so close, and I was crying, begging him and my body to both give in.

Then he squeezed my clit, pinching the bud between his fingers and making me scream through an orgasm. It was so strong, my muscles finally gave in to the fatigue, giving up holding my weight. Jackson caught me, pulling my chest back toward his until I winced from the pressure on my knees. I was definitely feeling those scrapes.

I felt more than heard him chuckle, purring loudly as he worked one-handed to zip himself up and then somehow manage to stand, from his knees, while holding me like I was a front backpack.

This type of multi-week workout I could get behind.

Chapter Twenty-Two

Two weeks and six days later

I was a fucking bundle of nerves.

It didn't matter that Eve had me wait as long as possible to shower in the hope that I could wash off the clinging scent of emotions. I couldn't hide what I was feeling, and I wasn't able to distract myself from what was about to happen.

My interview with Presley was in less than an hour. Eve was doing all the tactics that the OC taught her to calm omegas down, except I wasn't stressed about anything that could be easily soothed with a sarape and my favorite smoothie. Not that I didn't appreciate her attempts to help me.

"That's it," Eve said, standing up from the little metal chair she deemed was good enough for her. "I'm getting one of your mates."

Words were impossible to get out, but I was looking in a mirror, and I watched my head nod. Then I was alone.

The room that the studio gave me to prep for the interview was small yet filled with every necessity. A tiny shower with complimentary bottles to wash. A couch with a back-up sarape that Eve had told the company I preferred. A vanity where I could do my hair and makeup. There was also a small cabinet of dry foods and a tiny fridge with cold drinks. The thermostat was for just this room so I could make it any temperature I wanted. There was even a little gift when I arrived, and that I tore into seconds after I saw it.

My mates were in my room in seconds considering they were simply outside the door, waiting for the opportunity to be let in. They'd started the afternoon in here with me, but then Adam had wanted a word, thanking me for showing up and my emotions had gone haywire. That meant they were forced to wait outside the room so no one could have another excuse to come in and bother me. However, Eve was right—I needed them more than I needed everyone else to leave me the fuck alone.

It was Sebastian that reached me first, turning me around and pulling me into a hug. I heard the door shut again, only this time, Eve was on the other side, hopefully able to keep anyone else away. It was harder for a beta since the alphas didn't seem to respect her at all. Still, I appreciated the effort.

"Do you think I'm ready?" I mumbled against Seb's neck.

"Yes." There was no hesitation in his confirmation. "Despite her personal opinions, Presley is an expert interviewer. In some ways, that'll help because she isn't going to be led into topics we haven't covered."

Han came up behind me, rubbing his hand over my back, as he said, "She'll no doubt start you off easy. Once she realizes she isn't getting the responses she wants, she'll throw out the script."

"Her omega's here," Zeke added. "Hopefully that'll be enough to keep her scent in check."

"She brought her omega?" I asked. To me, it felt weird, like she'd brought her omega in to watch his doom unfold. Maybe he was one of those rare omegas that was content with the way things were. He had mated Presley and her pack after all.

My alphas did their best to stay close to me, all of us in a huddle. This close to my mates, I was finally able to calm down, my thoughts not able to permeate beyond the loud purring coming from them.

At least until someone softly knocked and Eve stuck her head in the room. "Are you almost ready, Hannah? They want you to get seated so they can mic you up."

I nodded. Still, I hesitated to leave my mates, to finally commit to this act that had consumed so much of our lives lately.

All the exercising and mock interviews had led to this moment. All the research Seb tried to explain to me, and the stories Eve had told me.

My tongue felt heavy in my mouth. Would I even be able to get the words out? Any words at this point?

"Should I do this? I know we've been working toward it and planning on it, but this is it. Our last chance to stop it before we've gone too far. We're going to have to face the OC's wrath, we'll have to deal with Adam, his pack, and every other employee in this building just to leave, and that doesn't even consider the social ramifications—"

"You're spiraling, rebel." Jackson cupped my face in his hands, his thumbs caressing my cheekbones. His gaze was intent on mine, not letting me look away from his brown eyes. "All of this is your choice. You know that. We tried behind the scenes and that didn't work. Now we're trying out front. If that doesn't work, we'll try something else."

I took a deep inhale, thankful that everyone ignored how shaky that breath sounded.

Eve led the way, with Jackson right behind her, Han and Zeke on either side of me, and Sebastian behind all of us. We all had a role to play in this, especially in front of so many gazes. Despite being surrounded by my mates, I still saw all the glances in our direction, and I was working to keep my stride confident, focusing on ensuring my hips had a slight sway.

Seb chuckled, and I winked at him over my shoulder, mercifully managing not to run into anyone.

The area where the interview was set to take place was brightly lit, my feet automatically slowing down as we neared it.

At least it didn't look sterile. Two club chairs sat facing each other, lined with fabric I knew would be soft, ensuring any sweat from my palms would soak into the material's arms, staining it. Between the seats was a decorative rug with a small table set in the middle. It was decorated like a furniture showing with books that didn't actually have titles laid on top, some fake candles, and even two place settings as if we were going to have some drinks with us while we chatted.

Overhead, dozens of lights dangled and angled themselves to illuminate the whole space. This area was literally warmer than the rest of the room, which I knew wouldn't help with my already present stress sweats.

Off to the side, I finally saw Presley and her omega. The latter was sitting in a chair with Presley's name on the back while the former stood, getting her last-minute details done to her hair and makeup. They looked good together, the kind of opposites that somehow perfectly complimented each other.

Presley was all blonde, with long curly hair that elegantly rested over her shoulders. Her eyebrows were dyed a brown color but that was the boldest thing about her. From her outfit to her slightly pink cheeks, she looked soft. Nothing was bold or form fitting, almost reminding me of a doll.

My own outfit was a black suit. I'd had it tailored so that it was almost form fitting. Underneath my coat, even my shirt was black, and my black heeled boots were making a hard thud sound as opposed to the clacking of heeled shoes. Koda had helped with my hair, dying it pink last night, and Zeke had cut it this morning, creating my new signature heart over my scar.

In my humble opinion, I looked badass. I could have been soft and sweet if I wanted, but I'd always been someone with an edge. The last thing I wanted was to appear different than myself as if I'd been coerced into whatever I was about to say. I had to appear normal. This was my normal, even if the suit was technically new.

Presley looked up from the other side of the room, her lips moving as she spoke to her omega, yet her gaze never dropped from our eye contact. She might have been dressed like a pretty little gift, but she was a predator. She was an alpha.

Eve was suddenly in front of me, blocking my view of anything except her. "Well, I can't smell your scent now, so you're a little bit calmer. That's good. Are you feeling good?"

In the face of Eve's panic, I was actually calming down. My own instincts always demanded that I comforted people I cared about, and Eve had quickly become a close friend of mine. Reaching out, I grabbed her hand, giving it a squeeze to reassure her.

"Right. Goodness, I'm nervous and I'm not even the one going on camera. Now, I'm supposed to have you sit on the chair and one of the sound producer guys talked me through how to put a mic on you. Once I do that, everything you say will reverberate throughout the room. Ready?"

"No. Let's do it."

I kissed my mates, none of them complaining about the pink stains from my lipstick before taking my designated spot. Sitting in the chair, I worked hard to get myself comfortable before giving up. The fabric was as soft as it looked, the thickness under it surprisingly firm.

Eve started moving around me, tucking what she

called the sound pack against my hip, and hiding the mic's cord behind my jacket. Her nerves were making her scent bloom, and her fingers just barely shook as she continued touching and adjusting the pack and cord and mic over and over again.

"Thank you, Eve." My whispered words echoed through the raised volume of the microphone, making me jump. I stared wide-eyed at my mates who were unsuccessfully hiding their smiles at the fact that I'd scared myself. Glaring at them, I pretended to turn my nose up.

Then Presley sat down, draining all the humor from me in an instant. For just a moment, I slumped, before I remembered that I was a bad bitch. I had to truly dig deep inside myself for those positive feelings, but I grabbed them with both hands, and used them to roll my shoulders back, posing like I was cocky and not at all intimidated by this alpha.

So close, she smelled like … milk. Her alpha scent reminded me of shoving my nose in a gallon that was close to its expiration date to make sure it was still good. Like a mix of milk and plastic. Honestly, it wasn't the worst alpha scent ever. It wasn't my preference, but I would take milk over salty water or black pepper any day.

"Good evening, omega," Presley said, speaking around the beta that was currently arranging her sound equipment. "We'll make sure this wraps up on time so you can get home before the curfew."

I was pretty sure she didn't mean her words maliciously. After all, she was still looking over her notes, barely even paying attention to the beta in front of her, let alone watching my reaction to her words.

I had no idea what to say, since the words, 'thank you' were definitely not coming out of my mouth at that comment. Fortunately, it didn't look like she was expecting me to answer anyway.

Turning my gaze to my alphas, I was asking them with my eyes if they'd just heard what she said. Sebastian gave me a look that told me to settle down while Han moved his hands around his chest in a gesture for me to breathe.

"Ready?" someone asked.

"Ready," Presley said.

There was a moment of silence before that same previous voice asked, "Ready, Hannah?"

"Oh, ready."

Almost directly in front of me, just off to the side of Presley's head, a large light turned on. I flinched at seeing it, my hands tightening around the arms of the chair as I waited for the light to get closer. It didn't.

From the peripheral of my vision, I saw Presley look up, watching me have a small melt down from a camera light. "Just relax, you need to focus on me, not the camera. Like you're gossiping with an old friend."

"One minute marker," someone yelled. Their voice was distant, yet it only served to make my memory stronger, to remind me of what happened then—

I was caught in a stare off with an inanimate object until a hand waved in front of it. Jackson was standing next to the camera, his thick corded arms crossed over his chest as he stared right at me. He was protecting me, standing by the thing that had scared me in order to remind my instincts that he wouldn't let anything hurt me.

The tension drained from my body as someone ran toward Presley, grabbed her notes, and the countdown from ten began.

Nine.

Eight.

Seven.

Six.

Five.

Four.

Three.

Two.

Ready or not—one.

"Good evening, everyone, thank you for your viewership," Presley started. Her voice was softer than I've heard in other interviews, and I had no idea if that was supposed to be for my benefit or the viewers.

"Tonight, I am interviewing a very special guest. For the first time ever, an omega is in the chair opposite me—Hannah Zeal. How are you doing, Hannah?"

"I'm good, especially since my alphas are nearby."

"Of course. If you're ready, I'd like to jump right into the hard stuff."

Taking a deep inhale, I gave her as much of a smile as I could. "I'm ready."

"Perfect. I'd like to start off in the timeline order, having you tell me about the first incident at Representative Adam's restaurant. How did you find yourself there?"

"If I'm being honest, I don't remember. I have no recollection of going into the restaurant, or even arriving at the shopping center. Even more, I didn't know the restaurant existed until my mates told me what had happened."

"What did your mates tell you?"

"That I'd been tackled. My head hit the pavement, cracking open a portion of my skull, and I was transported to the hospital."

"Tackled? That almost makes it sound intentional."

"I don't remember that part either. All I know is

what bystanders saw."

"How far back does your memory loss go? Do you remember the night before? Six months?"

"Years, actually. I, um—" I was getting choked up as I tried to get the words out in front of people. It was dumb to be sad about forgetting something I couldn't really remember, yet here I was. My hand came up the back of my neck, touching the only mating bite exposed. "I don't remember bonding with my alphas. Getting their claiming marks."

"An argument could be made that your attacker took those from you. How are you handling the effects of such a traumatic event?"

"My mates and I got to know each other again, and I can say, without a doubt, that I'm glad I'd bonded with them. I'd do it again if I could."

Presley laughed like I'd told a joke, so I did my best to smile like that had been my goal. "That's great to hear. Omegas need good alphas to support and protect them, especially in your case when it seems that you've become a topic of interest to a lot of people. Not all of it good."

"You know, I think a lot of people spend time daydreaming about what it would be like to be famous. I certainly used to. Having your moment of fame when you're in a hospital room doesn't give that fun, fulfilling vibe I'd always imagined. I was missing a chunk of hair after my surgery to fix my scalp, my whole body ached like my blood was sore as it traveled everywhere, and then there were all the emotions, the desire for strange alphas, fear of being in the hospital."

"It sounds overwhelming."

"It was." I almost winced as I said that since my words were hard to pivot to a new discussion.

"No doubt the experience you had with the press a

few weeks back has only added to your emotional distress."

I nodded, not really sure how to answer that statement, before I remembered that I wasn't supposed to do that.

"I was watching over the clips of what happened, and a lot of questions were thrown out about politics."

I bit my lip, then stopped, remembering my lipstick. For the last few weeks, I'd literally practiced on how to keep from making meaningless gestures and I was already messing up, but I had no idea how to respond to her statement. My gaze quickly glanced over to Jackson, my only alpha easily in my line of sight. He was too far for me to take any comfort in his scent, but just being able to see him helped me relax.

"I know that omegas typically stay out of the political world, but your circumstances are unique. You've almost been forced into it, and I know everyone is wondering your opinions. For instance, do you think the betas at the protest where you were injured should be held responsible for the damages incurred by you?"

"No." Fuck, I wish I'd said that louder—more confident. I tried again after quickly clearing the embarrassment from my throat. "No."

That got Presley to lean forward, her face never losing that kind look as if she wasn't actually fazed by my answer. "You have a kind, forgiving heart, then. How about your alphas, though? Surely, they think that some sort of punishment should be allotted for putting you in a hospital?"

"Well, sure, but that wasn't what you asked before."

The smile she gave me was condescending.

As soon as I saw her mouth about to open, I quickly added, "You asked about punishing the betas who were protesting. That wasn't who attacked me. All the accounts I've heard were about an alpha peace officer. That he pulled me from behind with too much force."

"That's quite a version of events. I've covered protests before, and things get out of hand. An alpha's instinct is to protect omegas, I imagine that's what any peace officer was trying to do in an event as volatile as that."

"Except I was tackled hundreds of feet from the building. Sprinting away from the protest."

For just a moment, I watched Presley's smile turn sharper, as if she'd realized I wasn't just a boring omega to pass the time, but some interesting prey for her to play with. "The peace officers were called out only after several hours had passed of the restaurant losing revenue. It's most likely possible that you got caught up in the crowd or that your alphas were far enough away that an alpha noticed an unattended omega. Where were your alphas during the incident?"

A trick question with a trick answer. "The emergency personnel struggled to get my alphas out of the way once they arrived. Apparently, I'd blacked out moments after my skull cracked. It really worried my alphas despite our bond."

"Being newly bonded myself, I can understand their fear. If that was me, I would be wondering how I could have prevented such an injury to my mate. If I should have been closer."

This time, it was my turn to change the topic, because I knew an argument about how my alphas shouldn't be blamed for someone else hurting me wasn't going to go over well. Alphas thought it was their duty to protect omegas. I figured alphas should just learn to control themselves since they were the prominent cause of omega related injuries. Especially unbonded alphas and omegas.

"My mates always stay close," I admitted, "that's the only reason I wasn't completely overwhelmed when all the reporters tried to get their answers on my date."

"If I remember correctly, several alphas from the orchestral band had to come help you both into the elevator."

I wondered how many times she'd watched those videos, all of them the same, just from different angles, making a note of each slight head movement I had. She made it sound like she had just glanced at the video, but I knew her question was rhetorical. She knew.

"I'm very grateful to those alphas," I told her.

"How come you were out alone with just one of your alphas? After what you'd been through, I would have kept my own omega on lockdown. And if he needed to go out, it would be with the whole pack."

"We've never had an issue out in public before all this—"

"That you can remember. With years lost from your memory, you can't really say for certain that this instance hasn't happened before."

"Maybe. Maybe not. But omegas shouldn't be forced to live in fear of going outside." I was getting too riled up, making it harder to keep my tone in check.

"I agree. Although a certain level of protection needs to be appointed to omegas. Like this bill proposed by representative Adam. In limiting the times that omegas are out in society, it ensures that the peace officers will be able to maintain proper surveillance. It was one of the hallmarks of Adam's proposal."

She didn't ask a question because she wanted me to simply nod my head along. Sebastian had warned me about that—stopping my natural tendencies in a conversation to simply acknowledge when someone was talking.

"Omegas are supposed to be protected to the point of allowing us out. If you keep us locked up for safety reasons, it seems more like an insult to the alpha, claiming they couldn't protect their mate."

"In extreme cases, the worst can happen. Look at you—"

"Exactly. Look at me. My alphas have protected me again and again. We were at a shopping district for the first attack, I might not remember how or why or when we got there, but I could imagine I wanted to go shopping so my mates came along. Then I went on a date, with my alpha, and again, he protected me. Now I get to sit here because the worst didn't happen."

"It's impressive how you stand up for your mates. I don't know a lot of omegas who would be brave enough."

"Do you know a lot of omegas?" As soon as the words came out of my mouth, I regretted them. Not their meaning, just their tone. "I just mean that I spent years in the OC, I've met hundreds of omegas at events and in housing. Just as much as alphas want to bond, so do omegas. We're just as territorial, just as loving, putting in just as much effort to be happy together."

"Of course," Presley agreed.

I wish I could smell her alpha scent. At this point, I had no idea if I was imagining her eyelid squinting on the edge as frustration. There were simply too many smells in here, and I was so focused on paying attention to what I was saying that I didn't want to distract myself by seeking her milk scent out.

"A lot of times, those alpha protective instincts come out through laws. Most representatives are alphas, so it's easy to see how the best interest of omegas is constantly put forward in proposed bills like

Representative Adam's. Have you read it?"

"My mates went over it with me after the temporary ban was put in place."

"Then you probably noticed your influence in the bill." Her smirk was back, and this time, I knew I wasn't imagining it.

"I'm not sure I understand."

"I've spoken with several co-writers on the bill, and I know that Representative Adam has made it clear that the bill's portion about building ownership and the restriction of certain designations allowed into a business based on the owner's preference came from the incident at his own restaurant with you. He wanted to ensure that you and other omegas were safe to eat at his business."

"What about packs that have betas?"

"Statistically speaking, very few packs ever bond with a beta."

"But some do. Are they simply banned from dining with their mates?"

"Do you have any plans to bond in a beta to your pack? You seem very passionate about this topic."

Fuck, I was totally messing up. I hadn't even noticed that I was leaning forward in my seat, that I was getting louder as I spoke. It felt like pure common sense to me that someone could be an ally to something they weren't a part of, but I knew that wasn't the image of me Presley was attempting to paint for our viewers.

My pause had been too long.

I tried for a nonchalant answer. "I have several beta friends. If we can't meet up at Representative Adam's restaurant, we'll go somewhere else. Easy as that."

"How is that? Being friends with betas, I mean. Most omegas tend to feel threatened around unbonded betas since they aren't familiar with the innate instincts that come naturally to us. Do you work around that feeling?"

"No." It was almost a question because I didn't feel threatened around most betas so long as they were respectful—but I immediately realized my mistake. It sounded like I'd answered that last question. I was getting sloppy the longer the interview went on.

"Most omegas find that difficult, and I'm pretty sure that's why most alphas are proponents for a separation from betas. Without betas, you wouldn't have been accidentally hurt at a protest, wouldn't have been swarmed by reporters. When you look at most of what's happened to you, the actions fall to the hands of betas."

Be fucking calm, Hannah. "I think that's a gross simplification. You could blame the laws that were unjust causing the betas to feel the need to protest in the first place. And when it comes to the reporter incident, I think it makes more sense to blame the industry that those specific betas are a part of. Or maybe we should blame the viewers who watched the video of me giving whichever broadcasting company more viewership or more incentive to keep continuing their actions."

I had to pause for a moment to breathe before I continued. "It wasn't the first time someone was swarmed with cameras in their face, demanding answers. It was just the first time that someone couldn't handle it. I'm not a celebrity, I didn't expect anyone to care about me if I went outside. It was a shock."

"That would be quite overwhelming. It was a good thing then that the members of the orchestral group were alphas and able to scent your distress."

"Good people do good things. Designations don't determine that. My best friends are betas, my lovers are alphas, and I'm an omega. The people in my life are a mix and we're more than our base instincts."

"In some sense, sure. But there's nothing stronger than instincts. As much as you might want to be able to ignore designations, that won't stop you from going into heat and pulling your mates into a rut. Your designation is simply part of who you are. Unless you hate being an omega?"

"We are our designations, sure. We're also so much more than that. My heat is just a part of me, like most omegas. That doesn't mean all omegas are alike. We have unique nests, unique comforts, unique mates. Each of us reacts differently in different scenarios. Some omegas don't like going outside the month of their heat, some need to be closer to nature. Grouping us together, even by our instincts, doesn't work."

"I totally agree," Presley said, immediately making me wonder how she was going to twist my words for her use. "Not all omegas are fit for every pack. That's why funding the local OCs are so important. Scent matches and personality matches, it's all part of forming permanent pack bonds. How was your experience at your OC?"

"I actually met one of my best friends when she was working there. She was sent out by the OC to check on me when I was in the hospital."

"A beta, then?"

I nodded.

"You've made quite a few statements this evening as a proponent of keeping the designations mixed. Does your opinion still stand when betas are taking the places of omegas? Bonding with alphas? Surely your instincts chafe against that, no matter how much you respect betas."

"Unless betas are murdering omegas and wearing their skin, I don't consider them taking anything from omegas. Each member of a pack decides who they want to be with. If that happens to be an omega or a beta or staying just with alphas, then I don't see a problem."

"What happens if there aren't enough alphas for omegas to bond with? Should omegas be forced to endure heats by themselves? Or should betas in packs allow their alphas to rut omegas without bonding them?"

"Have you ever been through a heat?" I had to work to contain my own smile, knowing that I was trying to set her up.

"I've seen my omega through one."

"But you haven't gone through one yourself."

"I've been in a rut."

"Exactly. A rut, not a heat. You don't know what omegas go through, except your own. If you gave us a chance, omegas could tell you our opinions about everything. There isn't a need to guess about laws or packs or heats, because we can tell you."

"Tell me now."

It wasn't what I meant, and she knew it. I knew it. I also knew I wasn't giving up this opportunity even if I could hear Seb's and Han's training in my head telling me to redirect the topic. "Omegas aren't territorial over alphas, we're territorial over our mates. Whoever that is. Instincts might help us find our mates, but those instincts are different for each person, for each designation. And when it comes to our heats, we should always be allowed to choose who or if we want someone to help us through it. Forcing sex on anyone, for any reason, should never be allowed."

"I think that's a very optimistic look at our society, and maybe one that most omegas share with you. Which is probably exactly why omegas aren't meant to make the tough decisions. Your alphas have done an excellent job of protecting you from the worst of society, of the people that have been repeatedly trying to take advantage of you, and I admire them for that."

An ache was forming in my jaw from how hard I was clenching my teeth. She was such a condescending asshole, talking down to me like I was a little kid who wanted world peace. As if my opinions were less because I was an omega.

"And they have my thanks for letting you come out and speak with me this evening." This was it, the last bit of my interview, the closing remarks.

Despite wishing for more time, I was glad it was done. My body finally relaxed, tension I hadn't even realized I had during the interview draining away. As of yet, I didn't have any regrets.

I wanted to stay here in this moment. Without the stress of the interview and before I learned about the effects of whatever was said.

"I wish you the best, Hannah. And for all our viewers, thank you and don't forget that the curfew for omegas is still active. Head straight home, wherever you are. Goodnight."

All at once the lights turned off. Presley didn't have even a moment to say anything to me before I was surrounded by all my mates. Their scents of pride were so strong that I felt the familiar burning sensation behind my eyes as I held back my tears for just a little longer.

I was so tired. Exhausted, really, from all the emotions I felt. My mates didn't linger, dragging me along with them as we left.

I needed a nap. I needed more time before the vote that week for the temporary ban to become permanent. I needed to know that I hadn't made things worse for my designation.

I wondered, for all my effort, if I'd even made a difference.

Epilogue

A few days later

The vote for nays, for refusing the permanent movement ban, was just barely higher than the yeas, but the number was still counting.

At this point, no one was even talking. Koda and her alphas were over, as was Eve, but we were all watching the TV in the living room.

I was sitting on Zeke's lap, but I wasn't truly aware of where the rest of my mates were except that each one was touching me somehow. A hand on my shoulder, my neck, my knee. All of our gazes locked on the screen as the count for each representative kept going up.

The space smelled of stress and worry with only a tinge of excitement.

Before the count had started, my face had been everywhere. On most news channels, social media, even on the hidden sites. An omega that spoke out was big news, especially one with controversial statements.

Both sides had used whatever clips suited them best. If anyone watched the interview, I felt like it would be obvious that the short, put together head nods and words were taken out of context. And as much as I raved about that fact, there was nothing to do about it.

I was officially at the whims of the media. A face for the omegas whether you supported more freedoms for them or supported stricter restrictions.

No one said anything as the lead for nays got bigger, not wanting to jinx the outcome.

These last few days had been more stressful than the entire weeks that led up to the interview. Both Han and Seb's families reached out, and neither of those conversations had gone well. The studio where we had filmed the interview receives fan and hate mail for me, because apparently while my face was public, my address was still hidden.

My secret app was blowing up. Luckily not with recognition—although some people had guessed correctly. Mostly, it was filled with last-minute protests, ideas for where to live if the ban did go through, certain loopholes someone might be able to use in a court against the potential law. It was all useful, just extremely pessimistic, so I'd been avoiding it.

It was hard to not feel like the decision, either way, was influenced by me. I had seen the clips both sides were using in their favor, and I was an emotional mix of pride and guilt.

I was still doing my classes, even if all my mates agreed it was fine if I dropped it. School and homework and tests weren't really my thing, yet I couldn't convince myself to stop taking them. I wanted the satisfaction of finishing it, of picking a major and passing like any other designation in society. Maybe I would even pick a communications degree to help with my public speaking so I didn't get tongue-tied on any other future interviews.

The biggest surprise came with the fact that none of us had heard from Representative Adam. Of course, he was completely alive and present for the vote, his one of the first yeas to be counted.

For some reason, I'd thought he'd come back to our house, raging at me for what I said. It was Zeke who suggested that he'd probably wait to throw his proverbial tantrum until after the vote in case my interview didn't change any minds. I thought a man with his amount of pride wouldn't have been able to withstand an omega talking shit—no matter how politely I'd done it.

As the count neared the final numbers, Koda stood, starting to pace. It was so close, nays and yeas going back and forth. If the nays won, we'd celebrate. If the yeas won, I was pretty sure Koda's mates would take her home, Eve would leave, and I'd cry in my nest for a long time.

That wasn't what I wanted. I wanted the party, the happiness. I didn't want to be forced to stay in my home, no matter how much I loved it. I wanted to keep going on dates. I didn't believe that you could truly know everything about a person, nevertheless I wanted to learn as much as possible about my mates.

I wanted freedom, choices, equality.

Eve's scent was growing stronger, showing how distressed the beta was about what she was watching. Reaching out with my free hand, I fumbled for hers, offering the small amount of comfort I could manage.

"How many votes left?" Eve asked.

"Ten," Aidan, one of Koda's mates, said.

I couldn't look away. Didn't even dare blink.

The nays were ahead, by one. Then none. Then one again.

Hands touching me got tighter, scents grew stronger. Koda stopped pacing, standing in place under the TV like she was worried there would be a delay in information if she was as far back as the couch.

Tears were pooling in my eyes, I just didn't know if they were from happiness or fear. I wanted the nay result so bad, I would have wished on a shooting star, rubbed a lamp, anything to make it happen.

Then it was done.

By one vote, the nays had it. The temporary movement ban wouldn't become permanent.

The crowd on the TV cheered, we all screamed. I was jumping up and down, letting the tears fall as I hugged all my mates before turning to Koda and Eve, pulling them into a tight hug with my arms around their necks, our heads banging together painfully.

"Fuck you, Adam," I yelled at the screen. "Fucking fuck you and your ban, you asshole."

"Yeah, what she said," Koda agreed.

"And to everyone else who voted with you," Eve added. She might not have been as affected by the movement ban as omegas, but we all knew that if this one had passed, so too would have more extreme laws separating betas from society.

This law was a test to see how the other representatives were feeling. It wasn't too much of a leap to propose stricter laws for omegas since some were already on the books. If this had passed, then it would be easier to suggest beta laws too.

Instead, Adam had made enemies and lost the bill. I only wished that his constituents would boot him out for losing—although I was doubtful of that. His voters worshiped him to a creepy extent that was strange for a person, let alone a politician.

"Now we party," I told everyone.

One of my mates changed the channel, and I was dragged into the kitchen to help start plating foods. We dumped chips into bowls, dips into containers, ordered delivery, and got several different types of desserts.

Seb even made drinks for everyone, letting me have the one he made for himself since his was weirdly so good. It even had edible glitter in it which I was thinking I wanted in all my future drinks.

We partied for hours. Not crazily, just enjoying the company of friends, being lighthearted for the first time in weeks, if not months. There was no mention of politics or Adam or anything beyond jokes and laughter and even Sebastian and Aidan telling stories about each other when they were both young.

Eve was the first to leave, then Koda and her pack to have their own, intimate celebration.

Then it was just me and my pack. The tension surrounding us was taut and brittle, ready to break if anyone so much as moved.

There was a lot to clean up—the food, the dishes, even just replacing all the pillows and blankets and chairs to their designated spot. Instead of doing any of that, I turned and ran up the stairs, forcing all my mates to run after me.

Adrenaline flooded my system. I was panting hard at the top of the stairs, but I didn't stop, running toward my nest. Jackson got to me first, half slamming me down onto the nest's soft floor, his playful growl adding to the arousal already building low in my belly.

"Strip," Jackson demanded.

He turned me around, so I was on my back, and he was hovering over me, blocking me from moving. I wiggled around, desperately trying to rip my clothes off as quickly as possible. It was made even harder by the fact that Jackson refused to move. Around me, I knew my other mates were stripping, but my first alpha was simply watching me, his gaze never wavering.

"Present," Jackson barked.

I scrambled to get into position, raising my hips high, spreading my knees apart, and pressing my chest onto the floor. Zeke was in front of me, on his knees, his cock already hard as his hand slowly ran up and down his length. My mouth watered in anticipation of tasting him, wanting his berry flavor on my tongue.

Behind me, Jackson started playing between my legs, tracing his fingers along my pussy which was already leaking slick.

Reaching for Zeke, my mate sat back down on his

heels so his cock was at the perfect height for me to suck on. I licked at his head, and down his length, completely focused on enjoying my mate in my mouth.

I felt one finger press inside me, then another, thrusting in and out of me gently, teasing me.

Han came up behind Zeke, the former wrapping his hands around Zeke's chest. One of Han's hands came down to Zeke's cock, slowly jerking him off, his fingers bumping my lips where I was pressing my tongue against the bottom side of Zeke's head. Between the two of us, Zeke's head was thrown back, groaning with pleasure from Han and I working him together.

I was missing Seb, but I wasn't able to pull away from Zeke's dick to beg for him.

Jackson was still using his hand on me, and I whimpered, wanting more. Multiple scents of arousal bloomed after the noise escaped, heightening the sexual atmosphere, taking us from desperate to frantic.

I finally felt the head of Jackson's cock at my entrance, shoving inside me in a single powerful thrust.

I screamed around Zeke's cock, the pleasure of finally being filled the way my body was begging, almost overwhelming. My orgasm was already threatening from the rhythm of Jackson's thrusts, the taste of Zeke, and the scents of all my mates' arousal.

Zeke came first, the taste of his cum coating my tongue. He didn't lock into my mouth this time, letting Han massage his inflated knot. It was a lot to drink down, some of it spilling down my chin and onto the nest floor.

As Zeke fell back, Han's face was in front of mine, licking up the cum on my chin and lips, before kissing me, shoving his tongue into my mouth so I could taste the mix of him and Zeke. I groaned, the dirty kiss pushing me over the edge toward my first orgasm.

Jackson came inside me, too, also not knotting

me, not that I could have begged for him with Han's lips almost glued to mine, making it hard to breathe.

Hands ran down my back, and even without looking, I knew they were Seb's. He was positioning himself differently than Jackson had, letting me know his intentions we're to fuck me in a different hole than my first alpha had. With his knees between my own spread legs, I felt him use his fingers to spread my arousal from my core to my ass.

When he pulled me back, slowly pushing his way inside me, I was more sitting on his lap than actually on all fours. The piercing on Seb's tip felt even better in my ass, the tightness making him constantly hit every nerve ending in existence. Han followed, keeping his mouth on mine and letting our tongues play together. Since I was sitting up more, I could see that Han had his hand wrapped around himself, squeezing tight as he jerked his length. He started playing with my breasts with his free hand, squeezing them, pinching my nipples, running the pads of his fingers around the underside of each breast, never stopping the back-and-forth motion for his own pleasure.

Han's touch was gentle compared to Seb's pounding in my ass. I was trapped between them, simply being used for their pleasure and it felt so good.

Dropping one of my own hands down to my clit, I rubbed the nub, feeling my second orgasm growing.

"Does this feel good, princess?" Seb asked, his soft words kissing my ear.

Han backed up, lowering his mouth to my breasts, sucking on the hard points of my nipples, even biting the sides of my breasts, leaving marks.

"Yes," I hissed, not just to his question, but to all of it. The pleasure, the sensations, the scents, the love.

I came then. My mouth open, my eyes closed, the

pleasure zinging throughout my body, tensing my muscles, stopping my breath.

Seb followed after, shouting his release as I tightened around him. Han was last, spilling his seed on my stomach as Seb held my body slumped against him. I'd just come twice, yet not one of my mates had knotted me. My instincts were not pleased.

"I need a knot," I admitted, looking at all four of my mates.

"Don't worry, rebel, we have all night."

Jackson pulled me from Seb, turning me so we were chest to chest, face to face. I could scent the emotions coming from him, his excitement and pride and arousal, yet also his fear and worry and anxiety. For all of us, this was a celebration, but we hadn't won yet. We just hadn't lost.

At least for tonight, in this nest, we were going to ignore the outside world. I would make sure of it. "Knot me, alpha."

He did. Then all of my mates did. The five of us falling asleep hours later, smelling of sex, covered in sweat, and smiling until our cheeks hurt and we couldn't physically keep our eyes open anymore.

The End

EVERNIGHT PUBLISHING ®

www.evernightpublishing.com